WIND CHIME SUMMER

A WIND CHIME NOVEL

SOPHIE MOSS

Dear Debbi,

Here's to many more
years of a healthy Chesapeake
Bay!

♡ Sophie Moss

Sea Rose
Publishing

Published by Sea Rose Publishing

ISBN-13: 978-0999358900

For the memory of my great-grandmother
Helen M. Murray
"Nan"
1908-2002

ONE

*I*zzy Rivera didn't notice the marshes. She didn't notice the tall reedy grasses that swayed into the beams of her headlights with every gust of wind. She didn't notice the wildflowers that lined the narrow strip of road through her rain-streaked windshield, or the way her whole car shook with each thunderclap from a storm that only seemed to grow worse the closer she came to this place at the end of the earth.

What she noticed were the pine trees. Or what was left of them. Hollow, broken stumps of pine trees glowing ghostly white in the strobes of lightning that splintered the sky.

That was how she felt now.

Dead. Broken. Empty inside.

She reached for her worn, Army-issue handkerchief and pressed the cloth to the back of her neck. It was already damp. Cold from the sweat she'd soaked up a few minutes ago.

She'd had to pull over three times since crossing the drawbridge to Heron Island. She'd passed through the tiny village about a mile ago, spied a blurry outline of an ice cream shop, a bookstore, a café, a school...and then nothing. There was nothing at all out here.

Nothing but her and those trees.

The memories crept in, threatening to swallow her whole. She forced them back as another flash of lightning lit up the sky and she spotted a lone structure in the distance, an old yellow farmhouse rising up from the end of this soggy, sinking spit of land.

She nearly stopped the car again, nearly turned around. But she wasn't a coward.

Broken? Yes.

A coward? No.

She willed her foot to stay on the gas pedal, to keep pushing the car forward. The wiper blades scraped sheets of rain from the glass, providing intermittent glimpses of a circular driveway filled with cars, a wide front porch covered in potted plants, and a waterlogged garden edging the base of the house.

There were lights on in the downstairs windows. She could see people moving around in the rooms. She eased her car into the last empty spot in the driveway and sat with her foot on the brake, watching them.

She wasn't good with people anymore. She didn't like the way they looked at her, the questions they asked. The smallest exchange of pleasantries—*How's it going? How are you today?*—could set her off now.

She wanted to scream, to throw things, to break things.

I'm fine, was all she ever said, but she wasn't fine. She was as far from fine as she'd ever been in her life.

Shifting the car into park, she cut the headlights and felt a moment of panic when the darkness closed in around her. It was the kind of darkness that could seep through your skin, sink into your bones, spread through your mind until there was nothing left but madness.

Her hand shook as she reached for her water bottle. Somehow, she managed to unscrew the cap. She drank until the dryness in her throat gave way to the familiar pulsing knot of rage that lived inside her.

It was the only thing that kept her going now.

Tossing the empty bottle onto the floor, she lifted her gaze to the yellow house. The colors dripped and melted, the image distorted through the wet glass, until the corners warped and the roof tilted. She was supposed to spend the next three months here. Three months with people like her—people who needed to heal.

As if there were any hope.

She'd read the mission statement on the website. She understood the purpose of this program. Will Dozier and Colin Foley weren't the first Navy SEALs to start rehab programs for down-and-out veterans. It seemed like a perfectly noble goal from the outside. But she'd encountered her share of SEALs overseas. Most of them were arrogant pricks who thought they were better than everyone and knew everything.

They probably thought fixing her would be a breeze.

Sliding the key out of the ignition, she grabbed her pack, flipped the hood of her raincoat up to cover her tangled mass of black curls, and opened the door. An unfamiliar scent rushed toward her. It was muddy, tangy, and smelled faintly of saltwater.

The Chesapeake Bay, she mused. She'd read about that on the website, too. The big body of water that surrounded this island was supposed to help with the healing process. Their fearless leaders were probably going to take them out kayaking and bird watching. Maybe they could hold hands and skip afterwards.

Stepping out of the car, she slammed the door and made her way to the porch. If they even mentioned the words 'group therapy' later, she was going to lose it. Mentally preparing herself for one of those big, cocky SEALs to answer, she knocked on the door. She was pretty sure she'd read somewhere that one of them was the son of the Governor of Maryland.

She could only imagine how big his head must be.

The door swung open, she took one look at the person on the other side, and the speech she'd rehearsed in the car froze on her lips.

He wasn't military.

He was...

A dog barked, slipping out of the gap in the open door and launching itself at her. She sucked in a breath as seventy pounds of wet dog wrapped around her legs in a sniffing, wiggling mass of brown fur.

"Sorry." The man grabbed the dog's collar, pulling the animal back to his side. "She's usually more polite than that." He glanced down at the dog, gave her a scolding look. "Sit."

The dog sat immediately, her tail thumping on the floorboards, her whole body quivering with excitement.

The man looked up at Izzy and offered her a sheepish smile. "This is Zoey. She's part of the welcoming committee."

No, Izzy thought as her heart rate struggled to return to normal. He was definitely not military. His stance was far too casual, far too relaxed. His build was tall and lanky, more like a long distance runner's, and he wore a faded T-shirt and jeans, both of which were streaked with mud.

"You must be Isabella." He smiled and held out his hand. "You're the last to arrive."

"It's Izzy," she corrected, glancing up at his face again. There was a small smudge of something that looked like white paint along his left cheekbone. His hair was a thick, tousled mess of sun-streaked blond. And his eyes were the palest shade of gray she'd ever seen.

Not the gray of storm clouds; they were lighter than that.

Like the calm after the storm, the calm leftover as the last of the clouds blew away.

She took his hand. A warm, pulsing sensation spread up her arm. Not sparks of electricity, not wild currents of sexual energy, just warmth and peace and complete and utter calm.

"I'm Ryan," he said, releasing her hand. "Can I help you with the rest of your bags?"

"No," she said, mentally shaking herself. What was wrong with her? She held up her backpack. "This is everything."

His gaze lingered on her small pack and an unspoken question swam into his eyes. But he kept his thoughts to himself. "Come on in," he said, nodding for her to follow him into the house. "Everyone else is in the kitchen."

The moment Izzy stepped inside, the feeling of home wrapped around her like a hug. She tried to fight it, but it was impossible not to feel the love and attention that had gone into every detail of the renovation of this centuries-old farmhouse. She took in the collection of black and white photographs that lined the hallway leading into the next room—family portraits, children at various ages, people from all walks of life.

To the left of the entranceway, a cozy sitting room was filled with overstuffed armchairs and floor-to-ceiling bookshelves. To the right, a polished oak stairwell led up to the second story. The floors were wood as well, thick planks that felt strong and sturdy under her feet.

Ryan took her wet coat, hung it on one of the hooks by the door, and snagged a towel off one of the tables, handing it to her to dry off with. It was big and plush and cozy and made her want to weep.

Stop, she told herself. She didn't need comfort. She didn't want comfort. Comfort would make her soft, would make her face things she'd locked up deep inside. The fact that those things were starting to leak out through the cracks didn't matter. She could patch herself together. At least for the next three months. At least until she could return to Baltimore. She could fall apart there. Where no one could see her.

She handed the towel back.

Ryan dropped it into a hamper. "How was the drive?"

"Fine."

"You didn't run into too much water on the roads?"

There had been a few bends in the road where the water had reached the underside of her car, but she'd powered through them, as she did with everything in life now. "I managed."

"Summer storms can be rough out here. We had one a few years ago that washed out the road completely."

Izzy didn't doubt it, and wondered why anyone would choose to live here, in this place that looked like the next high tide could wash it away. A jingle of dog tags drew her gaze down to the chocolate lab, who had unearthed a tennis ball from beneath one of the tables in the hallway and was looking terribly pleased with herself.

"Ready?" Ryan asked, gesturing for her to follow him into the kitchen.

Izzy nodded, but her throat tightened when she spotted the crowd gathered in the next room. There had to be at least fifteen to twenty people in there. She forced her shoulders back and her spine straight as the first few curious eyes swung her way. *Don't let them see any weakness. Don't ever let anyone know that you're afraid.*

She stepped into the room and her own gaze automatically gravitated to the stove, where steam rose from the top of a large cast-iron pot filled with something that smelled amazing—earthy and spicy with a rich tomato and beef broth. Her fingers curled around the straps of her pack as she struggled against the urge to walk over and see what was inside.

"Are you hungry?" Ryan asked.

"No."

"I'll let Colin and Will know you're here," he said, slipping into the crowd.

Izzy took in the gleaming stainless steel appliances, wide chopping block counter, oversized farmhouse sink, and impressive collection of copper pots hanging from an iron rack mounted to the ceiling. It was the kind of kitchen that was made for cooking big meals that took all day to prepare and inviting everyone you knew over to enjoy them.

There was a time when she would have dreamed of having a kitchen like this in her own home.

She looked past the bar, where a few burly guys in their late-twenties were wolfing down big bowls of soup, and took a quick inventory of the rest of the people in the room. Besides the middle-aged woman tending to the soup on the stove, there were only two other women. One was in a wheelchair. The other was missing the lower half of her right arm.

She was the only female veteran still in one piece.

That should make her feel better, right? She didn't look broken, so she must be fine. That's what everyone else thought. Most of the time, it was easier to let them.

One of the women offered her a tentative smile, a small offer of friendship. Izzy looked away. She didn't want friends. She didn't need friends.

They wouldn't want to be friends with her anyway once they found out the truth—that she wasn't a real soldier.

She was just a cook. A woman who'd worked in the kitchen. And now she couldn't even do that.

"Hey," Ryan Callahan said, putting his hand on Will Dozier's shoulder. His best friend from childhood turned. "Izzy's here."

He nodded across the room to where the woman stood, looking like she was ready to bolt.

"Thanks," Will said, extracting himself from a conversation with an ex-Marine. "I know Colin's been anxious to get started. He was hoping to be halfway through the introductions by now." He walked away, heading toward Izzy.

Ryan's gaze followed his friend's path across the room. He couldn't help it. It was impossible not to look at the woman again. Izzy Rivera was captivating in a rough-around-the-edges, mistrustful-like-a-cat kind of way. Her thick black hair was pulled back in a ponytail, but a few wet curls had slipped loose, framing an exotic, golden-skinned face of either Spanish or Latina descent. Her body was all female, with soft round curves that had drawn the attention of more than one man when she'd walked into the room.

But it was those eyes—big and amber and filled with emotion —that made him unable to look away.

Jesus. Those eyes. He'd never seen a pair of eyes like that.

A sudden hand on his arm startled him and he flinched.

"Somebody's jumpy tonight," Della Dozier commented.

Reluctantly dragging his gaze away from Izzy's face, Ryan looked down at Will's aunt.

"That's not like you," Della said, her blue eyes concerned. "Is everything all right?"

That was a good question, Ryan thought. He hadn't expected to be attracted to any of the women who'd enrolled in this program, especially not one who would be working for him. Obviously, it went without saying that any woman on his payroll was strictly off limits. She had come here to heal, *not* get hit on.

Ryan's gaze swept over the rest of the faces in the room. When he'd offered to provide temporary employment to some of the veterans in this program, he'd been so focused on the mutual benefits—he needed the workforce to help his new business succeed, and they needed something to do with their hands to get their confidence back—that he hadn't really considered the full impact of what he was taking on.

Every person in this room had something in common that he didn't—they'd served in the military. He didn't have a clue what it felt like to be shot at, to put on a uniform, to be shipped overseas and spend years away from your friends and family. He had no idea what it felt like to come home after multiple tours and try to fit in with the people you'd left behind.

What if he couldn't relate? What if he couldn't offer them what they needed?

He looked at Della. "I guess it just hit me—what's at stake. I don't want to mess up."

"You're not going to mess up," Della said, giving his arm a squeeze. "I have faith in you, in *all* of you. And I know that you haven't eaten anything tonight, so I fixed up a container of soup for you to take home afterwards. It's in the fridge, on the top shelf."

"Thank you," Ryan said, and felt some of the tension dissolve. Della had never had any children of her own, but she'd been like a mother to a lot of people on this island. People on Heron Island took care of each other. They looked out for each other. Now that these eleven veterans were staying here for the next twelve weeks, they would look out for them, too.

"Welcome, everyone," Colin's deep voice cut through the room, silencing all conversation. "I think I've gotten to meet most of you by now. We'll go around the room in a minute and let you all introduce yourselves, but I'd like to point out a few key people first. Most of you have probably met Will Dozier. He and his wife, Annie, and their daughter, Taylor, live in the private wing on the north side of the house."

From their spot by the fireplace, Annie and Taylor smiled and waved to everyone.

"Della?" Colin asked.

"Over here." Della waved an arm, her short frame dwarfed by a wall of taller men who parted to let her through.

Colin smiled warmly at the gray-haired woman wearing an apron with the words *Kiss the Cook* embroidered across it. "Everyone, this is Della Dozier, Will's aunt and the best cook on Heron Island. Let's give her a round of applause for making this incredible batch of Maryland crab soup for us tonight."

Everyone applauded and Della beamed.

"Della wanted to be here tonight to personally welcome you all to the inn," Colin continued, "but she works at the Wind Chime Café in town, which Annie owns. From now on, you'll be responsible for preparing the meals we eat together." He motioned to a large chalkboard hanging on the wall. "Every week, we'll assign new jobs to each of you. You can see the first week's breakdown here. We'll go into this in more detail after the introductions, but as you can see it's all the basic housekeeping chores: cooking, cleaning, laundry, grocery shopping."

Colin looked out at the crowd. "For those of you still recovering from injuries, we have a physical therapist who will be meeting with you at her office in St. Michaels. We'll arrange the transportation, so let us know when you've worked out a schedule with your employer and we'll make sure you get there on time. We also have a social worker on call twenty-four seven. She'll be reaching out to each of you individually to set up your first appointment. These sessions will be private and completely confidential between the two of you, but we expect you to attend a minimum of at least one a week."

Ryan saw a few guys wince and figured most of them weren't too excited about the prospect of talking about their feelings. He understood why it was a mandatory part of the program, but he didn't blame them.

"For those of you who are interested—and we expect

everyone who is physically capable to participate—Will has put together a rigorous exercise program that he'll be leading twice a day." Colin glanced up, catching Will's eye across the room. "And I can tell you from personal experience that it won't be a walk in the park." The two former SEAL teammates smiled, sharing an inside joke.

"Lastly, over the next few weeks, we'll both be meeting with each of you individually to go over your résumés, skillsets, and employment interests so we can find you a permanent position closer to your families and hometowns. As for your jobs on the island, we've secured temporary employment for each of you at a local business, which you'll be starting first thing tomorrow."

Colin glanced down at his notes, reviewing the list of assignments. "Troy," he said, looking back up and meeting the eyes of a short, stocky veteran near the front of the room, "you'll be working with Don Fluharty at The Tackle Box."

Troy nodded, as if he remembered seeing the small general store at the foot of the drawbridge when he'd driven by it earlier that night.

"Zach." Colin's gaze swept through the crowd, landing on a tall, brown-haired man near the middle of the room. "You'll be working on Bob Hargrove's charter boat as his first mate."

Zach lit up. "I get to work on a fishing boat?"

Colin nodded and glanced down at his notes again. "Megan, you'll be working with Lou Ann Sadler at Clipper Books."

Megan's face broke into a smile. The pretty brunette in the wheelchair was pleased with her assignment as well.

"Kade," Colin continued, "you'll be working with Gladys Schaefer at The Flower Shoppe."

A few people snorted as they tried to stifle their laughter, but most failed, and even Ryan's brows lifted at that one.

Kade McCafferty was the second tallest person in the room after Colin, which put him somewhere around six-foot-three. He was built like a linebacker, probably weighing close to three hundred pounds, and he was completely bald, like one day he'd just woken up and said 'screw it' to his hair and shaved it all off. Dark tattoos covered both arms and another huge tattoo on his left calf spelled out the word, 'MARINES.' He'd been one of the first to arrive at the inn that night and Ryan had spent some time talking to him earlier. He'd served five tours overseas as an infantryman. Front lines.

The Flower Shoppe?

That just seemed wrong.

But Colin was already forging ahead. "I know some of you have already met Ryan Callahan." Colin nodded to where Ryan stood and everyone turned to look at him. "Ryan is a marine biologist whose research has transformed the field of coastal ecology. He has a Ph.D. from MIT's joint program with Woods Hole Oceanographic Institution, and he's spent the past ten years fighting to mitigate the effects of climate change and pollution on our most endangered waterways. Last year, he moved back to this island to open a nonprofit to educate the public on how to become better stewards of the Chesapeake Bay and help his father, a fourth-generation waterman, expand his oyster farm. They've recently combined the two operations into a single company with a big vision and they're going to need a lot of help to get where they want to go."

"What's an oyster farm?" one of the women asked.

Colin looked at Ryan. "Go ahead."

"It's an environmentally sustainable process of growing and harvesting oysters," Ryan explained. "They start out as seeds, which we purchase from a hatchery, and then we plant them in the water like a regular farmer would plant seeds in the ground. It takes about a year-and-a-half for a farmed oyster to grow to market size, which is when we pull them out and sell them to restaurants, seafood markets, and wholesalers."

"Don't oysters grow in the wild?" one of the guys asked. "Why do you need to farm them?"

"The wild oyster population in the Bay was almost completely wiped out twenty years ago," Ryan said. "Right now, it's at about one percent of historic levels. There have been efforts to reestablish it, and it's starting to make a very small comeback, but it still has a long way to go. Oyster farming is a way of continuing a centuries-old tradition of harvesting seafood from these waters without affecting one of our most important natural resources. We don't take anything out that we don't put there ourselves."

"Which brings us to our last two groups of people," Colin said, segueing easily back to the point. "Hailey and Ethan, you'll be working on the nonprofit side of Ryan's operation. Paul, Jeff, Wesley, Matt, and Izzy, you'll be working on the farm."

"No," Izzy said.

Seventeen heads turned to face her, and Izzy's eyes widened, as if she hadn't realized she'd said it out loud.

Colin glanced over at her, surprised. "Is there a problem?"

She looked like she wanted to shrink into the wall, to disappear completely, but knew it was too late. "I'd rather not work... on a farm."

"Why not?"

She straightened her spine, visibly mustering her courage. "I would like to request to switch with someone."

"I'll switch with her," Kade said.

A few people laughed.

"I appreciate the team spirit," Colin said dryly, "but we put everyone in each position for a reason. If something changes over the next few weeks, we can make adjustments. Right now, we're confident that everyone is where he or she is supposed to be. Let's move on with the rest of the introductions and the tour so that those of you who are working with Ryan can make it an early night. You'll be leaving here before sunrise tomorrow to get to the farm by 0500." Colin looked over at Ryan, making it clear that the discussion was closed. "Is there anything else your staff should know?"

Ryan watched Izzy squeeze the straps of her pack. He caught the flash of fear in her eyes, and then something else, something that looked like anger, as if she were somehow offended by the assignment.

What could she possibly have against working on an oyster farm?

Suppressing the urge to speak up, to tell Colin that they should give her another job, he reminded himself that he wasn't in charge of this program. He was just one of the employers. He had to trust that Will and Colin knew what they were doing.

They were the ones who had served. They were the ones who could relate.

A wet nose brushed against his fingertips and he looked down as Zoey, his chocolate lab, nuzzled his hand. "Wear gym clothes," he said, "because you're going to get dirty."

TWO

The next morning, Izzy woke, her heart racing, her hair drenched in sweat. Fumbling for the lamp on the bedside table, she found the switch, almost knocking it over in the process. A small circle of light filled the room. She blinked, taking in the unfamiliar surroundings. Pale blue walls. Gauzy white curtains. A small wooden desk beneath the window.

She was at the veterans' center, she remembered. On Heron Island. She took a few deep breaths, slowly peeling back the sheets. Her limbs felt heavy and awkward, still tethered to the memory of the nightmare—the same one she had every night. Her clothes were soaking wet and sticking to her as she climbed out of bed. Goosebumps rose on her bare arms when a blast of air conditioning hit her. She shivered, searching for her pack, rooting through it for a change of clothes.

She pulled out a clean T-shirt and a pair of cotton shorts. Still holding them in her hands, she turned and spotted the dark outline of sweat on the sheets. Shame rolled through her. It didn't matter when this happened at home. At home, she could hide it. At home, no one needed to know. But, here, if anyone found out that she'd been waking up in a pool of her own sweat for the past nine months, they'd know something was wrong.

Checking the clock on the bedside table, she saw that it was only 0415. Maybe no one else was up yet. She stripped the sheets, balled them up in her arms, and slipped quietly out of the room. The house was dark, but there was a nightlight in the stairwell, and a small table lamp burned in the entranceway. She made her way to the laundry room, remembering where it was from the tour the night before. Finding the door open, she turned the corner and froze.

There was someone else in there. A man. One of the other veterans—the massive ex-Marine covered in tattoos—was holding his own set of sheets, which were completely soaked through.

"Night sweats?" Kade asked.

Izzy said nothing, mortified.

He held out his hand. "It's a big washer. I'll put them both in."

Her arms tightened around the sheets, unable to hand them over, unable to accept help.

Sensing it, he walked over and took them from her. He shoved them into the washing machine with a double dose of soap. "I won't tell if you won't," he said gruffly, then brushed past her and headed up the stairs.

Izzy stood, unmoving, listening to the sound of his footsteps on the stairs, then the upstairs hallway, then the faint creak of a bedroom door opening and closing, until there was nothing but the low thrum of the washer beginning to fill with water beside her.

She wasn't the only one.

She hadn't expected to relate to any of the other veterans in this program. She hadn't expected...to care.

She didn't want to care.

But knowing that there was at least one other person

suffering through the same hell as she was each night, especially someone who looked like Kade, made her feel a little bit less ashamed.

Backing out of the laundry room, she walked down the narrow hallway and paused in the doorway to the kitchen. In the past, whenever she'd been upset about something, she would have headed for the kitchen. She would have cooked something.

The simple act of putting food together had always soothed her. But not anymore. Not since...

A woman's place is in the kitchen.

The voice—the same voice that haunted her dreams every night now—had her shuddering. She took the stairs two at a time, retreating to the safety of her room. She shut the door and leaned against it, feeling much more rattled than she wanted to admit.

All she'd ever wanted was respect. All she'd ever wanted was to matter, to *not* be invisible. She'd never asked anyone for a handout. She'd never asked anyone for anything without giving twice as much in return. She'd spent twelve years in the Army working her way up from the bottom of the ladder. Only to be knocked off it again, violently, by a man whose life she had saved.

Now, she was back to being invisible. And working on a farm.

Walking slowly over to the clothes she'd pulled out of her pack earlier, she picked them up one by one. She wasn't a stranger to farm work. She'd spent most of her childhood working on farms—picking onions in Arizona, apples in Colorado, just about every vegetable that could be grown in Texas. She'd joined the Army at eighteen to put the memories of that life far behind her.

And she'd never once looked back.

For the first time since she'd begun picking alongside her mother and grandmother at the age of seven, she'd had a job she could be proud of, a job that people would respect. She'd built a life for herself in this country, an honorable life, a life of service and sacrifice, so she could have a future that was better than the one her mother and grandmother had left behind in Mexico.

She'd had no idea how easily it could all be taken away.

Peeling off her wet clothes, she changed into the clean ones and washed up in the small bathroom. Not even bothering to glance at her reflection in the mirror, she pulled her hair into a ponytail and crossed the room to the window.

Expecting the same view—those same haunted, broken trees she'd seen in the storm the night before—she was surprised to find that it looked nothing like that now. It had stopped raining. The slightest hint of sunlight was lightening the horizon, and the water stretched out as far as she could see in every direction.

A row of condensation from the heat and humidity clung to the glass. She slid the window open. A solitary heron glided over the shoreline. A few songbirds were waking up, cheerfully chirping from the branches of the leafy trees in the yard. It was so quiet. And so peaceful.

She jumped when someone knocked on the door.

"Yo." Kade stuck his head into her room. "Your van's outside. Better get moving."

He disappeared back into the hallway, but she noticed that he left her door open a crack. Closing the window, she tucked her wet clothes into a laundry bag on the floor of the closet and followed him down the stairs. She spotted the blue van in the driveway and walked outside. A few of the others turned to look at her, then looked away.

She wasn't surprised. She knew that a group of them had stayed up after she'd gone to bed the night before, hanging out in the living room, getting to know each other. They were already forming into sub-groups. Finding commonalities. Forging friendships, alliances.

She didn't need to form alliances. She wasn't here to make friends.

"Is this everyone?" the guy in the driver's seat asked, counting heads as they filed into the van.

Izzy climbed into the back, taking a seat in the corner.

"I don't know," one of the guys in the middle of the van answered. "Is Kade coming with us?"

"No, he's going to The Flower Shoppe," another commented. "Remember?"

A few people laughed.

"I don't know about this oyster farm thing," the guy in the passenger seat said, "but it's got to be better than working in a flower shop with some old lady."

More laughter broke out as the van began to move.

"If he's not coming with us, what's he doing up so early?" The guy sitting beside Izzy checked his watch. "It's not even 0500 yet."

"Maybe he wanted to practice his arrangements," the guy in the passenger seat joked.

"Make a wreath for his hair," another piped in, inciting more laughter.

The van bumped over a pothole and Izzy looked out the window, tuning them out. There was a time when she would have jumped in, dishing it out with the best of them. But she didn't have it in her anymore. She couldn't remember the last time she'd joked around with a group of guys, let alone laughed.

"You ever eaten an oyster?" one of the guys in the middle asked the guy beside him, after they'd finished ragging on Kade.

"Naw, those things are nasty. You?"

"Yeah, one of my buddies ate, like, a hundred in a contest once. He threw up afterwards."

A few people laughed.

"Aren't they supposed to be some kind of aphrodisiac?" another guy asked.

"Only if you eat them raw," the guy in the passenger seat shot back.

More people laughed, provoking a fresh string of jokes and comments, each rowdier and raunchier than the last.

The guy in front of Izzy twisted around to face her. "You ever eaten an oyster, Izzy?"

Izzy watched a fox streak through the grasses, its bushy red tail betraying its position until it ducked into a gap between two fallen trees, disappearing completely. "I can't remember," she lied.

RYAN WATCHED the van turn up the driveway. Beside him, his father, Cooper "Coop" Callahan, leaned against the shed, smoking a cigarette. "You know you're nuts for trying to pull this off."

"Thanks for the vote of confidence, Dad."

Coop took another drag. "I can keep selling to Dusty. I'm fine with the way things are."

"Well, I'm not," Ryan said. "And you shouldn't be either."

Ryan couldn't help the spark of frustration he felt toward his father. Was it wrong to want more, to believe in more? Oyster farming was still relatively new in Maryland, but he had watched it take off in other states—California, Washington, Massachusetts, Rhode Island. Even Virginia, their neighbor to the south, was claiming a healthy stake in the aquaculture industry. He'd been studying the business models of the most successful farms for over a year now and he was hungry to follow in their footsteps.

If they could pull this off, it would mean more jobs for the islanders, a revival of the waterman culture that was fading away, and reestablishing a precious natural resource that had been devastated from decades of overfishing.

Coop dropped his cigarette on the ground, crushed it with his boot, and left it there. Ryan bent down, picked it up, and handed it back to his father. He pointed to the aluminum can on the ground marked, "butts."

His father rolled his eyes and tossed his cigarette into the can. "You should be working on a research paper to present at some fancy conference to a bunch of other smart people like you—not hanging out here with me."

Ryan ignored him. It was the same argument they always had. When Ryan had quit his position at the lab in Baltimore, his father had accused him of throwing away his future. But all Ryan had ever wanted was to move back here and work on the water again. The higher he got in academia, the more papers there were to write, the more pressure there was to publish, and the more conferences there were to attend. He didn't want to work in a lab and analyze data on a computer screen for the rest of his life.

When he'd purchased this property to expand his father's bare-bones operation six months ago, along with a bunch of used equipment from another farmer whose operation had folded, he'd known it was a risk. Most oyster farms failed within a few years. It took a considerable amount of upfront capital, the stamina to endure long hours working outside in extreme temperatures, and the stomach to roll with the mistakes you would inevitably make by growing a crop in an environment that was constantly changing.

But most farms didn't have what he had. His father's resistance to change might drive him crazy, but he was a hell of a waterman. He knew how to run a boat, how to manage a crew, how to navigate these waters, and how to protect the crop that was down there. And, despite what he said, he cared about what he did.

"Go easy on the two guys going out with you today," Ryan said, as the van pulled to a stop in front of the shed. "It's their first day and neither of them have much boating experience."

"Better be fast learners," Coop said.

Ryan gave his father a sideways look.

"I'll go easy on 'em." Coop offered his son a craggy smile. "As long as they pull their weight."

Ryan shook his head. His father wasn't going to go easy on any of these veterans. He would push them, push them hard, and probably forget to thank them for it at the end of the day. But for some reason they would show up the next day, determined to impress the leathery old man of few words who led by example. He knew, because he'd grown up desperately trying to do the same thing.

Watching the veterans file out of the van, he hoped he'd chosen the right two guys to go out on the boat. He'd given a lot of thought to each person and which job they would be taking on. He'd poured over every application and consulted his decisions with Will and Colin. He was fairly certain he'd made the right decision about everyone.

Everyone except for one.

Izzy was the last to get out of the van. Something inside him twisted at the sight of her. Even in an oversized T-shirt and running shorts, she was stunning. Her golden eyes were guarded, wary, as they swept over the property.

He knew she didn't want to be here. It wasn't just that she didn't want to work on the farm—and he still didn't know what that was about—she was the only one who hadn't applied to this program. The only reason she was here was because she'd gotten into some trouble with the law recently, and the judge who'd presided over her sentencing hearing had granted her probation in exchange for her enrollment in this program.

Ryan had some misgivings about the arrangement, but Izzy's

lawyers must have made a pretty compelling argument on her behalf for Colin and Will to pass over hundreds of other applications to let her in.

He hoped his friends knew what they were doing. He had to trust that they did. Seven of the eleven veterans in this program were working for him, which meant that this farm and his nonprofit were the backbone of the employment structure. He might not know how to help these veterans heal, but he did know how to get people excited about working on the Bay. His friends were counting on him. His father was counting on him. He wasn't going to let them down.

He walked out and smiled. "Welcome to Pearl Cove Oysters."

THREE

*T*his doesn't look like any kind of farm I've ever been to," one of the guys said, looking around.

No, Izzy thought, it didn't. A rustic shed with faded, chipping green paint led to a wooden pier, where a few workboats were tied to the pilings. Another larger structure—white with a red tin roof—lay to the left. Between the two structures was a smattering of picnic tables, and beyond them, one of the most beautiful views she'd ever seen.

"Most of the actual farming takes place out on the water," Ryan explained. "We lease acreage from the state, where our oysters grow in cages that sit on the bottom. We pull the cages up periodically to wash and re-sort the oysters until they're big enough to sell. Harvest starts at daybreak, as soon as the sun crests the horizon." He glanced over his shoulder at the sky, where the faintest hint of gold was beginning to melt through the blue. "Matt and Wesley, the two of you will be going out on the boat with my father. Dad?"

The crusty, middle-aged man leaning against the shed eyed the two men who stepped forward. He looked them each up and down, then nodded toward the bed of a beat-up Ford truck parked a few yards away. "Find a pair of boots and bibs that fit, and meet me on the dock." Without another word, he turned and left.

The two men scrambled over to the truck, as if they'd been given an order by a four–star general.

"My father's not one for small talk," Ryan explained. "Most people call him Coop. He'll answer to that, or Cooper, or Captain. Just don't ask him too many questions until he's finished his second cup of coffee or he might push you over the side of the boat and say it was an accident."

Izzy watched Matt and Wesley each grab what looked to be a pair of orange rubber overalls from the bed of the truck, pull them on over their clothes, and awkwardly adjust the stretchy shoulder straps until they were snug.

She wished she were going out on the boat. She didn't want to talk. She didn't want to ask any questions. She just wanted to put her head down, do her work, and get through the rest of the week without drawing any more attention to herself.

"Everyone will get a chance to go out on the water at some point," Ryan said, as if reading her thoughts, "but Matt and Wesley will be the main boat crew."

The two men traded their sneakers for a pair of rubber boots and then disappeared into the shed, leaving the remaining five vets in the driveway.

"I thought you were only supposed to eat oysters in the fall and winter," one of the guys said.

"That's true for wild oysters," Ryan said. "Wild oysters spawn when the water temperature warms and they use up most of their energy to reproduce, so they're stringy and not very tasty in the spring and summer. Most farmed oysters are selectively bred to have an extra set of chromosomes, which makes them infertile. Since they don't have to waste any energy on reproduction, they grow faster than wild oysters and you can eat them all year round."

"Which means you can *sell* them all year round," the guy standing beside Izzy said.

"That's right," Ryan said, meeting the eyes of the man in his late-twenties with two prosthetic legs who'd just spoken. "Unfortunately, right now, we only have one client—another oyster farmer who runs a much bigger operation a few miles south of here. He's been buying our oysters and passing them off as his own when he can't meet the demands of his orders. But I'm hoping that you, Paul, can help us change that."

Paul looked back at him, surprised.

"My father's been"—he paused, searching for the right word—"resistant to the idea of building a brand and marketing himself. But he says he'll go along with it as long as he doesn't have to do any of the actual self-promotion. I understand that you studied marketing in college."

"That's right," Paul said slowly.

"And you have some experience in website and graphic design?"

He nodded.

"You're familiar with all the latest social media platforms and how to use them?"

"Of course."

"Good. We'll talk more later, but you're head of marketing."

Paul blinked. "Seriously?"

Ryan nodded.

"Wow." Paul grinned. "Cool."

Ryan turned to face the rest of the group. "We'll head out to the dock in a few minutes, but just to give you a sense of what you're looking at now..." He patted the side of the shed behind him. "Most of the cleaning, sorting, bagging and processing of the oysters gets done in here. Over there," he said, pointing toward the larger, newer structure on the other side of the picnic tables, "is the environmental center where Hailey and Ethan will be working."

Hailey and Ethan nodded, eyeing the building with interest.

"And behind us," Ryan finished, pointing across the yard, "is the office."

Everyone turned, taking in the simple but inviting two-story house with a screened-in porch that hugged a thin grove of pine trees.

"The inside could use a paint job and we don't have much furniture, but there's a full-sized kitchen, two bathrooms, Wi-Fi, and the best part—it's air conditioned."

"Beats a cubicle in a city," a redheaded man who looked to be in his early-thirties commented.

Ryan smiled. "I'm glad you think so, Jeff." He waited until the man had turned around to face him. "As our operations manager, you'll be spending most of your time in there."

Jeff's eyebrows shot up. "Operations manager?"

Ryan nodded. "Organization is not my strong suit—or my father's. I'm counting on you to set up a system for every aspect of how this farm functions. I need you to analyze the day-to-day operations, from the biggest picture to the smallest detail. Anything you see that's not operating efficiently, fix it. I've already set up a meeting for you with our bookkeeper for this afternoon. I want you to sit down with her and take a good, hard look at our finances. See what we're spending our money on and how we can better manage our resources."

Jeff puffed out his chest. "I know how to get things in order."

"That's what I heard," Ryan said, smiling. "You and Paul each have an office on the first floor. There's not much in either of them yet but a desk and a laptop, but what we lack in furniture, we make up for with the view."

Nodding for everyone to follow him into the shed, he led

them straight through a dark, mostly empty room, which housed a large metal machine in the shape of a cylinder with holes in it that emptied onto a conveyor belt, a rudimentary washing system with hoses that hung down from the ceiling, and two large white boards on the walls filled with markings and numbers that looked like some kind of complex tracking system.

Izzy was the last to step out of the shed and onto the dock. The sun had crested the horizon, revealing a clear, cloudless blue sky. The larger workboat holding the three men had already pulled away and was cutting a slow path toward the marshy shoreline across the channel.

There were a few other workboats out on the water, filled with cages she imagined would be used to catch different kinds of seafood. She wondered if the men behind the wheels all looked like Ryan's father—weathered and salt-crusted, their faces lined and leathery from decades of working in the sun.

Or if any of them looked like Ryan.

Ryan was definitely not leathery.

Tucking that observation away, because she didn't want to think about her boss in that way—she didn't want to think about any man in that way ever again—she trailed after the others to where two aboveground troughs sat at the edge of the pier. Both were hooked up to a sophisticated system of PVC piping, and she could hear the sound of running water as she made her way closer. It looked like some kind of elaborate science experiment.

"As I mentioned last night, we purchase our oysters as seeds from a hatchery," Ryan said, reaching into one of the troughs and scooping up a handful of creatures that were barely the size of a pinky nail. "These are our newest crop of baby oysters."

Hailey leaned closer, her eyes widening. "Those are oysters?"

Ryan nodded. "Go ahead. You can touch them."

Hailey reached in hesitantly, pulled out a handful of baby oysters, and marveled at how small they were in her palm.

"Oysters are filter feeders," Ryan explained. "They purify the water while they're eating it, filtering out any pollutants or harmful nutrients from their food source—which is mostly algae and phytoplankton—before releasing it back out into the Bay. It's estimated that a single adult oyster can filter about fifty gallons of water a day."

"Fifty gallons?" Hailey echoed, gazing down at the specks on her fingers in awe.

Ryan nodded. "The Chesapeake Bay used to be filled with so many oysters that they could filter the entire body of water in a matter of days. Now, these waters are so polluted and the oyster population is so depleted, it would take over a year to complete that process."

Izzy looked over his shoulder, at the tilted pilings at the end of the pier where several cormorants and seagulls were drying their wings. Beyond them, there was nothing but open water, the glittering sunlit surface stretching on for miles. It was hard to believe there could be anything dirty or damaged about this place. But she should know, better than anyone, that surfaces could lie. The truth was always a few layers deeper, hidden from sight.

"Every oyster we put into the Bay is purifying it of toxins, making the water cleaner and safer for fish, crabs, and other underwater life." Ryan set the handful of baby oysters back into the trough. "Once they go out to the lease, we can't track their growth and check for signs of mortality like we can when they're in the nursery, which is why caring for the baby oysters is one of the most important jobs at the farm."

Walking across the pier to a small wooden box, he switched off the electricity, cutting off the flow of water to the tanks. "Izzy, could you hand me that hose?" He nodded toward the hose lying by her feet.

She picked it up and handed it to him.

Walking over to the tank, Ryan opened a valve, letting the water drain out. "We drain and clean the tanks twice a day," he explained, spraying at the brown and green gunk congealed to the inside walls. "They can take a pretty heavy blast, just don't spray so hard that the oysters bounce out of the buckets. We don't want to lose any of them."

He released the nozzle and looked up at her. "Think you've got the hang of it?"

Izzy stared back at him. *Got the hang of what...how to use a hose?*

"You'll be spending most of the summer helping me with the nursery," Ryan clarified. "Could you finish up while I get everyone else settled into their jobs?"

Izzy looked down at the brown gunk congealed to the oysters as a sinking feeling formed in the pit of her stomach. "What exactly is this that I'm cleaning?"

"Well, like I said, oysters are filter feeders, so they have to let out what they filter in."

"So...it's crap."

"Yes," he admitted, giving her another one of those sheepish smiles. "Basically."

Fantastic, she thought. Paul got to be the head of marketing. Jeff got to be the operations manager. Hailey and Ethan got to play around in the environmental center, because, really, how much work could that be? And she got to spend her time washing oyster poop out of a tank.

Reaching for the hose, she gritted her teeth. "There's nothing I'd rather be doing."

TWENTY MINUTES LATER, Ryan walked back out to the pier to

check on Izzy. He found her looping the hose around one of the pilings. "All finished?"

She glanced up and nodded.

He walked over to the tanks and inspected her work. He made a few minor adjustments to some of the pipes, then motioned for her to come closer. Unscrewing the L-shaped portion of one of the PVC pipes, he held it up so she could see the small screen still filled with algae. "Next time, take these off and give the screens a really good scrub."

"Okay."

Ryan waited for her to ask a question or make a comment about the process, but she just stood there, staring back at him, as if she were awaiting her next order. He felt a prick of disappointment. He hadn't expected her to jump for joy at the task of cleaning the upwellers, but most people thought the baby oysters were pretty cool. He'd given her one of the most interesting jobs at the farm and she didn't seem to care at all.

He wasn't used to people not caring.

Fitting the pipe back into place, he tried not to let it bother him. Logically, he knew he wouldn't be able to convert every new employee into a glorified oyster nerd, but he'd hoped they'd be able to get into it, at least a little bit.

Maybe he just needed to give her some time.

"Ready to see the next step in the process?" he asked, doing his best to stay upbeat.

"Sure," she said, without an ounce of enthusiasm.

He nodded for her to follow him to the end of the pier, where the rest of the oysters were growing in a larger upwelling system suspended beneath a floating dock. The tide was still relatively low and the floating dock was a few feet below the pier. He stepped down and turned, offering her a hand. She ignored it, jumping down on her own, and immediately took a step in the opposite direction.

Ryan frowned, studying her across the small platform. He couldn't remember the last time he'd had this effect on a woman. Maybe he'd gotten a little spoiled over the years, but most women had a tendency to gravitate *toward* him, rather than away.

Was it something about him, specifically, that turned her off? Or was it men in general?

Lifting the wooden cover to expose the first row of submerged buckets, he gave her a quick run down of the system. "This is basically a larger version of what's happening in the tanks on the pier. We're still pumping water up, through the oysters, and back out again, but the force of the tide and the current increases the pressure of the water."

He knelt down and pulled out a handful of oysters that were twice the size of the ones in the tanks on the pier. "It's all about maximizing the rate of water flow, so they grow as fast as possible. The sooner we can get them to about a half inch in size, the sooner we can get them out to the lease."

Izzy nodded, and Ryan dropped the oysters back into the water.

"Could you hand me those hooks?" he asked, pointing to the two metal hooks he'd set on the end of the pier.

She handed them over.

He showed her how to feed each hook through the sides of the bucket, then handed one to her. "We're going to pull it up together," he said. "It'll be heavy. Are you ready?"

She nodded.

Water poured out of the screen in the bottom as they muscled it up out of the silo and set it down on a flat portion of the dock. Impressed with her ability to keep the heavy container steady on her first try, he asked if she could handle a few more. She nodded, and they hauled up the rest.

"Nice job," he said, when they'd finished.

She said nothing, and didn't offer him even a hint of a smile.

This was supposed to be fun, Ryan thought. It was supposed to be interesting. Yes, it was hard, physical, repetitive work, but they were doing something important. They were doing something that mattered. And they were doing it outside.

At least they weren't stuck in an office building, crunching data and drafting research papers that only a handful of academics would ever read.

Setting the hooks on the pier, he reached for the hose and dragged it over to the row of buckets. "We don't have to scrub these every day like we do with the ones on the pier, but we should give them a good rinse every time we pull them up to sort them."

He nodded toward the edge of the dock where he'd stacked a few empty bins, a plastic scooper, and a piece of mesh screen. "It's a pretty low-tech system. You set the screen on top of one of the bins, scoop the oysters over the screen, and shake the screen so the smaller ones fall through. The bigger ones can go into a new bucket so they have more room to grow. The smaller ones that fall through can go back into the original bucket."

"Got it," she said, grabbing the bucket he'd just washed and dragging it over to the edge of the dock. She set up a grading station efficiently, as if she'd done it a hundred times, and without any questions, got to work.

Trying, again, not to let it bother him, Ryan started to spray down the next bucket. He was just here to offer her a distraction, he reminded himself. He was supposed to give her something to do with her hands and keep her busy. Every hour of work that she gave him—that any of these veterans gave him—brought him one step closer to achieving his goal. That was all that mattered. That was all he should be focusing on right now.

He finished washing the buckets and knelt down, picking out a few oysters that were showing signs of distress. But he kept a close eye on Izzy. And, while she appeared to be going through the paces, he couldn't help noticing that, every few minutes, she would pause and glance down at her watch.

He could tell she was distracted, that she wasn't really focused on the task. If she couldn't focus one hundred percent of her attention on this, he'd have to give her a different job. The nursery job was too important.

He sat back on his heels. "I feel like you're not that into this."

She stopped working and looked at him. "Am I doing something wrong?"

"No," he said. "I just feel like you're not all here, like you're not really into it."

"Do I need to be *into* it?" she asked. "Can't I just do the job?"

"I think it's important that you care. That you understand why we're doing this."

Izzy set the screen down on the bin. The sun illuminated her face, turning her eyes an even lighter, more exotic shade of gold. "Okay," she said, with a hint of impatience. "I get that you're trying to save the Bay, but is *this*"—she gestured to the oysters —"really going to make that big of a difference?"

"Yes," Ryan said. "Over time, it will make a very big difference. Change isn't going to happen overnight. But we have to start somewhere. Introducing sustainable ways of harvesting seafood is a step in the right direction. Teaching people how to take better care of the Bay through our nonprofit is another."

"What people?" Izzy asked, looking around. "We're in the middle of nowhere. Who's even going to come here?"

"Lots of people come here," Ryan said, his brows drawing together. "They come on the weekends to get away from the city. They come in the summer to eat crabs and go fishing. They come for the wildlife, for the scenery. A lot of people are interested in what's going on with the Bay right now. They want to know how they can help, so that they, and their children, can continue to enjoy it year after year."

Izzy looked out at the water, her gaze tracking the path of an osprey. "You really think people care that much?"

"Yes, I do," Ryan said. "And if they don't, it's only because they don't know any better."

Izzy picked the screen up, scooped another batch of oysters over it, and went back to ignoring him.

"Look," he said, trying a different approach. "Most of the people who live on this island are watermen. The Bay is their primary source of income. Without a healthy, functioning ecosystem, they won't be able to make a living off these waters anymore. This island won't be able to survive."

She said nothing, gave him no reaction at all.

Ryan took a deep breath. "I don't think you're grasping how dire this situation is."

"Probably not."

"Over the past ten years, every major species of fish in these waters has experienced a rapid decline," Ryan said. "The wildlife that depend on those fish for food—the animals that live in these marshes and the birds that fly through here on their annual migrations—are suffering because they can't find enough to eat. There are dead zones in the Bay now, pockets of water with little to no oxygen, where the fish literally suffocate when they swim through them. We need to find a way to filter these waters and clean them. We can't just keep doing things the way we've been doing them. We have to find another way to make this work."

Izzy looked out at the water again, and was quiet for so long, he thought she must finally be absorbing what he'd said. But when she looked back at him, her eyes were completely devoid of emotion. "Sounds like a lost cause to me."

Ryan stared back at her. "You can't be serious."

"I'm dead serious," she said, reaching for an empty bin, and sliding the one that was full away from her. "Not everything—or everyone—can be saved."

The dock continued to rock gently beneath them, but the feeling of buoyancy, the lightness he usually felt while working on the water, never came. Were they still talking about oysters...or her?

If they were talking about her, then they had a much bigger problem on their hands.

A man cleared his throat from the end of the pier and Ryan glanced up. He spotted Paul, the guy he'd put in charge of marketing.

"Am I interrupting something?" Paul asked, looking back and forth between them.

"No," Ryan said. He stood and walked over to the pier and hiked himself up on the wooden planks.

Paul knelt down beside him and opened the laptop he was carrying. "Is this your website?"

Ryan glanced at the screen. "Yes."

"It sucks, man."

Ryan blew out a breath. "Thanks."

Paul clicked on a few of the tabs. "Who designed it?"

"I did," Ryan said wearily.

Paul looked back at him, a pained expression on his face. "It really sucks, man."

"Well, why don't you change it?" Ryan suggested.

"Yeah?"

"Yeah."

"I'm going to need some pictures," Paul said.

"There might be some on the hard drive," Ryan said, then glanced over his shoulder at where his father and the two veterans in the workboat were hauling cages out of the water. "Or you could take one of the kayaks out and get some shots of the guys working now."

"Really?"

"Really."

Paul grinned and stood up. "Awesome."

"Take a life jacket," Ryan called after him.

Paul gave him a thumbs up before ducking into the shed.

Ryan looked at Izzy. Why couldn't it be that easy with her? Why couldn't he figure out what to say to get through to her? Pushing to his feet, he wiped his wet hands on the front of his pants. "I'm going to check on Ethan and Hailey. I'll be back in a few minutes to help you put the rest of the buckets in the water."

"I'll be here," she said, without even bothering to look up.

Izzy waited for Ryan to disappear into the environmental center, then she sat back on her heels and let out a breath. She wished she could believe him. She wished she could believe that by spending the next three months scrubbing down shellfish, she could actually make a difference.

There was a part of her—a small part, deep down—that admired his passion and idealism. And there was a time, not too long ago, when she would have thrown her whole heart into helping him bring this vision to life. But she wasn't that person anymore.

She picked the screen up again and started to shake it, focusing on the sound of the tiny bivalves dropping into the bucket. Until her mind was completely empty. Until she felt nothing again.

As long as she felt nothing, as long as she stayed completely detached, no one could hurt her.

Three hours later, when the workboat came in, she was too hot to think about anything but getting a drink of water and a few minutes to cool off in the shade anyway. She joined the others—Jeff, Paul, Ethan, and Hailey—under the awning that covered a small portion of the dock where it connected to the shed, while Ryan helped his father secure the lines to the pier.

The guys who'd been on the boat were dirty, sweaty, and sunburned, but they were smiling as they followed Ryan's father into the shed to wash and bag the oysters they'd harvested. Ryan grabbed a half dozen from one of the baskets and motioned for everyone else to follow him over to the picnic area. "Come on," he said. "I want you all to try one."

They gathered around one of the tables, watching him slip the top of a knife into a groove in the shell and pry it open. He handed the first one to Paul.

Paul looked down at it warily. "People actually eat these things raw?"

Ethan glanced over his shoulder and made a face. "They look like snot."

"Great. Thanks," Hailey said, elbowing him in the ribs. "Now there's no way I can eat one."

"Aren't you supposed to put cocktail sauce or lemon juice on them...or something?" Ethan asked, hesitating when Ryan handed him one.

"Try one without first," Ryan urged.

There were a few more murmured protests, but eventually, Paul, Ethan, and Hailey slurped theirs down.

Ryan grinned. "What do you think?"

"Not bad," Hailey said, surprised. "I thought they would be gross, but they taste really clean, really fresh."

"Good," Ryan said, smiling as he took her shell back and tossed it in a small bucket for recycling. "That's what I like to hear."

"I think they taste kind of sweet," Paul said.

Ryan nodded. "What else?"

"I don't know," Paul looked down at the empty shell in his hand. "Maybe kind of...buttery?"

Ethan washed his down with a long drink of water, making it clear that he wasn't as thrilled with the prospect of becoming an oyster connoisseur as the other two. "I think they taste as gross as they look."

Ryan laughed. "It's an acquired taste for some people. You'll come around."

He shucked two more, handed one to Jeff, and one to Izzy. When she reached for hers, their fingers brushed and she felt that same calm, peaceful feeling flow through her as she had the night before, when he'd offered her his hand in the doorway at the inn.

She held his gaze for a few beats before breaking the contact and glancing down at the shell. She paused, surprised, because it looked nothing like the stringy, grayish-brown oysters that usually came from this region, which were more fit for stews and frying. This one was plump and fully formed with pale ivory-colored flesh, resting in a deep round-cupped shell—pretty enough to deserve a moment of respect.

She lifted it slowly to her lips, inhaled the earthy scent of the Bay, and let it slide into her mouth. The texture was perfect—soft and silky, but with enough meat to sink her teeth into. The taste was mildly salty, buttery, and sweet. The fact that it had been pulled out of the water a few hundred feet from where she stood made her feel suddenly energized, awake, alive.

She thought about the elaborate system of pumps, tanks, and piping, how much effort went into caring for the baby oysters each day, how much time it took, even after they moved out to the lease, for them to grow to full size, and how hard the men on the boat had worked—and were still working—to get them ready to ship out.

She looked at Ryan again, thinking about what he'd said earlier, that all he was trying to do was introduce a new method of harvesting a dying resource that blended modern science with the centuries-old traditions of this island. She felt a faint stirring, deep inside her, as another memory fought to resurface. There was a time when she had wanted to do something similar. Her dream had been to bring the traditional recipes of her grandmother's village in Mexico to Baltimore, but with a fresh, innovative twist all her own.

The dream reformed, slowly taking shape inside her. She grasped onto a thread of it, wanting, needing, just for a moment, to remember who she had been before—a woman who'd been filled with joy, with passion, with a dream. A woman who'd known, without a shred of doubt, what she'd wanted. A woman who'd been willing to do anything to succeed.

"So?" Ryan asked, still smiling from everyone else's reactions. "What do you think?"

"It's an oyster," she said, tossing the shell into the bucket for recycling and stuffing the dream back down, where it belonged. "They all taste the same."

FOUR

*H*ey," Grace Callahan said, walking up the steps to Ryan's house later that afternoon.

Ryan glanced up from a report he'd been reading about a local oyster restoration project, surprised to see that his twin sister was still on the island. "I thought you were heading back to D.C. today."

"I was." Grace paused to pet Zoey, who thumped her tail appreciatively against the floorboards. "I was halfway to the bridge when I got a call from Senator Crawford's office. He finally agreed to let me interview him about his decision not to run next term."

Ryan raised a brow, impressed. "You've been working on that one for weeks."

"I know," she said, smiling. "He wants me to meet him at his summer house in St. Michaels tomorrow. I figured I'd crash here tonight and head back to the city afterwards."

"Fine by me," Ryan said, always happy to have his twin sister nearby. Born only a few minutes apart, they were about as close as two siblings could be.

"Do you have any more of those in the fridge?" she asked, pointing to the cold beer in his hand.

He nodded. "Help yourself."

Grace walked inside, grabbed a beer, and came out again, settling into the wooden rocking chair beside him. Propping her feet up on the porch rail, as comfortable here as she was in her own apartment in Capitol Hill, she twisted the cap off her bottle. "So...how was your first day?"

Closing the report he'd been reading, Ryan shut his laptop and set it on the table between them. "Rough."

"What do you mean?" she asked, surprised. "What happened?"

"I think I bit off more than I can chew."

"I doubt that," she said. "Did Dad say something?"

"No. Dad was fine."

Grace studied her brother more closely, concern knitting her brows. "Are you sure?"

"Yes," Ryan said, lifting his hand to wave to a neighbor who was just getting home from work. "You should have seen the two guys I sent out on the boat with him today. They're already half in love with him."

"Of course they are," Grace said, rolling her eyes. "And I bet he worked them to death, too."

Ryan nodded. "They're going to be in so much pain tonight."

Grace shook her head, because they both knew that their father's style of motivation, though frustrating, netted impressive results. As a single father, Coop Callahan had raised two extremely successful children—both of whom would have happily traded every bit of that success for even an ounce of the unconditional love and affection that other children got from their parents. "If it wasn't Dad, then who was it?"

Ryan leaned back in his chair. "Remember that veteran I was telling you about—the one who's here on probation?"

Grace nodded.

"I don't think she's too happy about the situation."

"What do you mean?" Grace asked.

"I was at the inn when she drove up last night," Ryan said. "She only brought one bag, like she was planning to stay for a week, not three months. She barely said two words to any of the other veterans and she made it clear today that she only sees this program as some kind of penance she has to pay to stay out of jail, not an opportunity to get her life back on track."

"Huh," Grace said.

"I didn't have a chance to study her résumé like I did with the others, so I wasn't sure which job to give her. I decided to put her in the nursery with me, thinking I could keep an eye on her. I mean, I'm all over the place, making sure everyone's settling in and explaining how everything works, but it's like she's just...checked out. Like she doesn't care about anything anymore."

"Do you know what she was arrested for?"

"Assault."

Grace's brows shot up. "Assault?"

"Apparently, she shot someone."

"Who?"

"I don't know," Ryan said. "Colin was pretty vague on the details."

"Want me to find out?"

It was a tempting offer, Ryan thought. If anyone could dig up the truth about someone, it was his sister. As one of the top political reporters for *The Washington Tribune*, Grace had access to resources that went way beyond a simple Google search. But he wasn't sure he was ready to make Izzy the target of one of his sister's investigations. At least, not yet, anyway. "No," he said, "but if I change my mind, I'll let you know."

Grace studied the label of her beer. "I guess if Colin and Will let her into the program, they must have thought she needed to be here. Maybe give her some time."

Ryan nodded, because he'd been trying to tell himself the same thing all day. But everyone else seemed to recognize how lucky they were to be here. Everyone else seemed eager to make the best of the experience. He had kept a close eye on Izzy throughout the rest of the day and he was really concerned.

She had shown no interest in the business. She had shown no interest in making friends. The few people who'd tried to strike up a conversation with her had been shut down instantly. And yet, every so often, he'd get a glimpse of something, like a spark, deep in her eyes, that wanted to come out, but she was too afraid to let it. "She's got these eyes, Grace. I've never seen anything like them. It's like...they've seen so much."

"I bet most of these veterans have seen things you and I could never dream of," Grace said.

"Yeah, but it seems different with her," Ryan said. "With the other vets, you can see a kind of resignation. There's a sadness in their eyes, and you can tell they've experienced things that will haunt them forever, but with Izzy, it's like whatever happened just happened yesterday. Like she hasn't even begun to process it yet."

"Maybe she hasn't."

"But most of our soldiers pulled out of Iraq and Afghanistan years ago," Ryan said, still trying to make sense of it. "If whatever's bothering her is connected to something that happened overseas, shouldn't she have at least developed some coping mechanisms by now?"

"I think PTSD can manifest in a lot of different ways. If it's left untreated, it can only get worse," Grace said. "Have you talked to Will or Colin about it?"

"I called Will a little while ago. I'm waiting to hear back."

"Well, there's a social worker who's going to meet with them, right? Whatever it is, she'll be able to help her process it."

"True," Ryan said, but he wasn't entirely convinced. He had a feeling it was going to take a lot more than a few hours of therapy to get Izzy Rivera to open up.

Grace was quiet for a few minutes as they listened to the sounds of the neighborhood—two kids playing catch in the yard next door, the clatter of tools on pavement as a teenager worked on the engine of his truck in his parents' garage, the occasional bark of a dog wanting to go outside.

When she looked back at her brother, and he continued to stare blankly out at the street, she frowned. "Hey," she said, tapping the arm of his chair. "Haven't you got enough on your plate without taking on somebody else's problems?"

"Yes," Ryan admitted.

"Then don't," she warned. "You need to be able to separate yourself from these people emotionally if you're going to be working alongside them for the next three months. I know you've been working like crazy trying to get everything ready for the launch of this program. When was the last time you took a day off?"

"It's been a while."

"Why don't you come up to D.C. on Saturday? We could go out, check out the new bar that just opened down the street from my place. I've got a few single friends I could introduce you to." She wiggled her brows.

He smiled, but shook his head. "I don't think so."

"Come on," she urged. "You can't keep hiding out down here and nursing a broken heart forever. It's been over six months since you and Julia split up. You need to get out there, start dating again."

Absently, Ryan reached down to scratch Zoey behind the ears. He knew it was pointless to argue with his sister, because she couldn't possibly understand. The truth was, he hadn't been in love with Julia. He'd enjoyed her company, but *he* was the one who'd broken things off.

Like he always did when things got too serious.

He was starting to wonder if he was capable of opening his heart to a woman in that way. He wasn't sure why he couldn't take that next step with anyone. Maybe he'd just never met anyone he'd thought was worth the risk.

At the sound of a screen door opening and closing, he glanced up. Across the street, his neighbor, Tyler Gannon, walked out of his house carrying a bag of charcoal. Tyler emptied the contents into the grill and lit the coals, before lifting his hand in a friendly wave and wandering back inside to join his wife and daughter.

All around the neighborhood, people were doing the same thing—prepping for dinner, talking about their days, chasing their kids around the yard. He was the only person on this street who wasn't married, who wasn't even in a relationship.

It was hard to believe he was still single at thirty-three when all he'd ever wanted was to settle down with a wife and a couple of kids.

But maybe some people weren't meant to have that life.

Maybe some people were destined to be alone.

As if sensing his depressing mood, Zoey rolled over and stretched all four paws up into the air. Ryan smiled and rubbed her belly with his foot until her tongue lolled out of the side of her mouth. This was all he needed, he reminded himself. He had his dog. He had his friends. He had this island. And whenever he got really lonely, he could always distract himself with the farm and the environmental center.

"Fine," Grace said. "I won't bug you about your love life, but will you promise me something?"

"What?"

"That you won't turn into Dad."

"I'm not going to turn into Dad." Ryan laughed, clinking the neck of his bottle against hers to seal the deal. But he couldn't help wondering, as he took a long swallow, if that wasn't exactly what he was doing.

BY THE TIME Izzy stepped out of the shower, it was close to 1800 hours. She'd managed to scrub most of the oyster muck out of her hair, but her skin still carried a faint scent of the briny filter feeders. It was going to take more than a bar of soap to wash away the smell that had permeated every inch of her body throughout the past twelve hours.

Picking up the cell phone that was lying on her bed, she saw that she had one missed call. It was her probation officer, checking in to see how the first day had gone. Fantastic, she thought, tossing the phone back onto the bed. She couldn't wait to tell her all about it.

Right now, she had more important things to do.

Slipping her laptop out of her pack, she walked over to the desk beneath the window and sat down. She clicked a few buttons to bring up the spreadsheet of over two hundred female soldiers whose names she could recite in her sleep. Scanning the list on the left, she found the row where she'd left off two nights before, and copied the next name over to Google, preparing to spend the next few hours learning everything she could about Private First Class Jennifer Sanders.

She had been tracking the movements of every woman who'd served under Colonel Bradley Welker for over four months now. So far, she hadn't found anything that would raise a red flag. Most of the women were still serving, some had been honorably discharged, a few had gone into officer training programs. They all seemed to be living normal, healthy lives. She hadn't noticed any bizarre, erratic behavior, or anyone else suddenly dropping off the face of the earth.

But she wouldn't stop looking. Not until she knew, for sure, that what had happened to her hadn't happened to anyone else. She needed to know that her silence wasn't putting other female soldiers at risk.

"Yo," Kade said, opening the door to her room without knocking.

Izzy snapped her computer shut.

He raised a brow. "Am I interrupting something?"

"No," she said quickly.

"Then what are you doing up here with your door shut?"

"I'm...decompressing."

"Well, come downstairs and decompress with the rest of us."

"No, thanks," she said, turning back around.

"Come on, Izzy," Kade coaxed. "It's not healthy to sit up here all alone. The two guys on dinner duty are just starting to cook. Maybe you could give them a few pointers."

A familiar smell floated up from the kitchen—onions simmering in butter and garlic. She could hear voices downstairs, the sound of knives chopping on cutting boards, the muffled clatter of pots and pans. Remembering how easy it had once been to lose herself in the rhythms and repetitions of preparing a meal, she struggled against a sudden, desperate urge to follow Kade downstairs and ask if there was anything she could do to help. "I don't cook."

"What are you talking about?" he asked, confused. "You said last night that you enlisted in the Army as a cook."

"I don't cook," Izzy repeated. "Not anymore."

There was a long pause. "Have you mentioned that to Colin and Will?"

"No."

"You might want to let them know that before it's your turn in the kitchen."

"Thanks for the tip," she said. "Will you please leave me alone now?"

"Okay," he conceded, "but whenever you're done feeling sorry for yourself, you should come downstairs and join us." He turned to leave, then paused. "Oh, by the way, I checked the board downstairs earlier. We're on dish duty tonight."

"I know."

"Unless, you've given up doing dishes, too...?"

She twisted around. "Seriously?"

"Hey." He held up his hands, grinned. "It was a valid question."

He walked away laughing, and she noticed that he left her door open again, the same way he had that morning.

"Hey, Rosie," she heard one of the guys downstairs say when Kade made it to the kitchen. "How was your first day at The Flower Shoppe?"

"It was peachy," he said dryly. "Thanks for asking."

"Did you bring any flowers home?" the same guy asked. "Want to make an arrangement for the dinner table?"

A few people laughed before another guy piped in, "Do you have any spare ribbons? Want us to tie one in your hair?"

"Oh, right," the first guy said. "You don't have any hair."

Kade laughed good-naturedly. "I'd rather be bald and working at a flower shop than stink like you three do. What'd you do at the oyster farm all day, roll around in the mud?"

"Hey," the second guy said defensively, "the farm's actually pretty cool."

"Well, good luck getting a woman to go out with you smelling like that," Kade shot back.

Izzy heard what sounded like chair legs scraping against a wooden floor and imagined Kade settling his big body onto one of the stools. Turning back to face the window, she spotted a circle of people stretching in the yard, getting ready to go out on an afternoon run with Will. One of the men still recovering from shoulder surgery was in the pool with a physical therapist, being coached through a series of exercises. On the other side of the lawn, Hailey was playing fetch with Taylor's yellow lab, Riley.

More laughter drifted up the stairs, and she looked over her shoulder at the open door that led into the hallway. What would happen if she went downstairs, if she pulled out a stool at the bar and just hung out? What would happen if she went outside and talked to Hailey, who had tried at least a dozen times to strike up a conversation with her today?

As soon as the questions popped into her mind, she felt foolish for thinking them. Even if there was something to this program, even if there was a small chance that she could benefit from it, she shouldn't be here. She didn't deserve to be here. The only thing that mattered was making sure that the man who'd attacked her wasn't planning to hurt anyone else.

There was no way she could live with herself if that happened.

FIVE

*R*yan knew he should heed his sister's warning, that he should steer clear of Izzy before he got tangled up in a mess he had no business getting involved in, but he couldn't seem to stay away. He felt drawn to her with the same irrational intensity that he'd felt twenty-three years ago, when he'd snuck out his bedroom window, climbed into his father's wooden rowboat, and paddled out to Pearl Cove. There'd been a full moon that night.

The same way there would be tonight.

He looked out at the water, at the calm, quiet surface that had nearly swallowed the underside of the pier. He didn't need a tide chart to tell him that the water level would rise a few more inches before it slowly began to recede, or that, when the moon rose over the Bay tonight, the surface would swell even higher to meet it.

He always knew when the moon was full.

He could feel it in his bones, in his blood, in the familiar restlessness that had plagued him since he was a child. Looking back at Izzy, he watched her gather the materials to assemble the next oyster cage with the same quiet efficiency that she'd devoted to every task he'd given her that week.

She'd barely spoken two words since she'd arrived in the van with the others, but he thought he'd detected a slight shift in her attitude—a tiny crack in the shell she kept so firmly closed around herself. Part of that might have to do with the fact that he'd decided not to push her anymore, not to force her to care about something she clearly had no interest in. Her apathy about the environment still bothered him, but he couldn't shake the feeling that she was wrestling with a bigger demon than anyone realized.

"Hey, Ryan," Paul called out from the office across the lawn. "Do you have a minute?"

"I'll be right there," Ryan said, bending the flat sheet of coated wire mesh over the side of the picnic table to create the first edge of the cage.

"No, stay where you are," Paul said. "We're coming out."

Ryan smoothed his end of the cage toward Izzy's until their hands met in the middle, but he was careful to draw his hand back right before their fingertips brushed. It hadn't taken him long to pick up on the fact that she preferred not to be touched—a preference he found troubling, to say the least.

Helping her flip the sheet around to create the next three sides, he tried not to notice how small and feminine her hands were as they moved along the edge of the cage, how much of the smooth skin of her legs was visible beneath her cotton shorts, or the way her thin T-shirt stretched across her breasts every time she shifted positions.

He'd been trying not to notice those things all week.

When the door to the office opened and Paul and Jeff walked out, Ryan stepped back from the table, grateful for the distraction. "Let's take a break," he suggested to Izzy. "Why don't you grab some water, cool off in the A/C for a while?"

"I'm fine," she said, reaching for the zip ties to begin the process of securing the top of the cage to the sides.

Of course she was, Ryan thought as he wiped at the sweat on his brow. It wasn't even midday yet and the temperatures were already climbing into the nineties. It was going to be a scorcher, but the woman across from him seemed completely immune to the heat. She was a hard worker. No one could deny her that.

Leaving her to it, Ryan followed Paul and Jeff over to a neighboring picnic table.

Paul set his laptop down and opened the screen. "I've been playing around with the website. I came up with a few design options and wanted to run them by you."

"Sounds good," Ryan said, grabbing a bottle of water from one of the coolers and taking a long sip. He was surprised that Paul already had something to show him. He'd assumed this task would take at least two or three weeks.

He sat down in front of the computer and clicked on the first site. Expecting a rough template with lots of blank spaces and placeholders, he was floored to find a fully designed website with an eye-catching home page and multiple tabs, each filled with photographs, headers, text, and a blended color scheme.

Ryan looked up at the man he'd put in charge of marketing only a few days ago. "Wait...you made three of these?"

Paul nodded, watching him apprehensively. Beside him, Jeff was grinning.

Looking down at the screen again, Ryan clicked on the other two sites. "This is incredible, Paul. I don't even know what to say."

"We'll work on refining the language later," Paul said. "This is just about getting a quick first impression on the design. And I want you to be honest—really honest. If you don't like any of them, it's no big deal. I can start over from scratch. I just need to get a sense of what you like and don't like so I know what direction to go in next."

"I highly doubt I'm going to reject all three of these," Ryan said, clicking through the three websites.

The first had a modern, sleek feel that focused more on sustainability and science. He might have leaned toward something like that if he were running the farm alone, but he wanted to make sure his father's heritage as a waterman was respected and the history and culture of the island were firmly woven into the narrative from the very beginning. The second site had a more corporate, streamlined feel, which gave the impression that they'd been in business for years, but it lacked character. The third, Ryan thought as a slow smile spread across his face, was exactly what he'd been looking for.

The entire site was tinted in sepia tones. It had a gritty, nostalgic feel that captured the perfect balance of merging the old with the new. There were candid shots of him and his father working on the water. There were pictures of workboats against marshes, of boots caked in mud, of ropes hardened from years of use, coiled around tilted pilings that had weathered hundreds of storms. Each page drew you further into this world, until you felt like you were there, working alongside the watermen and the farmers, with an emphasis on the quiet beauty and enduring spirit of the Chesapeake Bay.

"This is the one," Ryan said, sitting back.

"Yeah?" Paul asked nervously. "Are you sure?"

"Absolutely," Ryan said. "It's perfect."

"I told you, man," Jeff said, clapping Paul on the back. "I knew he'd love it."

Still not convinced, Paul looked over at the environmental center. "Are Hailey and Ethan around? I want to get their opinions, too."

"I'll go find them," Jeff said, already starting across the lawn.

Ryan noticed that Paul didn't ask Izzy for her opinion, and she didn't offer it. Twisting around, he saw that she was busy working on another cage. "Want to take a look?"

"No, thanks," she said, concentrating all her attention on bending a few ragged edges down with a pair of pliers.

Reminding himself of his decision to let her be, Ryan turned back to the screen and clicked through the tabs on the site, more slowly this time. "Where did you find all these images?"

Paul lowered himself to the seat beside Ryan, carefully threading his two prosthetic legs through the gap between the table and the bench. "I took a few shots yesterday, but most of them were already on the hard drive. They're just placeholders for now until we get some with higher resolution."

"They look pretty good to me," Ryan said.

"Those are amateur shots."

"Amateur shots?"

"There's a difference," Paul said. "Trust me. I want to hire a professional photographer to take a series of shots of you and your father. I've got a few names, but I wanted to make sure we were on the same page before I contacted any of them for a quote."

If the current images were Paul's idea of 'placeholders,' Ryan had a feeling he was going to be blown away by the final product. "If Jeff thinks there's room in the budget to hire a photographer, I say go for it."

"I already ran it by him and he said we should do it."

Of course he had, Ryan thought, smiling to himself. He had a feeling that when these three months were over, he was going to have a hard time letting go of Paul.

"Once we have the website set up, I'll design a logo and then we can build out the rest of your social media sites from there," Paul continued. "We want to have the same feel on everything, give people an idea of what they can expect from this farm, what an experience here would be like."

Ryan could hear the excitement in his voice. He could hear his confidence growing with every word. And he didn't want to take that away from him. But he couldn't help wondering how he'd managed to pull this off so fast. "You didn't work on this after hours, did you?"

Paul lifted a shoulder. "I might have played around with it a little."

A *little,* Ryan thought as realization dawned. He'd probably been up all night. "I don't want you to take work back to the inn with you."

"I bet you take work home with you," Paul said.

"Yeah, but I'm the owner," Ryan said. "That's what I signed up for. I'd rather you get a full night's sleep and be ready for work during the day than stay up late finishing something you could do here."

"I don't really sleep much, so it's no big deal."

A shadow fell across the table as Jeff returned with Hailey and Ethan. The three of them had caught the tail end of their conversation, but none of them seemed fazed by what Paul had said.

Wondering how many others had trouble sleeping at night, Ryan hardly noticed when Hailey sat down beside him and started poking around the site. Her delighted squeals and Ethan's enthusiastic exclamations didn't allow him to worry for long, though. Paul tried to shrug off the attention and act like it was no big deal, but it was. And they all knew it. He'd done an incredible job and Ryan could see from his face that he was proud of his work.

Feeling a small swell of pride of his own, Ryan thought for the first time since everyone had arrived earlier that week that maybe—just maybe—they were actually going to pull this off.

"Here's my only issue with the site," Paul said, turning to face Ryan. "We need to work on your story. We'll play up the environmental center, your Ph.D. in marine biology, and the fact that your father has been working these waters his entire life. But a lot of farms in this area have hired watermen, several have marine biologists on their staff, and some even have a nonprofit component. We need to stand out, do something different. What sets you apart?"

"Isn't that obvious?" Ryan asked, looking around. "You guys."

"No." Paul shook his head. "We're temporary labor. In three months, we'll be gone and you'll get a whole new group of people. We're just here to help you get started, right?"

"Well, yeah," Ryan said. "But..."

"You can't build a brand around temporary workers. You need something permanent, something that people will remember. And it's got to be unique—something that'll set you apart from the other farms in this area angling for a piece of the same pie."

"This isn't really my area of expertise," Ryan admitted.

"I think we should focus more on the island," Paul said, "on the water where we're growing the oysters. Sort of like vintners do with wine. You know, how the grapes pick up the different flavors of the soil where they're grown?"

Ryan nodded. He liked the sound of that.

Paul shifted on the bench and pulled something out of his pocket, setting it on the table between them. "I found this old map on a bookshelf at the inn last night." He unfolded the crinkly, yellowed paper, smoothing it out so Ryan could see.

Ryan recognized the map immediately and felt a touch of uneasiness.

"This is where we are, right?" Paul asked, pointing to the mouth of Pearl Cove on the map.

"That's right," Ryan said slowly.

Paul moved his finger about an inch on the map, to a curve of land about halfway up the cove. "There's a spot here," he said, pointing to the letters faded from years of overuse. "I can barely make out the words, but I think it says, 'Selkie Beach.'" He looked up at Ryan. "Is that right?"

Ryan nodded, careful to keep his voice neutral. "It's just an old beach that eroded away years ago. I think it's completely underwater now."

"What's a...selkie?" Paul asked, sounding out the strange word.

Ryan was vaguely aware of Jeff and Ethan staring down at the map from behind him, as interested in his answer as Paul.

"It's just an old folk tale," Ryan said. "It's a story that some of the watermen tell to the tourists who come to the docks in the summer to buy crabs."

"A folk tale?" Paul asked, lifting a brow. "Like a legend?"

"Yeah," Ryan said, "something like that." Feeling trapped, he considered coming up with something for them to do, just to distract them, but he could tell that everyone was listening to him now, hanging on his every word. *Don't make a big deal of it*, he thought. *If you make a big deal of it, they'll know something's up.*

"Will you tell us?" Hailey asked eagerly.

Ryan looked out at the water, at the high tide swelling against the shoreline, spilling into the marshes, filling in all the spongy gaps in the soil. Across the channel, his father and the other two veterans were hauling up cages in the mouth of Pearl Cove, a location they'd chosen not only for its convenience, but for its mysterious ability to produce abundant seafood harvests for fisherman since the early 1900s.

"The legend," Ryan said, as he watched his father reposition the workboat to catch the angle of the current, "is about a fisherman who lived on this island about a hundred years ago. One night, he went out in his boat and got caught in a terrible storm. The seas were so rough that he got thrown off course and couldn't find his way back in the dark. Suddenly, there was a voice in the wind, a strange voice that he'd never heard before, and something inside him told him to follow it. It led him home, and when he returned, there was a rowboat washed up on the beach. Inside it was a woman."

He looked up at the faces of his new employees, remembering how he had felt the first time he'd heard this story, how he'd been practically obsessed with it as a child. "The woman was wearing only a dark leather cloak and a long strand of pearls around her neck," Ryan continued, sinking into the rhythm of the story that his mother used to tell him before bedtime at night. "Her hair was knotted with seashells and eelgrass. And the fingers on her right hand were webbed. She didn't know her name or where she'd come from, but she had a beautiful lilting Irish accent and she loved to sing."

He waited as Ethan and Jeff came around to sit at the table across from him. "There were some Irish immigrants living here at the time—early settlers to the region. They whispered that she was some kind of seal-woman, an enchantress who could shed her skin and transform into a beautiful woman on land. They warned the fisherman to stay away from her, that she would put a spell on him. They told him that he would be a fool to try to claim her, for she would never belong to him. She belonged to the sea— and only the sea—and one day she would return to it."

Absently, he picked up the map, his fingers tracing the faded letters over the cove. "The fisherman didn't believe them—or didn't want to believe them. And it was too late anyway, for he'd fallen in love at first sight, as any man would have if they'd been in his shoes. He convinced her to marry him and they moved into his home on the shores of Pearl Cove. They had three healthy children, and it seemed, for a time, that the Irishmen were wrong."

Ryan looked back out at the water. "But as the years went by, the woman became restless. She began to spend all her free time wandering the shoreline. She would get lost in the marshes, leaving her children alone for hours at a time. At night, she would slip from the house and wade into the cove and sing—deep, mournful songs of heartbreak and loneliness that had the rest of the islanders begging the fisherman to make her stop. But he never had the chance. Because one day, not long after, she disappeared."

"She left?" Hailey asked.

Ryan nodded. "Just as the Irishmen said she would. She took her rowboat and her leather cloak. And the only thing she left behind was a single strand of pearls, lying on the beach."

"Did he go after her?" Ethan asked.

"He tried," Ryan said. "But she'd disappeared without a trace, never to be heard from again. After months of searching, the fisherman finally gave up."

"What about her children?" Hailey asked.

"They were devastated," Ryan said, knowing far too well what it felt like to be abandoned by a mother, and not understand why. "Every year, on the anniversary of her disappearance, the fisherman and his children would walk down to the beach and drop a single pearl from her necklace into the water to try to lure her back."

"Did it work?" Hailey asked hopefully.

"No," Ryan said, looking up at her. "The woman never returned to the island, but the watermen swear she left a little bit of her magic in the cove, since it always produces the biggest crabs, oysters, and clams, year after year. Some say that if you walk into the marshes at midnight, you can still hear her singing. Others say that if you close your eyes when a storm's on the way, you can hear the faintest clinking of shells in the wind. But the strongest magic is when the moon is full; there's something about the way the surface runs through the marshes, the reflection of the moon is multiplied to make it look like a strand of pearls, rather than just the reflection of the moon."

When he stopped talking, no one said anything for several long moments. They just stared at him, speechless. Even Izzy had stopped building cages and had walked over to listen.

Ryan cleared his throat. "Obviously, this is Maryland, not Ireland. There aren't any seals here—the water is too warm—so there can't be selkies." He folded his hands in front of him on the table, as if he were perfectly relaxed. "Not that they even exist."

"Hold on." Paul stared at him, his eyes wide. "You're saying these women are like...magic or something? That they come *out* of the sea? And that they're so beautiful that men fall in love with them at first sight?"

"Yes." Ryan nodded slowly. "But...like I said, it's a fairy tale."

"A fairy tale that's connected to the cove where we're growing our oysters?" Paul asked.

Ryan shifted uncomfortably. He didn't like the way everyone was looking at him. He should have kept this story to himself. "Yes."

"Dude." Paul's face broke into a grin. "You need to tell that story to *everyone*."

"What?" Ryan regarded him warily. "I don't think—"

"This is what we're going to do," Paul said, grabbing his laptop and opening to a new document. "I want you to tell me that story again, word for word. I'm going to write it down, then we're going to come up with a marketing plan for two different oysters—one called Pearl Coves and the other Selkie Pearls. The Pearl Coves will be our main oyster, which we'll market to everyone—men, women, seafood markets, grocery stores, any restaurant that will take it. The Selkie Pearls will be our fancy, boutique oyster that we'll only market to high-end restaurants, five-star hotels with honeymoon packages, and swanky wedding planners. It'll be smaller. It'll be prettier. And we'll focus it entirely on women, on romance, and on the fairy tale." He smiled. "There's your tagline, man. Taste the magic. Taste the love."

"*Two* brands?" Ryan held up his hands, shaking his head. This was all happening too fast. It had been hard enough talking his father into promoting one. Two was asking too much. "I think we might be getting ahead of ourselves."

"Are you kidding me?" Paul said. "It's perfect! Everybody's going to want to eat these oysters!"

Ryan looked at the rest of the faces around the table. Everyone nodded.

"I think it's amazing," Hailey said, looking at Paul. "If I heard there was an oyster that could put some kind of love spell on a guy I had a crush on, I would totally try it."

Paul grinned back at her, nodding.

Hailey looked away and blushed.

Feeling cornered, Ryan glanced at Izzy. She seemed like the last person in the world who would believe in fairy tales. But she was staring down at the map, her expression as captivated as the others. For the first time since he'd laid eyes on her, her guard had dropped completely.

"What do you think?" he asked.

"I think," she said, with an oddly nostalgic tone to her voice, "that if I owned a restaurant, and you walked into my kitchen and told me that story, I'd want to buy your oysters."

SIX

*F*airy tales, Izzy thought as memories of long, hot days in the fields swam back to her. She still remembered the stories her mother and grandmother had told while she'd trailed behind them, her nimble fingers plucking vegetables from vines. There'd been other children in the fields, and they'd listened, too, following the Rivera women up and down the rows, picking as close to them as possible so they could hear.

She hadn't known, then, that children weren't supposed to work alongside their parents. Or that the tales her mother and grandmother told were simply a way to distract them all from the backbreaking labor.

No. She hadn't known any of that.

Those stories had defined her childhood in a way very few people could relate to. They'd been the building blocks of her education, a stepping-stone into a new language, a bridge between two worlds. At night, in the ramshackle camps that slept eight to a room, bone-weary workers had gravitated to their kitchen, crowding into the tiny space, hoping to hear more of the magical tales that reminded them of home.

It was there, in the camps, where she'd first learned how far food could stretch, how many mouths you could feed with a pound of dried black beans, and to never let anyone go hungry. But it wasn't just the amount of food, or the stories her mother and grandmother told, that brought people back, night after night, to their kitchen. It was the way the food tasted, and the way it made them feel afterwards, like all their troubles had washed away.

Just like the women in the fairy stories, who could spin straw into gold, the Rivera women were known for creating their own kind of magic in the kitchen. They knew, instinctually, which combination of flavors could ease a restless mind, which spices could soothe a shattered spirit, and how three chili peppers seared over an open flame could heal a broken heart. With access to only the most basic ingredients, they could prepare a meal that could bring tears to a grown man's eyes.

Izzy had taken that talent with her into the military, transforming bulk shipments of second-rate ingredients into extraordinary meals for the soldiers. She had worn her chef's apron over her uniform with pride. And she had made a name for herself with the knowledge she'd inherited from generations of Rivera women who'd come before her.

Stepping back as Ryan rose, she remembered something that Colin had said on their first night at the inn—that Ryan's father was a fourth-generation waterman. If Ryan had returned to carry on that legacy, that would make him the fifth.

Five generations of Callahan men working these waters.

This wasn't just a business to him. It was in his blood—the same way cooking was in hers. Was that what he'd been trying to tell her yesterday? That the Bay was dying and he was fighting to save it, because losing it would mean losing himself?

His eyes met hers briefly before he turned, and the emotion in them nearly stole her breath. While everyone else at the table gathered around Paul's computer, searching for images of pearls and oyster shells and magical seal women, Ryan quietly withdrew to the water's edge, where he stood for a long time with his hands in his pockets, gazing out at the cove.

For the first time since meeting him, she wanted to go to him. She wanted to ask him what happened. She wanted to know why that story made him so sad. But no one else seemed to notice, and she didn't know how to approach him without drawing attention to herself. So she stayed where she was, watching him as he turned slowly, and made his way over to the pier. Without so much as a glance back in their direction, he untied one of the small, flat-bottomed boats, stepped into it, and motored out to the mouth of Pearl Cove.

He spent the rest of the afternoon on the water, helping his father work the rows of cages. And by the time she and the rest of the vets piled into the van to return to the inn, and he gave them a halfhearted wave goodbye, Izzy had no doubt that there was more to that story. There was something he wasn't telling them. And whatever it was, it had caused him a great deal of pain.

Five minutes later, when they rolled to a stop in front of the inn, she was still lost in thought.

"Izzy Rivera?"

Stepping out of the van, Izzy glanced up and spotted a woman in the driveway who looked to be in her mid-forties. She was wearing a long, flowing cardigan over a soft knit top and linen trousers. Her strawberry blond hair fell in soft waves around her slim shoulders, and a pair of rectangular-shaped eyeglasses framed a pair of striking cobalt blue eyes. "Yes?"

The woman held out her hand. "I'm Erin Delancy, the social worker Colin and Will hired to meet with everyone."

Izzy stiffened. Glancing over her shoulder, she searched for someone to use as an excuse to slip away, but there was no one else in the driveway. She'd been the last one to get off the van.

"Hello," she said guardedly, taking the social worker's hand. The rest of the vets climbed the steps to the porch, disappearing into the inn. Behind her, the van pulled away with a crunch of tires on oyster shells, leaving the two of them alone.

"I was hoping we could set up a time to meet," Erin said, smiling.

Izzy released her hand. "Maybe later this weekend."

"All my slots for the weekend have already filled up. Any chance you have time now?" Erin glanced at her watch. "I could squeeze you in before my six o'clock."

No, Izzy thought. She'd let her guard down today and too many emotions were rising up to the surface. It was one thing to try to hide the truth about what had happened nine months ago from the other vets; it was another to try to hide it from a trained professional. "I need to take a shower," she said, gesturing to her dirty clothes. "I'm covered in mud."

"From the look of the group who walked in before you, the showers are going to be tied up for a while."

That was true, Izzy thought, racking her brain for another excuse. A movement on the porch drew her gaze up and she saw Colin step into the doorway. He gave her a pointed look and crossed his arms over his chest. He must have found out that she hadn't signed up for an appointment yet. He'd made it clear on their first night that the sessions were mandatory. If she didn't follow all the rules, he could report her to her probation officer and she could lose her place in the program.

As much as she didn't want to be here, it was better than going to jail.

"I promise it'll be painless," Erin said, her smile friendly and inviting.

Izzy took a deep breath. You can do this, she told herself. You don't have to tell her anything you don't want to. It's only one hour. Just get it over with. "Okay," she said. "I can meet now."

"Great," Erin said, motioning for Izzy to follow her across the lawn to the three private cottages by the water—far enough away from the main house so that no one would be able to hear them speak. They stepped into the one surrounded by pale pink peonies and Erin led her through the cozy living area to a small sunroom overlooking the Bay.

Izzy took in the plush blue sofa and matching armchair. Late afternoon sunlight reflected off the tiny sea glass and silver mobiles spinning from the ceiling. A book of glossy photographs lay open on the coffee table, inviting visitors to leaf through the shots of workboats, marsh scenes, and wildlife.

Everything about this cottage mimicked the feeling of the Bay —calm, peaceful, and serene. But it did nothing to put Izzy at ease.

Erin gestured to the sofa. "Make yourself comfortable."

Izzy sat, awkwardly, perched on the edge.

"Would you like some water?" Erin asked. "Tea?"

"No, thanks."

Erin walked into the kitchen, and came back out with a cup of tea and a glass of water. She set the water on the table in front of Izzy. "Have you ever spoken to a counselor before?"

"Not outside the Army," Izzy said, making the clarification because she knew there was a difference. The mandatory post-deployment sessions for military personnel were often just proce-dure, another box to check on a form where the counselor was more concerned with relieving the Army from any further responsibility than finding out if the service member was in actual need of support.

She had a feeling Erin had been hired to dig a lot deeper than that.

"Well," Erin said, settling into the chair across from Izzy, "we have a whole hour and we can talk about anything you want."

Izzy uncrossed, re-crossed her legs. She shifted on the sofa, running her hands along the seams of the cushion until she found a loose thread. She wrapped it around her index finger. Unwrapped it. Wrapped it. Unwrapped it. She looked up, met Erin's eyes, and immediately looked away—at the floor, at the ceiling, out the windows. Anywhere but at the woman across from her.

"Why don't you tell me about your day?" Erin suggested, taking a sip of her tea.

Izzy let go of the cushion, folding her hands in her lap. They were pretty beat up after spending most of the day making cages. Her knuckles were covered in nicks and scrapes. There was dirt caked under her fingernails. And streaks of mud ran up both her arms. But she would have happily traded eight more hours of making cages for a single minute in this room. "It was fine."

"Fine?"

Izzy nodded.

Erin paused, waiting for her to elaborate. Outside, an osprey circled the shallow waters near the shoreline, its cries piercing the silence. When it dove, striking the surface with its claws, Izzy watched, fascinated, as it lifted an impossibly large fish out of the water and carried it over to a nest on top of a channel marker.

"Pretty amazing, huh?" Erin asked.

"Yeah," Izzy said, forgetting for a moment that she wasn't supposed to be interested in anything.

"I still remember the first time I visited this island," Erin said. "I was sixteen and my father dragged me out here from D.C. to go fishing. I'd been getting into some trouble at school and he thought it would be good for me to get out of the city for the weekend. I was a typical surly teenager. I spent most of the two-hour drive giving him the silent treatment. It wasn't until we got out on the boat and the captain handed me a rod with a fish on the end of it, that I realized how badly I *had* needed to get out of the city. Suddenly, all the things I'd been rebelling against didn't seem quite so important anymore. All that mattered was catching another fish."

Izzy had a hard time picturing the crisp, cool professional across from her out on a fishing boat. But she liked the direction this conversation was taking. Maybe, if she could keep the questions focused on Erin, and away from her, the next fifty-seven minutes wouldn't be so terrible. "Do you still live in D.C.?"

"No," Erin said, taking another sip of her tea. "I live in Annapolis. My office is only a few blocks away from the Naval Academy."

That must be how she'd met Will and Colin, Izzy thought. She'd heard that Will was a Naval Academy graduate and that Colin had been living in Annapolis for the past year since he'd left the SEALs. "Do you still like to fish?"

"I do," she said. "I run a small charity that organizes weekend fishing trips for wounded warriors. It's one of the first things I recommend to new clients when they come to see me."

"Do you see a lot of vets?"

Erin nodded. "My practice focuses mainly on veterans, their families, and post-traumatic stress disorder."

Izzy reached for the water on the table in front of her, trying to appear relaxed. "How come?"

"My husband was a Marine. He served two tours in Iraq. When he returned from the second tour, he struggled to cope with the things he'd seen, but he refused to get help. He signed up for a third tour—Afghanistan, this time. The morning he was supposed to ship out, he swallowed a bottle of pills and never woke up."

Izzy slowly lowered the glass back to her lap.

"But we're not here to talk about me, are we?" Erin asked, her tone shifting from friendly to no-nonsense professional. She reached for the folder that was lying on the table beside her, making it clear that the small talk was over. "I have a copy of your service record, Izzy. And I've spoken to both your probation officer and the lawyers who handled your case last month."

Erin opened the folder, revealing a thick stack of papers. "You were in the Army for twelve years. You served in both Iraq and Afghanistan. You were promoted to the rank of Sergeant within three years, and rose to the rank of Sergeant First Class before you retired. You have a Purple Heart, an Army Commendation Medal, and a Bronze Star for your bravery during an attack in Afghanistan, where you saved the lives of three officers —including a lieutenant colonel who'd been badly wounded —*after* securing the safety of your kitchen staff."

Izzy looked away. She didn't want to hear about the soldiers whose lives she'd saved. Those medals meant nothing to her now.

But Erin wasn't finished.

"After your tour in Afghanistan, you served as a personal chef for a four-star general, chosen from an extremely competitive pool of applicants. You earned an undergraduate degree by taking night classes while you were working full time. And, three years ago, you were selected to join the Army Culinary Arts Team, where you won a gold medal for the U.S. at the World Culinary Olympics in Germany." Erin held up the folder. "This is a *very* impressive résumé."

Yes, Izzy thought. It was. And hearing it all out loud only made it hurt that much more.

"Here's what I don't understand," Erin said. "After twelve years of exemplary service, you decided not to reenlist. With no plans for the future, you returned to Baltimore, where, according to your probation officer, you were fired from three different jobs in six months due to anger management issues. Then, on March 27th, you were arrested for assaulting someone." She held Izzy's gaze. "Something doesn't add up here."

No, Izzy thought. It didn't.

"Care to connect the dots?" Erin asked.

Izzy stood abruptly and walked to the south-facing windows. Flecks of sunlight dappled the water. A yellow fishing boat, with three men on board, had anchored near a crooked lighthouse. She watched the men reach for their rods, cast their lines into the water, and patiently wait for the fish to bite.

Izzy wished she were with them. She wished she had a rod in her hands. She wished she had something to do besides sit here and answer this woman's questions. Because she didn't have any answers, at least not ones she could give without causing harm to someone else.

"You know that these sessions are confidential," Erin said from behind her. "Nothing you say will ever leave this room."

The only way to keep anything confidential, Izzy thought, was to say nothing, and to trust no one.

"Will you take me through what happened on the night of March 27th?" Erin asked.

"You have my file," Izzy said, her voice blank, devoid of emotion. "You can read my statement."

"It says you pled guilty to assault with a deadly weapon—that you shot a man three times."

Izzy said nothing, continuing to gaze out at the water.

"Did you do it?" Erin asked. "Or did you just plead guilty to get the deal the prosecution offered so you could stay out of jail?"

"Does it matter?"

"Yes," Erin said quietly. "I think it does."

"Why?"

"Because the person who committed this crime doesn't match the one who's described in the first three-quarters of this file."

That was true, Izzy thought. But the person in the first three-quarters of that file didn't exist anymore. She would never have that same hope, that same belief in herself, that same hunger to succeed. Her bright future was gone, and with it, the dream her mother and grandmother had come to this country with so many years ago.

She would never again be the woman who enlisted in the Army to give her family a better life. She would never again be the woman who put on a uniform for the first time and stood in front of the mirror with such unbridled pride, believing she could accomplish anything if she worked hard enough.

"Izzy," Erin asked. "Why did you decide to leave the Army?"

She could feel herself shutting down again, the emotions that had begun to unravel earlier tucking themselves away, like black thread rewinding on a spool. "I just decided it was time to get out."

"I don't believe you."

"I don't really care what you believe," she said, reaching for the anger that simmered like a lifeline on the edges of despair. Anger was easier. Anger she could control. Anger was the only rudder she had in this shit storm of loss. "Are we done here?"

"It's only been fifteen minutes, and we still have a lot of ground to cover." Shifting through the papers, Erin pulled out a page in the middle of the file. "Why don't you tell me about your tour in Afghanistan, the one where you earned the Bronze Star? I think one of the men whose lives you saved was stationed at the same base where you were working in North Carolina last year." She glanced down at her notes. "Bradley Welker."

At the sound of his name, every muscle in Izzy's body tensed. "I don't want to talk about him."

Erin looked up, surprised. "He's been very complimentary of you."

Izzy turned slowly back around to face her. "You've *spoken* to him?"

Erin nodded. "I wanted to know if he had any insight into why you decided to leave the military."

Insight? The room started to pulse. Her therapist had asked her attacker if he had any *insight* into why she'd decided to leave the military? The air felt thick, like glue in her throat. "What did he say?" she asked, forcing the words out.

"He said that your performance had started to slip in the months after you decided not to reenlist, that he suspected there was a personal matter you were struggling with."

Izzy's fingers curled into fists at her sides. "A *personal* matter?"

Erin nodded again. "He said he thought it might have something to do with your family."

Her *family?*

Izzy couldn't stay here. She couldn't stay here and listen to these lies. Without another word, she turned, walked out the door, and slammed it behind her. Taking one look at the group of vets gathered on the front porch, she started to run in the opposite direction.

"Izzy?"

She heard a man's voice—Kade's voice—call after her. She ignored him. She needed to be alone. She didn't know where she was going, but she couldn't stay here.

She slipped through a gap in the blackberry hedges and came out on the other side. She couldn't go back to the inn right now. It was filled with people. Everywhere she went, all day, she was surrounded by people. She felt like she'd been dropped in a fish bowl, and every move she made was being watched, judged, recorded.

It was enough to make anyone want to run away.

She heard footsteps behind her—heavy, masculine footsteps. "Go away, Kade."

"I saw you get ambushed by that therapist," he said. "You shouldn't be alone right now."

She ran faster. "I'm not talking to you."

"Fine," he shot back. "I don't want to talk to you anyway."

They ran in silence, past the school and the village and over the drawbridge, until there was nothing but cornfields and wild-flowers lining the long stretch of road before them.

"I'm not going to stop anytime soon," Izzy called back over her shoulder.

"I'm a Marine, Izzy. I can do this all day."

He stayed with her, stubbornly following her for miles. She didn't know when she slowed down enough for him to catch up and start running beside her, or when he pulled ahead and began to lead. But when he turned down a long lane toward an old abandoned house overgrown with weeds and ivy, she followed.

"Where are we?" she asked, slowing down to a walk and breathing hard. "What is this place?"

Kade said nothing, leading her around to the back yard. A red punching bag hung from a tree branch. It was weathered and misshapen from years of neglect. He walked over to it and positioned himself behind it, holding it out for her. "Go ahead," he said. "Get it out. All of it."

She hesitated, just for a moment, before walking over and punching it. Hard. Dust and mold puffed out from the bag and her knuckles stung from the impact. But it felt good. Really good. She punched the bag again. Harder.

"Come on," he said. "You can do better than that."

She punched it again. And this time she pictured him—the man who had raped her. The man who had made her feel like she was nothing. The man who had stolen twelve years of her life in one vicious act of revenge.

She punched it again. And again. And again. The anger rose up, pouring out of her, until she heard something like a battle cry come out of her lungs, and she lunged at the bag, swinging at it with both arms until she fell to her knees in the grass. Sweat rolled into her eyes. Or maybe it was tears. Or both.

She didn't know. She didn't care anymore.

"Feel better?" Kade asked.

She knelt, breathing hard, her palms pressing into the earth. "I used to be strong," she said, her voice breaking. "I used to believe in myself. I used to know what I wanted to do with my life." Her arms ached, shaking with exhaustion. "I don't even know who I am anymore."

"You're Isabella Rivera. And you're here."

Her vision blurred, each blade of grass melting into a sea of green.

"You're here, Izzy. That's the first step."

"I didn't even choose to be here."

"So what? You're here. That's all that matters." He held out his hand.

She looked up at him. At this man who had come running with her, who had offered to switch jobs with her, who had washed her sheets for her, and who was giving her his hand to help her back to her feet, because God knows she was just beginning to realize that she couldn't do this on her own. "Why are *you* here?"

"Because I need help," Kade said. "When I came home after my fifth tour overseas, I started drinking. I turned my back on my family. I treated my wife and kids like shit. My wife kicked me out of the house and filed for divorce. I'm here because I lost everything. I'd been thinking about putting a gun in my mouth and pulling the trigger for weeks before I saw Colin and his father announce this program on TV. It gave me hope. I want to deal with the demons inside me and win my wife back. I want to win my kids back. I can't do that alone."

Izzy stared up at this massive, muscular infantryman covered in tattoos, floored by his honesty and vulnerability. She looked at the hand he was holding out to her, and she took it. He helped her up until they stood eye to eye. They looked at each other for a long time, two broken, battle weary souls, with so much more to say. But in the end, only one question popped out of her mouth. It was so simple, so small, but maybe that was all they could handle right now—the smallest of steps. "Does your wife like flowers?"

Kade nodded slowly, as if the thought had never occurred to him. "Um, yeah," he said. "She does. She loves them."

"When was the last time you sent her some?"

"I can't remember," he admitted.

"Maybe you should start there."

SEVEN

*R*yan knew he shouldn't be here. He should be at home, in bed, pretending to sleep. Not wandering through the marshes at midnight like a crazy person. But the story Paul had asked him about earlier that day had woken something inside him, something he'd buried long ago. And he knew he wouldn't sleep at all tonight, even if he tried. The moment he closed his eyes, the questions would haunt him—the same questions that had haunted him since he was a ten-year-old child.

There was a reason he'd chosen a career in science, and marine biology, in particular. He'd needed something to help him make sense of the mysteries that lay beneath these waters. His studies had been his anchor; his research the only tether he could trust to ground him in reality. He'd sought comfort in numbers and data, in conducting experiments based on hypotheses that could be validated and proved.

He'd spent most of his life looking for answers, searching for the truth. And while he'd built a hell of a name for himself in the process, he was still no closer to finding them now than he had been when he'd first started out.

The spongy earth tugged at his feet, suctioning to his waders. He could feel the pull of the cove, as strong as it had been that night, so many years ago. Resisting the urge to walk any further, he paused just long enough for Zoey to catch up. He reached down, stroking her wet fur. She was covered in mud, and he'd have to give her a bath before letting her in the house tonight. But he'd known better than to leave her behind. She would have started howling the moment his truck pulled away.

She always stayed close during a full moon.

Glancing over his shoulder, he looked at the farm, all sharp angles and dark shadows under a wash of silver light. The tide had peeled back, exposing the slick muddy shoreline, the spray of oyster shells, the roots of the marsh grasses. He could hear the water pumping through the tanks on the pier, feeding his latest experiment—an experiment that would be linked, now, to the one night from his childhood he wanted to forget.

But what could he do?

He had seen the way Paul and the others had reacted to the story. He had seen how excited they'd been, how eager they were to run with it. He couldn't ask them to stop without telling them what had happened. And he'd never told anyone. Not even his twin sister.

Looking back at Pearl Cove, at the curve of water shimmering in the moonlight, he wished he hadn't taken his father's rowboat out that night, twenty-three years ago. He wished he could erase what he'd seen and heard while the rest of the islanders had been asleep. But, most of all, he wished he hadn't woken up his mother when he'd returned and told her everything.

Because he knew, now, that *he* was the reason she'd left. *He* was the reason she'd vanished the next morning, never to be seen or heard from again. *He* was the reason his sister had grown up without a mother, and his father had lost his wife.

And he would never forgive himself for that.

Across the channel, a heron squawked, its prehistoric cry echoing through the night. A set of footprints, probably belonging to a fox, circled back toward the marshes. By his feet, a minnow flopped in a small puddle of water, abandoned by the ebbing tide. He bent slowly, holding Zoey back, and scooped up the small fish, tossing it gently into the deeper waters, where it shot out of sight.

No. He wouldn't ask them to stop using the story. He'd have to find a way to get used to it. He needed this farm to succeed. Their mission was too important. And he would never put his own interests ahead of that.

Besides, he thought, looking up at the moon, he was a man of science now. He didn't believe in fairy tales anymore.

And, yet...

He sensed the subtle shift in the water almost before it began —the way the reflection broke, dancing over the surface. The way the light melted, each drop clasping onto the next until the reflection reformed into a single strand of pearls.

He heard the voice, the woman's voice, the same voice he had heard all those years ago, as clearly as if she were standing right beside him, and in the distance, the sound of seashells clinking together on a windless night.

Izzy woke to the sound of wind chimes, of seashells suspended from strings. The faint, faraway clinking lured her from the deepest sleep she could remember having in months. Groggily, she reached out and switched on the lamp. The blankets shifted as she turned toward the window, toward the source of the sound. But it had already faded. And then there was nothing but darkness and silence and the occasional creak of the old house settling into its bones.

Convinced she'd imagined it, or dreamed it, or both, she breathed in—a deep restful breath—and looked down at her hands. Her knuckles were still swollen and bruised from hitting the bag so hard the night before, but the peace it had brought her inside was worth every painful band of color on the outside. She flexed her fingers, forcing the circulation to return to them, and started to peel back the sweaty sheets.

But they weren't sweaty.

They were dry.

Floored, she ran her hands over the pillows, every inch of them, just to make sure, then sat up slowly, almost afraid to believe it. She took in the clothes strewn over the floor, the empty water bottles caked in mud, the crinkled granola bar wrappers that had fallen out of the pockets of her gym shorts. Everything looked the same way it had when she'd turned out the lights the night before. But for the first time in nine months, she hadn't woken up from a nightmare. She hadn't dreamed about her attacker at all.

Feeling light, almost buoyant, she rose to retrieve her laptop. Relishing in the idea of crawling back under the covers, of being able to get back in bed without having to strip the sheets, she opened the screen of her computer and immediately sobered when she spotted the spreadsheet of female soldiers. She might have eluded her attacker for a night in her dreams, but he was still out there. He was still a threat. And she refused to be lured into a false sense of security just because she hadn't found anything suspicious yet.

Today was Sunday, her first full day off, and she planned to spend it catching up on her research. She had over a dozen new names to look into, and she wanted to do a quick follow-up search on the women currently stationed under his command.

They were the ones she was worried about the most.

She had already typed the first name into the search engine

when she heard a faint scratching at the door. Figuring it was probably Kade on his way down to the laundry room, she stood to answer it, but frowned when she heard a low whine, like the sound a dog made when it wanted to come in. Crossing the room, she cracked the door and a wiggling ball of fur squeezed through the opening.

"Well, hello there," she said softly as the dog licked her hands and wagged her tail. It was Riley, the yellow lab that belonged to Annie and Will's daughter, Taylor. Looking out into the hallway, Izzy expected to find the child bounding up the stairs after her, but there was no one there. "Your owner's probably looking for you," she said, reaching for the dog's collar to guide her back down the stairs.

Riley dodged her playfully, then ran around the room, sniffing every corner, before grabbing a dirty sock off the floor and jumping on the bed.

Izzy raised a brow. "I have a feeling you're not supposed to do that."

Riley wagged her tail, plopped herself down on the blankets, and started chewing on the sock.

Izzy walked over to the bed and tried to pry the sock from the dog's mouth, but Riley wasn't having it, so she gave up. Not sure what to do, because she didn't have any treats to tempt the dog with and she had a feeling Riley wouldn't listen to her without them, she decided to leave the door open and wait for Taylor to come find her. Sitting down beside the animal, she pulled her computer into her lap, and sure enough, a few minutes later, she heard footsteps on the stairs.

"Riley!" a child's voice whispered from the hallway.

At the sound of her name, Riley's tail thumped against the blankets.

A moment later, Taylor stepped into the doorway. She took

one look at her dog on the bed and narrowed her eyes. "Riley, come here."

Riley wagged her tail, but she wouldn't move.

"Riley," the child said more firmly. "Come."

Riley lifted the sock proudly, chewing it, blatantly ignoring her owner.

Taylor glanced over at Izzy. "Sorry," she said, taking a cautious step into the room. "Did she wake you up?"

"No," Izzy said, surprised the dog hadn't bounded off the bed when her owner had called her. Every other time she'd seen them together, Riley had been glued to Taylor's side.

Taylor walked over to her dog, wrestled the slobbery sock out of her mouth, and gave her collar a gentle tug to encourage her to jump off the bed.

Riley rolled over, demanding a belly rub.

Annoyed, Taylor took a step back and put her hands on her hips.

A smile tugged at Izzy's lips. "How old is she?"

"A year and a half."

"So she's still a puppy."

"I guess," Taylor said, looking a little hurt. "But she *always* comes when I call her."

"Maybe she's tired," Izzy said, not wanting the child's feelings to be hurt. "Do you always get up this early?"

Taylor shook her head, looking pointedly at the dog. "We were *supposed* to go crabbing."

Riley's tail thumped against the blankets. She was still on her back, her paws in the air. Resigned, Taylor sighed and gave her a belly rub. She was rewarded with a sloppy kiss on the face. "What are *you* doing up so early?" she asked Izzy. "Isn't it your day off?"

Izzy closed her computer, set it aside. She wasn't about to tell an eight-year-old that she woke up most days around this time covered in a cold sweat. Or that she'd planned to spend the morning searching for clues that might reveal if her rapist had attacked someone else. "I like to watch the sun rise."

"Me too," Taylor said. "Especially out on a boat."

Izzy took in the child's outfit—jeans, sneakers, a T-shirt, and a faded Navy ball cap pulled over her wispy red hair. "Who are you going crabbing with?"

"Mr. Haddaway," Taylor answered. "He's my teacher's dad. Ms. Haddaway usually comes with us, but she can't today, so it'll just be Ryan and me."

"Ryan's going?" Izzy asked, her thoughts immediately shifting to the story he had told them the day before, and the way he had withdrawn afterwards, retreating into himself.

Taylor nodded. "He's coming to pick me up. He's probably here now. Do you want to come?"

Izzy blinked, taken aback by the invitation. "I can't."

"Why not?"

"Because..." Izzy glanced at her computer. She had things to do—important things.

Taylor bit her lip.

"What?" Izzy asked.

"I think Riley wants you to come."

Izzy started to laugh, then stopped when she realized that Taylor wasn't joking. "You're serious?"

Taylor nodded. "I don't think she's going to leave this room without you."

"Of course she will," Izzy assured her.

To prove her point, Taylor walked out to the hallway, turned around, and called her dog's name. Riley wagged her tail, but wouldn't move from the bed. Taylor looked over at Izzy. "See? I told you. She wants you to come."

"She's not going to come for me either," Izzy said, standing and walking over to join Taylor in the doorway. "Riley," Izzy said, patting her legs. "Come."

The dog jumped off the bed and ran to her side.

Izzy stared at the dog, then looked slowly back up at Taylor. "That was...strange."

Taylor's big green eyes held hers. "I can't go out on the boat without Riley."

And I'm not going out on the boat, Izzy thought, looking fleetingly at her computer. But she didn't want to hurt Taylor's feelings. "How about I walk you to the car? Make sure Riley goes with you?"

Taylor brightened. "Okay."

Relieved that it was only the dog she cared about, Izzy glanced down at what she was wearing. "Hang on," she said, grabbing some clothes from the dresser. She slipped into the bathroom, changed, and slid her bare feet into a pair of flip-flops. "All right," she said. "Let's go."

They headed downstairs, with the dog trotting alongside them, and walked out onto the front porch.

"Wow," Taylor breathed, pausing mid-step.

The screen door slipped from Izzy's hand, slapping back into the frame. The moon, bone-white and twice its normal size, hung suspended over the marshes. The tide had risen to meet it, creeping into the yard, blurring the boundary between earth and water. A silvery haze of heat and humidity clung to the air, beckoning them down to the curved oyster shell driveway, where a man stood with his hands in his pockets, leaning against the bed of a pickup truck.

As soon as Riley caught sight of Ryan's chocolate lab, Zoey, she raced to the bed of the truck to jump in beside her. Taylor trailed slowly after her dog, her eyes fixed on the moon. But Izzy only had eyes for the man. Dressed in a pair of faded jeans, a gray T-shirt, and white boots, he looked so much a part of this place, so eerily perfect silhouetted in the moonlight and marsh grasses, it was almost like she was seeing him for the first time.

She felt suddenly lightheaded, dazed, as she walked down the steps and made her way over to the truck. He opened the passenger door for Taylor, and when the child hopped in and scooted over to the middle seat, Izzy climbed in beside her.

Ryan held her gaze, saying nothing as he closed the door gently behind them—like he'd known all along she'd be coming. This was a mistake, Izzy thought. She was only supposed to make sure Riley got in the truck, not go with them. But as Ryan rounded the front of the vehicle and slid behind the wheel, filling the cabin with the scent of salt and marsh and man, she realized there was nowhere else she wanted to be.

EIGHT

*R*yan felt the tension he'd been holding onto all night begin to dissolve as they motored out of the harbor. He always felt more relaxed when he was out on the water, like a weight had been lifted off his shoulders. All the expectations, the frantic need to prove himself, the obsessive drive to succeed— none of it seemed to matter anymore.

All that mattered was catching enough seafood to fill the day's quota.

It was a simple life, a romantic life, a life he would have wanted for himself if the Bay was still healthy enough to produce an endless supply of fish, crabs, and oysters—the way it had been over a hundred years ago when it had first put this region on the map as one of the seafood capitals of the world.

But that wasn't the reality anymore.

So he stole these nostalgic Sundays with Jake Haddaway as a reminder of what he was fighting for. The fact that Taylor wanted to join them, almost every weekend, fueled his optimism for the future. It meant a lot to him that she cared, that she wanted to learn about the traditions he'd grown up with as a child. One day, if he ever had a daughter of his own, he hoped to be able to do the same thing with her.

Looking over his shoulder, at where Taylor and Izzy sat huddled together on one of the coolers, he saw that Taylor was explaining the difference between the crab pots and bushel baskets piled up in the stern. Izzy was nodding and appeared to be listening, her free hand absently stroking Riley's soft fur. She'd had a hand on the dog almost from the moment she'd stepped on the boat, and he was glad to see that she didn't mind touching the animal or sitting so close to Taylor.

Apparently, it was only men she shied away from.

Determined to bridge that gap, to get her to trust him and not see him as some kind of a threat, he grabbed a spare hat out of one of the compartments and walked it over to her. "Here," he said. "You're going to need this when the sun comes up."

"Thanks," she said.

She twisted her hair up and tucked it into the hat. Ryan couldn't help feeling a little sad to see it go. It was the first time he'd ever seen her with her hair down, and nothing could have prepared him for the picture she made with those wild, unruly curls tumbling down around her bare shoulders.

In a white tank top and cutoff shorts, she looked different today, more approachable. Her skin had a glow to it that he'd never seen before. And when she lifted those striking tawny eyes to his, he saw, for the first time, a glimmer of the same heat and passion that he kept so carefully hidden from everyone else.

"Looks good on you," he said, nodding toward the camouflage trucker hat she'd just put on.

The slightest hint of a smile tugged at the corners of her mouth before she turned away, focusing her attention on Taylor again.

Ryan walked back to the helm where Jake stood with one

hand resting on the wheel and the other flipping through the pages of his logbook. "Where are we heading today?"

Jake nodded toward the marshy shoreline in the distance. "We'll check the traps off Nelson Point, then head up into the river and do some trotlining."

"Sounds good," Ryan said, reaching down to give Zoey a scratch behind the ears. Most watermen preferred to use one method over the other—traps or trotlining—but these outings were more for Taylor's benefit, so she could learn all the ways a person could catch a source of food from these waters, both commercial and recreational. "Want me to start getting the crab pots ready?"

Jake nodded. "Bait's in the cooler."

Ryan made sure there was fresh bait in each of the traps, then worked on a few knots in the trotline. He was aware of Izzy watching him, her eyes tracking his every movement. He didn't know why she was here, but he'd learned a long time ago not to try to make sense out of anything that happened during a full moon. It was still out there, a fading white disk retreating toward the western horizon.

As far as he was concerned, it couldn't sink fast enough.

He didn't want to think about what had happened the night before. He didn't want to think about what he had seen and what he had heard. He wanted to put it behind him, as quickly as possible.

Jake eased up on the throttle. The water churned beneath them as the heavy boat slowed. Turning his back on the moon, Ryan grabbed two pairs of waterproof gloves out of a basket and tossed them to Izzy and Taylor. "Ready?"

Taylor stood, fitting the bulky gloves over her small hands and making her way over to her usual position behind the culling table.

"What do you want me to do?" Izzy asked.

Ryan motioned for her to follow him over to the side of the boat as Jake lined them up to drift along the line of buoys marking the pots he'd set the day before. "I'll hook the traps and pull them up to the side of the boat. I want you to take them from me and empty them onto the tray so Taylor can cull them."

"Okay," she said, looking down into the shallow water a little apprehensively.

He dipped the hook in, grabbed the line attached to the first trap, and let the winch do the rest of the work. It came up alongside the boat dripping wet and filled with a half dozen crabs. "That's right," he said once she had a good grip on it. "Just pull it in, turn it over, and shake it over the table."

Izzy gave it a shake, but the crabs wouldn't budge.

"Harder," Ryan said. "You've got to get them to fall out."

Izzy shook the cage, hard, and jumped back as half of them fell out onto the table and the other half ended up on the floor. "Holy shit," Izzy said as they skittered in every direction, their claws scraping over the fiberglass.

Taylor laughed, chasing after the runaways.

"Maybe not *that* hard," Jake said, snagging one off the floor before it latched onto his shoelaces.

"Here comes the next one," Ryan said, not giving her a chance to catch her breath.

Izzy grabbed the crab pot, pulled it into the boat, and shook it over the culling table. Only two managed to fall onto the floor this time.

Taylor reached for the one closest to her, and tossed it into a bushel basket. Izzy did the same.

"Not that one," Taylor said, fishing it out. She turned it over so Izzy could see the dome-shaped apron on the underside of the shell. "This one's a sook." Taylor threw it overboard, then went off in search of the rest of the runaway crabs.

Izzy looked at Ryan, her expression bewildered.

"A sook is a female crab," he explained, passing the next trap off to her. "All the females go back into the water this time of year, so they can keep breeding. We only keep the males—the jimmys. And they have to be at least five inches long, or they go back, too." Ryan smiled as she peered at the crabs in the cage she was holding, trying to see the difference. "You'll get the hang of it."

And just as he suspected, it didn't take her long. By the time they'd pulled up the rest of the cages and laid the freshly-baited traps, she seemed to have found her rhythm. It almost seemed like she might be enjoying herself. They headed up into the river as the fog slowly receded, revealing the calm, glassy surface beneath. They passed an occasional workboat now and then, but mostly they had the meandering waterway to themselves.

It was his favorite time to be out on the water, Ryan thought. Great Blue Herons stood like pale statues on fallen tree trunks, scanning the surface for fish. Families of ducks paddled beside muddy shorelines, leaving small ripples in their wake. Behind them, the marsh grasses rustled, teeming with life.

He never questioned Jake's instincts on where to go to find the crabs. Like his father, Jake had been a waterman his entire life. He knew how to catch a source of food from these waters, the same way the Native Americans had centuries ago, when they'd had only their skills as hunters and gatherers to rely on to feed themselves. It was part of what had always made this area so special. Anyone, with a boat and some bait, could catch a meal for his family and make an honest living.

The methods and gear had improved a bit over the years, but it had always been more about earning the respect of these waters than anything else. You learned the habits of the fish, then figured out how to stay one step ahead of them. You learned how to work with the tides and the currents, how to adapt to the wind and the rain. You trusted that nature would always provide for you as you followed your catch up into the rivers and back out into the Bay from season to season.

"How long have you been doing this?" Izzy asked Jake, after they'd laid the lines down and were making their way back to the first one to run it.

"Since I was seventeen," Jake said, effortlessly maneuvering the big workboat around the narrow tributary. "Been working these waters for almost forty years."

"That's a long time," Izzy said.

Ryan glanced up, surprised at the note of respect in her voice. It was the first time she'd seemed even remotely interested in anything, or anyone, on this island.

At almost sixty years old, Jake was a quiet, unassuming man who mostly kept to himself. The only reason Ryan knew him so well was because Jake's daughter, Becca, was one of Ryan's best friends.

"Who taught you?" Izzy asked.

"My father," Jake said, nodding for Ryan to grab the line. "Same way his father taught him. And his father taught him before that."

Ryan hooked the first trotline and fed it over the prop stick while Taylor held a dip net over the side of the boat, waiting for the first crab to surface.

"Did you ever think about doing anything else?" Izzy asked, moving over to stand beside Ryan to watch what was happening.

"Nope," Jake said. "Never."

Ryan let Taylor take the lead as she netted the crabs, pulling them into the boat and tossing them into a bushel basket while Jake maintained a slow, steady pace along the line.

"How many crabs can you catch in a day?" Izzy asked.

"Good day's anywhere from fifteen to twenty bushels," Jake said, fishing out an ice-cold soda from the cooler by his feet. "But most days aren't that good."

"No?" Izzy asked, glancing back at him.

"Harvests aren't what they used to be," Jake admitted, cracking open the can. "I catch about a third of what I used to catch when I started out."

"A third?" Izzy asked, surprised.

Jake nodded. "Crab population's declined a lot over the years."

Izzy looked over at Ryan. He said nothing, wondering if the picture he'd painted on her first day at the farm was finally beginning to sink in. Maybe she'd needed this human connection to really understand how dire things were.

"It's getting harder and harder to make ends meet," Jake said matter-of-factly. "A lot of guys have given up—guys who've been out here longer than I have. But I could never walk away from this. It's the only life I've ever known. It's the only life I ever want to know."

Izzy watched Taylor net a few more crabs, then looked at the man behind the wheel again. "Do you come out here every day?"

"Every day I'm allowed to," Jake said. "The state regulates how often we can come out and how much we can catch."

"What do you do in the winter?" Izzy asked.

"Work the oyster beds," Jake said.

"With cages, like Ryan does?"

Jake shook his head.

"I hand tong for a couple months when the season opens, then switch over to dredging."

"On the same boat?"

"Same boat," Jake confirmed. "I rig it up differently for each season, depending on what I'm after. 'Course," he added, taking a sip of his soda, "the oysters are in worse shape than the crabs."

Izzy was quiet for a long time as they reached the end of the first trotline and Jake turned the boat around to repeat the process all over again with the second line. As soon as Ryan had slipped it over the stick and Taylor was poised to net the first crab, Izzy turned back to Jake. "Would you ever consider doing what Ryan and his father are doing?"

Jake shook his head slowly. "No."

"Why not?"

Jake looked over at Ryan and the two men shared a long look. "It's not what I want to do."

Izzy looked back and forth between the two men, sensing the sudden tension between them.

Not wanting to put Jake in an awkward position, Ryan spoke up for the first time since Izzy had begun quizzing his friend. "Not everybody likes what my dad and I are doing."

"What do you mean?" Izzy asked. "Why not?"

"Oysters are a pretty contentious subject in this state right now," Ryan said, picking up a smaller crab Taylor had accidentally tossed into one of the baskets and throwing it overboard. "Everybody agrees we need to do something drastic to bring them back, but there's a lot of debate about the best way to go about that. The idea of parsing the Bay into farms isn't sitting well with a lot of watermen. They don't want us chopping up the Bay, privatizing the water."

"Would that happen?" Izzy asked.

"If the state approves too many aquaculture leases, some fear there could be a domino effect," Ryan said. "A lot of watermen already feel there are too many restrictions on how much seafood they can catch, especially when it comes to oysters. More leases would further restrict their access to the water, and the few oyster bars that are left on the bottom."

"The state loves to spend money on oyster restoration projects," Jake said, shifting the course of the boat. "We've got one of the world's biggest man-made oyster reefs about a mile north of here. It's huge—over three hundred acres—and now they're working on building two more." He shook his head. "If the state wants to throw taxpayer dollars at something, they should focus on rehabilitating the wild oysters in the beds we can work instead of pouring more money into aquaculture and sanctuaries that we can't touch."

Izzy looked out at the water and Ryan wondered if she was beginning to see how controversial this was. Watermen, oyster farmers, environmentalists, politicians—they were all coming at it from a different direction, and arguably the watermen were the ones with the most at stake. But the Bay wouldn't be able to sustain any of them if they didn't start reversing the damage right now. These waters had to be saved, or everyone would fail.

"Look," Jake said to Izzy as they neared the end of the second trotline. "I understand why Ryan's father decided to make the jump over to aquaculture. The state's got us so choked up with regulations we can barely scrape a living from these waters anymore. But even if I wanted to follow in his footsteps, I couldn't afford to."

He made a minor adjustment on the throttle. "You've got to buy the seed, the cages, the equipment, the land. You've got to factor in a budget for marketing, legal fees, permits, labor. It takes almost two years from the time you plant your first crop to even think about making a profit. Most of the guys who are getting into this are college graduates, people with backgrounds in finance, people who've already had some success with a conventional career and want to try something different. Most watermen don't have that kind of money lying around."

Izzy looked at Ryan. "Where'd your father get the money to start his farm?"

Uncomfortable, Ryan looked away. He felt a wet nose nudge his hand, and he fished a piece of jerky out of his pocket, slipping it to his dog. When he glanced up again, he saw the moment the realization dawned in Izzy's eyes and knew she was finally beginning to put two and two together.

NINE

*I*t wasn't his father, Izzy realized. It was Ryan. He was the one who had taken on the risk. He was the reason his father had started the farm. He was the bridge between the two worlds—the solitary waterman tradition that ran in his blood, and a future, which relied on science, expensive equipment, and growing seafood in cages.

She felt the workboat begin another one of its slow-motion turns, and she imagined that it was Ryan behind the wheel. It was so easy to picture him there, with only his dog and the sunrise for company. It had taken her less than an hour on the water to see that this was where his heart was, that this was where he belonged.

She understood, now, what he had been trying to tell her the other day—that there was a culture here that was sacred, a way of life that was worth saving.

Maybe the idea of farmed shellfish wasn't as romantic as harvesting wild oysters, but it was a step in the right direction, wasn't it?

Jake evened out the course of the boat. "The state's been

subsidizing a loan program to try to get watermen to make the transition for a few years now, but the money only covers a portion of the start-up costs. And it's a loan, so you've got to pay it back. What if I'm no good at oyster farming? What if I kill half my crop in the first year? What if I can't find anybody to buy my oysters? I don't have the stomach to take on that kind of risk."

Izzy watched Jake reach for his soda, his calloused fingers wrapping around a can that was already beginning to sweat in the heat. "Would you ever consider working for another oyster farmer as an employee?"

Jake shook his head. "I'm not interested in being on someone else's payroll."

"Even if it meant a steady paycheck?" Izzy asked.

"I've been my own boss for almost forty years," Jake said, lifting the can to lips that were cracked from decades of working in the sun. "I'd rather take my chances with the way things are than let somebody else call the shots."

It was one thing to have a stranger calling the shots, Izzy thought. But family was different. How many men, like Jake, would be the last generation to carry on this legacy, simply because they had no one to pass it to? She thought of all the kids who would leave this area for college and never come back. Most of them would have seen the writing on the wall long ago.

Looking at Ryan, she thought about everything he'd accomplished in the years he'd been away. With his credentials, he could have gone anywhere. But he'd chosen to come back here. To invest in this island. To invest in his family. She watched him dip his own net into the river to snag a crab off the line that Taylor had missed—his movements so quietly tuned to the water and the boat. Wasn't that exactly what she'd planned to do for her own family?

Her decision to join the Army at eighteen had been as much for her grandmother as for herself. Her mother had already passed away by then, but the enlistment bonus had provided her with enough money to invest in a small house for her grandmother in Baltimore. Izzy had only planned to serve in the military for twenty years—just long enough to qualify for retirement benefits. Then, with a comfortable pension at thirty-eight, she would return to Baltimore, where she and her grandmother would open a traditional Oaxacan-style restaurant.

It had been a shared dream that the two of them had been working toward for years. Enlisting in the Army had been the first step. The military had offered security, stability—a steady income that her family could rely on for the first time in their lives. It had meant that they would never have to go back to working in the fields.

When she'd lost her grandmother to cancer three years ago, it had only made Izzy that much more determined to keep their shared dream alive. She had vowed to honor her grandmother's memory by carrying on the Rivera legacy in the only way she knew how.

Gazing down at her hands, she thought of the long line of Rivera cooks who'd come before her, and how that legacy would die with her now.

"Want to give it a shot?" Ryan asked.

Izzy looked up to see him holding the net out to her. There was compassion in his eyes, like he'd known she'd gone somewhere in her mind she hadn't wanted to go. He moved over, making space for her to join him at the side of the boat. She grasped the handle—the same way she had with Kade's hand the night before—accepting the olive branch.

"Just follow Taylor's lead," Ryan said.

Taylor netted the next two, then stepped back so Izzy could take her position.

Izzy watched the first wriggling crustacean appear beneath the murky waters, clinging onto the bait attached to the line.

"Try to grab it right before it surfaces," Taylor said from beside her.

Izzy reached down, scooped it off the trotline, and added it to the basket with the others.

"See?" Taylor said, smiling up at her. "Piece of cake."

The child's joy was so infectious that Izzy couldn't help smiling back at her. Behind her, Ryan maintained his post by snagging any crabs off the line that she missed. Izzy couldn't help noticing how he let Taylor take on the role of instructor. His management style at the farm throughout the past week had been similar, in the way he'd patiently explained each task, then stepped back to let whoever he'd put in charge take the reins. He'd been quick to dole out praise and give credit wherever it was due, but he'd never asked anyone to boost his own ego.

He was a natural leader, inspiring confidence and trust in those around him. Even Jake, who might not necessarily agree with the career path he'd chosen, clearly respected the man he'd become. She could tell by the way they interacted, the way they anticipated each other's next move, the way they spoke to each other without having to say a word.

She'd spent the past twelve years working alongside men in uniform—men who barked out orders and expected people to fall in line. She was used to big egos, short fuses, and raunchy senses of humor. She'd only known her new boss for about a week, but she could already tell he was the complete opposite of that.

The next time he reached into the water to scoop up a crab, her gaze drifted to his left hand. His ring finger was bare, which meant he was still single. She wondered how he'd made it this far in life without attaching himself to someone. He didn't seem like the kind of man who would float aimlessly from woman to woman.

Not that he would have any trouble attracting them.

She took in his rugged profile, messy, sun-streaked blond hair, and quiet gray eyes. He was tall, probably around six-foot-two, and the muscles that rippled beneath his T-shirt weren't the kind that came from the gym. Her gaze dropped back to his hands—those strong, calloused, workingman's hands—and a flutter stirred deep in her belly.

She didn't want to be attracted to him. She didn't want to be attracted to anyone, ever again. Because the thought of being intimate with someone now...

She shuddered, turning her attention back to the task at hand. Over the next few hours, she lost herself in the repetitive nature of the work, in the calming effect of floating. By the time they headed back to the island, the sun was almost directly overhead and they had close to five bushels draped in strips of wet burlap to keep the crabs cool.

They were almost to the marina when a man waved them over from the deck of a neighboring restaurant. Jake shifted direction and cruised up alongside him.

"I see you got the hydraulics working again," the man said, catching the bowline.

"Finally," Jake said as the boat drifted to a stop, rocking gently against the rubber tires nailed into the bulkhead.

The man looked under the canopy. "What? No Becca today?"

"She was up late last night prepping for summer school," Jake said.

"Already?"

"Starts in two weeks."

The man shook his head. "That daughter of yours works too hard."

"Takes after her father," Jake said, and Izzy could hear the pride in his voice.

Hard work, she mused. That's what they valued here. It was the same message that had been drilled into her head as a child. It was the one truth she'd always been able to depend on—work hard and you can achieve anything.

So much of what she'd believed in had been shattered that night, nine months ago. But what if she could reclaim this one thing? What if he didn't get to take *everything* from her?

"My brother's in town for the weekend," the man said. "He and his wife want to pick crabs this afternoon. Can you spare a half bushel?"

Jake nodded and Ryan handed the crabs over. The man slipped Jake a cash payment, then started to untie the line from the cleat. "A couple of tourists came by earlier asking where they could buy some crabs. I told them to head down to the docks around eleven and look for you. Big guy with a Steeler's cap on and a blonde in a sundress."

"I'll keep an eye out for 'em," Jake said as they pushed away from the deck.

The motor hummed, the heavy workboat propelling them forward as they made their way over to the marina. "We try to cut out the middleman as much as we can," Jake said to Izzy.

Izzy nodded, because it made sense. Looking out at the vast body of water, she thought about how far removed she'd been from the people who'd grown or harvested the food she'd prepared in the Army. Wasn't that what the farm-to-table movement was all about? Getting to know the people behind your food?

She had never owned a farm, but she had worked on plenty. And she knew firsthand that every migrant worker who picked the fruits and vegetables that ended up in restaurants and dinner tables all over this country had a story. Many of them had families. Most of them were struggling. And every single one of them had a dream.

Or they wouldn't be here in the first place.

They pulled into the same boat slip they'd left hours ago,

before the sun had even begun to rise, and Ryan stepped onto the dock to secure the lines. He tied the knots, looping wet ropes around metal cleats in a rhythm so second nature it was obvious he'd been doing it since he was a child. This time, when he offered her a hand to help her off the boat, she took it.

"Thank you," she said, thinking how strange it felt to be on solid ground again. How, for the first time in months, when she'd been out there floating, things had started to make sense. "That was..."

He smiled. "I think I gave you the wrong job."

"What do you mean?"

"How would you like to go out on the boat with my father one day this week?"

"I'd like that," she said, already feeling a tremor of excitement at the prospect of being out on the water again.

"I thought so," he said, releasing her hand.

They heard footsteps on the end of the pier and glanced over. A petite brunette in her thirties was heading toward them with a child about Taylor's age. They were both carrying fishing rods. "Hey," the brunette called out. "How'd it go out there today?"

"We got five bushels," Ryan said.

"Not bad for a Sunday," she said, waving at the two people still in the workboat.

"Hi, Ms. Haddaway!" Taylor said, hopping out with both dogs trailing behind her. "Look what Ryan gave me!" She held up an arrowhead.

"Another one?" the brunette asked.

"Mom's going to be so excited."

Izzy looked at Ryan quizzically.

"Taylor and her mom make wind chimes," Ryan explained. "They're working on a Native American-themed chime now, with arrowheads and eagle feathers. I found the arrowhead on the shoreline at the farm the other day." He turned toward

Taylor. "You know you still owe me an oyster shell wind chime."

"I know," Taylor said, her expression growing serious. "Mom and I are still working on it. We haven't perfected it yet."

"I'll try to be patient," he said, the corners of his eyes crinkling as he smiled. He looked back at the brunette. "We had to loan Izzy a pair of your boots."

"And the hat," Izzy said, remembering that it was still on her head. "Is this yours, too?"

Becca took in the camouflage trucker hat and bit back a smile. "No. That's definitely *not* my hat. And it's probably never been washed, so you're a brave woman for wearing it. I'm Becca." She held out her hand. "And this is Luke."

"Are you going fishing?" Izzy asked, after they'd finished the introductions.

Becca nodded. "Luke's uncle bought him a new lure yesterday. We're going to test it out, see if we can get a few perch to bite."

"Can I see it?" Taylor asked.

Luke showed it to her, and she inspected the shiny silver lure carefully.

"Do you want to take the boat out?" Jake asked Becca. "It'll take me about a half hour to get her cleaned up."

"No," Becca said. "We'll just cast off the end of the pier, keep you company while you work."

"Can I come?" Taylor asked.

"Of course," Becca said. "But you have to eat lunch first. Your mom sent sandwiches over from the café." She started handing them out. "Oh, and Dad? Colin just called. He and Will want to have crabs at the inn this afternoon. Can you hold a bushel for them?"

Jake nodded, setting his sandwich aside until he finished his work for the day.

Ryan turned to Izzy. "Want me to give you a ride back to the inn?"

The inn? She didn't want to go back to the inn. She wanted to stay here.

"It was nice to meet you, Izzy," Becca said, waving goodbye as she and the two children headed for the end of the pier with their sandwiches and fishing rods.

Izzy glanced over at Jake, who was already hard at work prepping the boat for the next day. If she stayed, she'd probably just get in the way. "You know what," she said, looking at Ryan, "I think I'll walk."

"Are you sure? I don't mind running you back."

"I'm sure," she said. She needed some time to herself, to think.

"I'll walk you up to the parking lot. I need to grab a few things from my truck."

Izzy said goodbye to Jake and they strolled past the row of workboats and pickup trucks to the silver Chevrolet they'd arrived in that morning. She paused, glancing over her shoulder, just in time to see Riley try to steal a bite of Taylor's sandwich. She heard the child laugh, the carefree sound echoing over the harbor. "She's really something."

"She is," Ryan agreed.

Izzy continued to watch her. "She said something this morning about Riley—that she couldn't go out on the boat without her. Do you know what that was about?"

Ryan looked back at her, surprised. "You haven't heard?"

"Heard what?"

"About what happened to her."

Izzy shook her head.

Ryan was quiet for several moments. "I guess if you're going to be spending the next three months here, you're going to find out eventually. I might as well tell you."

"Tell me what?"

"Do you remember the shooting that happened at the elementary school in D.C. last year?"

Izzy nodded slowly. Everyone had heard about that shooting. A man had walked into a second-grade classroom and killed seventeen children before turning his semi-automatic weapon on himself. Only one child had made it out alive.

"That was Taylor's class," Ryan said. "Taylor's school."

Izzy's jaw dropped.

"I know," Ryan said. "It's hard to believe something like that could happen at all, let alone to someone you know."

Izzy looked back at the child on the dock. Taylor was the sole survivor of the Mount Pleasant school shooting? But she seemed...so normal, so well-adjusted.

"She's come a long way," Ryan said, "but she still has setbacks from time to time. Annie doesn't like her going anywhere without Riley. Whenever she gets upset, the dog calms her down."

"Is Riley a therapy dog?"

"I guess that depends on your definition of a therapy dog. She's not trained, if that's what you mean. She's just a dog, and like most dogs, they can sense what people need. When Annie moved here last year, Riley attached herself to Taylor. After a while, it was pretty obvious that she'd picked a new owner, so I just let her keep her."

Izzy looked back at Ryan. "Riley was yours?"

He nodded.

"You gave her a dog?"

Ryan reached down, petting the older, mellower chocolate lab who'd followed them up to the parking lot. "Zoey and I still miss her sometimes, but Taylor needs her more than we do."

Something inside Izzy cracked open, widened. She thought about how attentive Ryan had been with Taylor out on the boat today, how patient Jake had been, how Becca had greeted the child at the dock with lunch. No wonder Taylor had healed so quickly. With this many people looking out for her, how could she not? "Was Will overseas when it happened?"

"Will wasn't in the picture then," Ryan said. "He met Annie last fall, the same time we all did, when she and Taylor first moved to the island. Will just happened to be here, getting his grandparents' place ready to sell."

"Taylor's not his?"

"Well, she is now," Ryan said. "Will and Annie got married two weeks ago, right before the veterans' center opened."

Two weeks ago? Annie and Will had gotten married two weeks ago? And they'd already opened their home to a group of strangers? Still struggling to wrap her mind around all of it, Izzy remembered hearing that Will had recently separated from the SEAL teams after ten years of service. Aside from that, she knew next to nothing about him...despite the fact that she was staying in his house.

A house that, apparently, less than a year ago, he'd been planning to sell.

Why would Will give up a position in one of the most coveted branches of the military to move home and open a veterans' center? Was it because he had seen what this island had done for Taylor? Was there something about this place that she hadn't been able—or willing—to see before now?

Ryan held her gaze and she swore she could hear it, the same sound she'd heard that morning—the faintest clinking of seashells over the wind. She'd been so ready to write him off the moment she'd found out he was a farmer. But he wasn't like any of the farmers she'd worked for as a child. He wasn't running a soulless operation focused on productivity and the bottom line, ready to exploit its workers at any cost.

He might be running a farm, but he was a waterman at heart. And the men who worked these waters loved these waters. Every one of them had a story to tell, a personal history stitched into this tapestry of tributaries and marsh grasses. All Ryan was doing was trying to stitch a new future into it—one that would last. And she knew exactly how she was going to help him.

She might not be able to reclaim her dream, but she could help Ryan achieve his.

TEN

*B*radley Welker could hear the hum of the air conditioner as it kicked on down the hall. The rest of the offices were quiet as most of his staff, including his assistant, took Sunday off. He often worked through the weekend—responding to emails, catching up on paperwork, taking the occasional off-the-record meeting with one of his soldiers who had a personal matter to discuss.

Today, he was meeting with Lieutenant Alicia Booker, an intelligence officer who'd found out, a few days ago, that her ex-husband was suing for custody of their seven-year-old son. She hadn't told him herself yet, but he made it a point to know what was going on with his soldiers...particularly the women.

If there was one thing he'd learned in his twenty-five-year career with the military, it was that information was power.

Leaning back in his chair, he studied her file. He was fairly certain the purpose of this meeting was to get his approval to defer her acceptance into Ranger School so she could remain on base until the dispute was resolved. He'd been surprised when he'd found out that she'd applied to the program—a grueling eight-week infantry leadership course that admitted a small number of soldiers each year to the elite special operations branch of the Army.

He'd been even more surprised when he'd found out that, once she completed the course, she planned to transfer to infantry. Apparently, she didn't want to be an intelligence officer anymore. She wanted to fight. And with the increasing number of infantry leadership roles opening up for women, there was a good chance that within a year or two, she could be cleared to lead men into combat.

It was laughable really, the idea of a woman leading a unit on the ground. It was bad enough that so many of them were already tucked away in offices, calling the shots. In the past year, thousands of direct-action combat jobs had been opened up to women. Even the SEALs and the Green Berets had been ordered to open their ranks to the weaker sex.

As if a woman could actually complete those courses without the instructors dumbing them down. He had no doubt that the people running those programs had been given orders to fill quotas, let things slide. He knew a thing or two about following orders. The Army had drilled that message in loud and clear from the day he'd stepped off the bus. He wouldn't have risen so far in the ranks if he hadn't learned how to toe a line he didn't believe in from time to time.

But this...*this* was taking it too far.

He didn't know what the hell was going on with their leadership at the Pentagon, but if no one else was going to do anything about it, he would take matters into his own hands. Someone had to remind women where they belonged—in support roles, caregiver roles, *domestic* roles. As long as they stayed in their place, the world could continue to function the way it was supposed to.

He closed the file, tossed it back on the desk. It was unfortunate that Alicia Booker had decided to step out of line. But he'd enjoy putting her in her place first, making sure she knew exactly where she belonged.

The same way he had with Izzy Rivera.

Just thinking about the way the fiery Latina had struggled had him growing hard. For seven years, he'd tracked her career, biding his time. For seven years, he'd lived with the humiliation of being saved by a woman. How many nights had he lain awake, wishing the spray of shrapnel from the rocket-propelled grenade had killed him rather than wounding him?

Instead, he'd had to suffer through dozens of interviews, field countless questions from reporters, and shrug off an endless string of jabs from his male colleagues about the female cook who'd saved his life. He'd played the part that was expected of him in public—showering her with praise, giving her all the credit she'd deserved. He'd even flown to Washington D.C. for the awards ceremony and posed for pictures beside her when she'd received her Bronze Star.

But she had paid her price in the end. And she would keep their little secret. He'd made sure of it.

She had no proof. No real evidence. If she ever tried to open her mouth, it would be her word against his.

And no one would believe her anyway.

In public, his record was squeaky clean. He'd been one of the biggest supporters of women in the military—promoting them, praising them, treating them with respect. He knew how to make the people above him happy by checking the right boxes. What happened *behind* closed doors was another matter entirely. The way he saw it, he was doing the military a service. Nobody wanted women on the front lines. Not really.

He was simply putting things back in order.

Footsteps echoed on the tiles and he glanced up at the clock. Right on time. Alicia stepped into his office, offered a crisp salute.

He smiled, taking a moment to admire the view—mocha skin,

full lips, ice blue eyes. She was a little exotic, just the way he liked them, with enough curves to show through her uniform. "At ease, Lieutenant."

She relaxed. "Thank you for seeing me, sir."

"Of course," he said, gesturing for her to have a seat on the sofa as he stood, walked to the door, and closed it with a subtle flick of the latch.

DELLA DOZIER WASN'T above being a little sneaky, particularly when it came to matchmaking. When Will had called earlier that morning to enlist her help with one of the veterans, she'd been happy to offer whatever assistance she could provide. Of course, her nephew hadn't asked her to meddle in anyone's love life. He'd only asked her to spend the afternoon at the inn, cooking a crab feast and doing her best to lure Izzy Rivera into the kitchen. But the request had gotten her wheels spinning in a different direction.

She'd noticed how Ryan had reacted to Izzy on the first night. He'd hardly been able to take his eyes off her. She liked to think she had a sixth sense about these things. And when she'd heard that Izzy had spent the day on Jake's boat with Ryan and Taylor, it had only confirmed her suspicions.

As far as she was concerned, Ryan was long overdue for his own happily ever after. He'd spent far too much of his life obsessing about work and not nearly enough time having fun. She was looking forward to spending some time with Izzy today, to get to know her a little better. But first, she needed to get her into the kitchen, and get everyone else out.

Glancing around the room, she decided to start with the two men at the bar. "How would you like to fire up the grill for me, Kade?"

"I'd be happy to," he said, sliding off the stool where he'd been sitting for the past two hours, making small talk with her while she cooked.

"Jeff, why don't you give him a hand?" Della suggested. "There's a bag of sweet corn in the fridge that could go on the grill as soon as the coals are hot."

"Sure thing," Jeff said, grabbing the corn and following Kade outside.

No sooner had Jeff and Kade stepped out than Zach, Wesley, and Matt walked in, sweaty and sunburned from spending the past few hours kayaking. "It smells amazing in here," Matt said, heading for the spread of food on the counter.

That was the problem with big kitchens, Della thought. Too many people could come in and make themselves comfortable. She was used to working in a kitchen that was about a quarter of this size, where every square inch of counter space was accounted for and people entered at their own risk. Zach reached for a slice of cheese, popping it in his mouth, as the other two headed for the bar stools which had just been vacated.

"How would the three of you like to move some tables together and set up a place for us to eat outside?" Della asked. "We're less than an hour away, so you could go ahead and spread some newspaper over them, too."

"No problem," Zach said, snagging two more pieces of cheese for the road. "Where can we find the newspaper?"

"I think there's a stack in the den," Della said, sending them on their way.

Giving her coleslaw a stir, she looked across the room at where Paul and Hailey were sitting side by side on the sofa, their heads bent together over Paul's laptop. "Don't you two want to get outside and stretch your legs before we eat? You've been staring at that computer screen all day."

"We're almost finished," Paul said, without glancing up. He

made a few adjustments on the track pad with his fingers, then turned the screen toward Hailey.

"No." Hailey shook her head. "I still like the other one better."

"The first one or the second one?"

"The second one."

"Okay, wait. What if I..."

Tuning them out, Della tucked the coleslaw into the fridge and kept her ear trained for the sound of footsteps on the stairs. She didn't know what Izzy could possibly be doing up there, but she'd been holed up in her room ever since she'd returned a few hours ago. She slipped a few buttermilk-battered drumsticks into a pan of sizzling oil—there were few people who could resist the smell of her fried chicken—and hoped they would do the trick.

"So," she said, dusting the flour off her hands as she turned to face Paul and Hailey, "who wants to cut some fresh flowers for the tables?"

"I can do that," Megan said as she wheeled in from the hallway with a tattered copy of James Michener's *Chesapeake*, which she'd found on one of the bookshelves in the den that morning and had been absorbed in for most of the day. She pushed her wheelchair over to Della, accepting the clippers and a few small glass jars to use as vases. "Anything specific?"

"Maybe just some daisies from the beds by the front porch," Della said, smiling at her.

Megan wheeled away and Della could tell that Paul and Hailey weren't going to budge anytime soon. She figured she'd done her best. If she tried any harder to get rid of them, they'd probably pick up on it and start to suspect something. The only way she was going to pull this off was if everything seemed as natural as possible when Izzy came downstairs.

Glancing at the clock on the oven, she calculated that she had about fifteen minutes until Ryan and Becca would get here with the crabs. She took in the scene in the yard, making sure everyone else was distracted, then sent Will a quick text.

It was now or never...

THE D.C. FOOD scene was exploding, Izzy thought as she finalized the list she'd spent the past few hours compiling, hit the 'send' button, and closed her computer. Gone were the stuffy, unimaginative menus that had catered to politicians, lobbyists, and back room attorneys for decades. Celebrity chefs from all over the world were moving into the city, opening restaurants, experimenting with new methods, competing with each other. Michelin's prestigious *Red Guide* reviewers had even visited the city for the first time last year, thrown a few stars around.

It would take a while before D.C. caught up to places like New York and San Francisco, which had long ago established themselves as culinary trendsetters, but the initial sparks were there. And the energy behind those sparks was a new wave of breakout chefs who were targeting young, hip, environmentally conscious consumers willing to pay a premium for the best locally sourced food.

The timing for Ryan and his father to get into this market could not be better. But they needed to act fast, and make a name for themselves now, before they became a blur in a sea of suppliers who would all be courting these chefs with their own stories and promises to provide the finest product. It was really only a matter of winning over a few of them. Because they all talked to each other. They all followed each other's social media accounts. And if the best of the best were sourcing with a specific supplier, everyone else was going to get on board.

It was a good thing she understood chefs, what they cared about, what made them tick. It was simple, really. Behind every chef was a deep-rooted need to comfort. It didn't matter how technically accurate they were or how artistically they presented a dish; that desire to comfort others, to heal them and nourish them was the most important ingredient.

The most successful chefs were the ones who had learned to transfer that emotion into their cooking. And if the ingredients they started with had been cultivated with the same love, the same passion and intensity that they brought with them into the kitchen every day, it would be a powerful combination.

The way she saw it, all they needed to do was get a few well known chefs out here, let them experience what she'd experienced firsthand today, and Ryan and his father would be receiving more orders than they had oysters to fill.

Pushing back from the desk, she stood and followed the mouthwatering scent of fried chicken into the hallway. She spotted Will at the foot of the stairs, reading a text on his cell phone.

He slipped the device into his pocket the moment he saw her. "I was just about to come up and get you."

"Oh, yeah?" she asked, making her way down the steps.

"I wanted to make sure you didn't sleep through the crab feast."

"I wasn't sleeping," she said, offering him a smile for the first time since she'd arrived at his house a week ago. "Have you seen Paul around?"

Will gave her a questioning look, then nodded. "He's in the living room."

"Thanks," she said, brushing past him and walking into the hallway that connected the foyer to the kitchen. She saw Della behind the stove, lifting pieces of crispy chicken out of a pan of bubbling oil and transferring them onto a plate. She could smell the sharp, yeasty scent of biscuits rising in the oven, the vinegar from a batch of coleslaw, and the subtle, citrusy aroma of key lime pie.

She stepped into the living room, spotted Paul and Hailey on the couch, and walked toward them. When they glanced up and saw her, surprise registered on both their faces.

"I sent you an email," she said to Paul.

"When?"

"Just now," Izzy said.

Paul opened his email and scanned through the message. He was probably wondering why she was talking to him when she'd barely said two words to him all week. "What is this?"

"It's a list of chefs," she explained, "to target."

He looked back up at her. "For the oysters?"

She nodded. "I've broken them into three groups. The first are the celebrity chefs. You'll probably recognize some of the names. If we can get even one person in that group to give us a chance, it'll be enough for everyone else to start taking us seriously." She pointed to the next set of names on the screen. "The second group is made up of mostly farm-to-table chefs. They're the ones who'll want to hear about the Selkie Pearls, because they care about the stories behind the people who are growing their food. I've studied each of their websites and found something we could use to appeal to each of them personally. I've made notes and linked to their sites so you can see what I mean."

She paused, waiting for him to scroll down. "The third tier is the largest, and represents most of the well-established restaurants and oyster bars in the area. Every chef on that list is working for a business with a solid reputation and a loyal customer base. I'd recommend pitching the Pearl Coves to them, because they're running fast-paced operations with heavy turnover, and their staff won't have time to explain what a selkie is. These restaurants will be our main source of income, simply because of the sheer quantity they'll be able to move. But getting into the ones owned by the chefs in the first two groups should be our highest priority. Those are the ones that will set us apart, that will make it clear that we're not messing around. The more top tier chefs we can get in with, the less we'll have to market ourselves to the rest. Ultimately, they should be coming to us, not the other way around."

Paul and Hailey both stared at her with their mouths open.

Izzy heard the sound of a pan clatter behind her, and she glanced over her shoulder. Alone in the kitchen, Della was muscling a heavy, cast-iron pan onto the largest eye of the stove. Izzy watched her fire up the heat, and noticed that she had almost every eye going now. It seemed like an awful lot of food for a crab feast.

Weren't crab feasts supposed to be about the crabs?

"Some of these chefs are famous," Paul said, scrolling through the list of names on the screen. "They have TV shows."

"I know," Izzy said.

He looked up at her again. "They're not going to give me the time of day."

"They will if you have something they want."

"But..."

"Look," Izzy said, sitting down next to him. "Take Nolan Reyes, for instance." She pointed to one of the first names on the screen. "He owns six different restaurants in D.C., and each of those restaurants has a different chef in the kitchen. All you need to do is find a connection with one of them."

"But...how?"

"I would start by following each of them on social media. Get to know their personalities and figure out what you might have in common so you can strike up a conversation when you just happen"—she made air quotes—"to run into one of them."

"But...where am I going to run into one of them?"

She smiled and pushed back to her feet. "You'll figure it out."

The timer on the oven binged and Izzy looked over at the kitchen. Della was still behind the stove, with both hands occupied. The smaller pan was starting to smoke, and she thought she caught a hint of something burning. She walked over to the oven, pointed to the timer. "Do you want me to turn this off?"

"Yes, thank you," Della said, a little breathlessly. "I-I'm sorry. I'm not used to working in a kitchen this size. Could you just grab those biscuits out of the oven?"

Izzy hesitated. She hadn't set foot in a kitchen apart from zapping something in the microwave since leaving the military. But the woman did look a little frazzled.

"Here," Della said, pushing a pair of hot pads toward her. "Use these."

Izzy took the hot pads and looked at the oven. The light was on, and she could see from the golden-crusted tops that the biscuits needed to come out or they'd overcook. She took a deep breath. It was only a tray of biscuits. All she had to do was pull them out and set them on the counter.

The door squeaked as she opened it. A blast of warm air hit her in the face. It smelled of butter, cheddar cheese, and Old Bay seasoning. She breathed it in, letting the comforting aromas soothe her heightened nerves. She slid the tray out, set it on the counter, and stepped back.

There, she thought. That wasn't so bad.

She started to back out of the kitchen.

"Have you seen my slotted spoon anywhere?" Della asked, frantically pushing things around the cluttered counters. When she couldn't find it right away, she started opening drawers, rattling through them. "There's got to be another one around here somewhere."

"Um... I think it's..." Izzy took two tentative steps back into the kitchen, picked up the spoon from where it was hidden beneath a layer of paper towels, and handed it to Della. "Here."

Della beamed, grabbed her hand, and dragged her over to the stove. She dipped the spoon in a large pot of boiling water and fished out a butter bean. "Will you taste this? Tell me what you think?"

Izzy held out her hand and Della dropped the large, cream-colored bean into it.

She wasn't cooking, Izzy thought as a curl of steam rose from her palm. She was just tasting. And no matter what it tasted like, she would tell her it was perfect. But when she popped the bean in her mouth, and bit into it, it wasn't perfect. It was bland. And she couldn't lie. Not to another chef.

"It needs something, doesn't it?" Della asked.

Izzy nodded.

"Salt?"

No. Salt wouldn't be enough. "Do you have any bouillon cubes?"

"Yes!" Della's face lit up. "That's it!" Her cheeks were flushed and her gray-blond hair was starting to curl wildly from the steam coming off the stove. "I usually cook the beans in chicken broth, but I ran out last night and I forgot to pick up a box at the store this morning."

Izzy looked around the enormous kitchen. "Do you know where the spices are?"

Della pointed to one of the cabinets to the left of the stove.

Izzy walked over and rooted around the collection of spices until she found a jar of bullion cubes. She pulled one out, unwrapped the foil, and handed it to Della.

"You're a lifesaver," Della said, making room for her in front of the stove. "Would you mind throwing it in, giving it a stir?"

Izzy paused, not wanting to get any closer.

Della slid the next batch of chicken into the frying pan. "I know it seems like a lot of food, but not everyone has the patience for picking crabs. You've eaten them before, haven't you?"

"I have," Izzy said, still holding the bouillon cube.

"Have you ever steamed them yourself?"

"No."

"Well, if you think you can stomach it, I could use the help," Della said. "Which reminds me..." She stepped back, wiping her hands on her apron. "I left my big steamer pot in the car. Can you keep an eye on the chicken for me? I'll just be a minute."

Izzy opened her mouth to say no, but Della was already on her way out the door. And before she knew what was happening, she was alone in the kitchen, with four pans bubbling on the stove.

She stood frozen, her feet rooted to the floorboards. She heard voices out in the yard. Zach, Wesley, and Matt were moving tables together. Jeff and Kade were manning the grill, laughing at something someone had said. Behind her, in the living room, Paul and Hailey were deep in conversation, but their words sounded muffled, far off.

Fighting to curb the panic attack that lay like a familiar gray fog at the edge of her mind, always ready to creep in at the slightest hint of weakness, she took a step forward. Then another. The oil popped and sizzled, splattering out of the pan holding the chicken. She reached over it and dropped the bouillon cube into the boiling water.

It sank, dissolving into the butter beans. She picked up the spoon, gave the broth a gentle stir. You can do this, she thought. You just have to stand here and make sure nothing burns. Della will be back any minute.

But the seconds ticked by. Then the minutes. Until the breading on the drumsticks began to crisp, turning a rich golden brown. She swallowed, lifting the spoon again, slowly turning each piece over.

"Something smells good in here."

The voice—deep and masculine and hauntingly familiar—

had the spoon slipping from her fingers, clattering to the floor. And just like that, she was back in North Carolina.

Izzy snapped to attention, honoring Colonel Welker's rank. He smiled and waved away the formality, as he often did when no one else was around. The rest of her staff had left hours ago, but she had stayed late to test out a recipe for an upcoming military cooking competition, which she was determined to win. It wasn't uncommon for Colonel Welker to wander into her kitchen after hours, so she relaxed, at ease in his presence.

"It's a Oaxacan chili sauce," she said, turning back to the stove. "My grandmother's recipe."

He walked up behind her, and she thought nothing of it when he leaned in, peering over her shoulder at the exotic mixture of spices and dried chilies, ground nuts and dark chocolate. Despite the fact that he outranked her, and that officers weren't encouraged to mingle with enlisted soldiers, they'd been friendly ever since the attack in Afghanistan. She liked to think that it had bonded them. That, in a war zone, when you were fighting for your life, rank didn't matter as much.

She added cinnamon and a pinch of aniseed, turned the heat up on the burner, just a touch, and was about to reach for the bar of chocolate when his hand snaked out, caught her wrist.

The action was so unexpected, so out of character, it took her a moment to react. Her gaze shot up to his. He wasn't smiling anymore. His eyes were cold. And there was a look in them she'd never seen before.

She started to step away, but he grabbed her other arm and twisted it behind her back.

"What are you—? Stop," she said. "What are you doing?"

His grip tightened. He yanked her back against him. "Teaching you a lesson."

She froze, paralyzed. Panic pooled in the pit of her stomach.

No. This wasn't happening. This couldn't be happening. "Stop," she said again.

He leaned down, his lips grazing her ear. *"I've been waiting a long time for this."*

Fear whipped through her, pumping through the shock. "Get off me," she said, then louder. "Get off me."

He laughed, a hollow sound echoing through the empty kitchen, reverberating through the deserted dining hall. There was no one around—no one to hear her scream.

She struggled, pushing against him, using every instinct and surge of adrenaline inside her to fight. She managed to get one hand free, jam an elbow back, into his ribs, before he fisted a hand in her hair and threw her down on the counter. She cried out when her forehead smacked against the stainless steel. Pain seared through her temple. The inside of her mouth tasted metallic.

But none of that was as horrifying as the sound of him unfastening his belt.

"Did you think you'd get away with it?" His words were hard and bitter. "Did you think I'd let you emasculate me?" She heard the hiss of a zipper, the pop of a button. "You're no hero. You're nothing but a whore."

His hand was pressed into the back of her neck, holding her down. She tried to kick, to shove against him, but he'd pinned her to the counter with his hips. And then his hands were on her clothes, yanking them off her.

She saw the knife, a blur of silver, but it was too far away.

If only she could reach it. If only she could...

"Izzy? Izzy, can you hear me?"

The voice—a man's voice, low and urgent—raced toward her, like a rope, unfurling down a well.

But the other man was still holding her down. And all she could hear was his voice, and his words—the last words he'd said before he'd forced himself inside her—*"A woman's place is in the kitchen."*

The pain was blinding. But the knife was still there. She could just make out the blade, glinting in the fluorescent lights.

"Izzy? Are you okay?" A hand curved around her elbow, pulling her back, away from the heat of the stove. "Can you hear me?"

She hadn't been able to reach it then.

But she could reach it now.

She grabbed it, wrapping her fingers around the handle like a dagger, and whirled.

ELEVEN

*O*ill pivoted, instinctively moving his body away from the arc of the blade—or what would have been the arc, if she'd brought her arm down. But the moment she turned, and their eyes met, she froze. He seized on that split-second hesitation by disarming her, swiftly, skillfully, and with as little physical contact as possible.

The knife fell to the ground and he kicked it out of the way. Far enough away so she couldn't reach it. Not that he suspected she would. He could already see from the expression on her face that the flashback was fading and reality was beginning to sink in.

He didn't dare touch her, knowing, somehow, deep down, that that was what had set her off. He stood with his arms at his sides, his palms facing toward her, making sure she could tell that he wasn't a threat. Adrenaline still surged through his body, carrying with it a hot rush of anger. Not at her. But at whoever had planted that fear inside her.

Someone had hurt her.

And, suddenly, all at once, her actions, her attitude, her isolation from the rest of the veterans made perfect sense.

Izzy's eyes were wild as they darted around the room, as she took in the faces staring back at her. "I... I didn't mean..." She trailed off when her gaze landed on the knife. She took a step back. Then another. Two more steps and she turned, pushed past the group of people in the hallway, and fled up the stairs to her room.

Will said nothing, because he knew what that felt like—how humiliating it was to have a flashback in public.

"My God, Will," Della breathed, her voice shaking. "She almost... You almost..."

Will walked to the stove, switched off the burners. He picked up the knife from the floor, set it on the counter, and crossed the kitchen to where his aunt stood. Reaching out, he put a hand on her shoulder and squeezed. They would talk later, in private, when he had the ability to offer her the comfort she needed. Right now, they had a mess to clean up. "I need you to go upstairs and make sure Izzy's okay. We're responsible for what just happened. She needs to know that it wasn't her fault."

Della wrung her hands. He could tell she didn't want to leave him, that the image of what had just happened would be seared into her mind for months. But she took a deep breath and nodded before turning and heading for the stairs.

In the hallway, Becca and Ryan parted to let her through. Ryan was holding Taylor in his arms. She was clinging to him, her head buried in his shoulder. He'd probably picked her up as soon as he'd seen what was happening. Will went to them, mouthed a silent "*thank you*" to Ryan, and carefully took his step-daughter into his own arms. "Hey, sweetie," he said, his voice gentling. "You okay?"

She nodded bravely, then wrapped her arms around his neck and just held.

He took a moment to savor it—the relief at knowing she was safe. It was the only emotion he would let himself feel right now. The rest would come later, much later. He had learned a long time ago how to push his emotions aside. How to focus on what needed to be done and deal with the implications later.

He had a feeling they were going to be dealing with the implications of this for some time.

He looked down at Becca. "Where's Annie?"

"In the garden," Becca said, the worry evident in her voice. "We saw her when we drove up."

"Good," he said. At least she hadn't seen what had happened. He needed to tell her as soon as possible, but at least she hadn't seen it with her own eyes.

He turned to face Paul and Hailey, who stood in front of the sofa in the living room, looking shell-shocked.

"You all right?" Will asked.

They both nodded slowly.

"When Izzy comes back downstairs, try to make light of the situation," Will said. "Joke around with her a little. The worst thing you can do is pretend like nothing happened or tiptoe around her like she's going to break. She needs your friendship, not your pity. Understand?"

"Yes," Paul said.

"Of course," Hailey said.

Taylor tightened her grip around his neck and he whispered a few soothing words in her ear before looking back at Ryan. "Can you get the crabs started? Tell everyone to go ahead and eat as soon as the first batch is ready?"

Ryan nodded, grabbed the steamer pot Della had left on the counter, and carried it over to the sink to fill with water.

"I'll help," Hailey offered.

"Me too," Paul said.

"Thank you," Will said gratefully. "Maybe one of you could try to salvage what's left of the food on the stove."

"I'm on it," Paul said, already walking over to inspect the contents of the pans.

Will headed for the doorway, pausing briefly beside Becca. "Find Colin," he said, lowering his voice. "Tell him to put a call in to Erin, see how soon she can get here."

Becca nodded. "Where are you going?"

He looked past her, to the front yard, where Annie was walking toward them with a basket of strawberries. "I need to talk to my wife."

Izzy GRABBED the last of her clothes from the bureau, shoving them into her pack. She walked into the bathroom, scooped her toiletries off the counter, and threw them in as well. It didn't matter if the tops came off, if the liquids leaked through her clothes. They'd probably confiscate all her belongings as soon as she got to the jail anyway.

Her limbs moved mechanically, her mind racing from question to question. Would they send a police car? Take her away in handcuffs again? Should she call her probation officer? Tell her what happened before she found out from someone else?

She opened the door to the closet, pulled out the basket of laundry, emptied it onto the bed. The last time the cops had come for her, she'd surrendered herself willingly. She hadn't even considered the possibility of a plea bargain in her future—the opportunity for a second chance. She'd been so numb back then, she wouldn't have cared if they'd told her they were locking her up for life.

But she did care now.

She had started to feel something today—the tiniest sliver of hope. She had actually started to think that she could contribute. That, even if she couldn't cook anymore, she could at least use the knowledge she'd picked up from years of working in kitchens to help Ryan understand his new clientele. That, maybe, it hadn't *all* been for nothing.

She grabbed fistfuls of laundry, shoving them into her pack. Stupid, she thought. Stupid, stupid, stupid, stupid, stupid. She should have known better than to think, even for a second, that things could be different. That she could actually belong somewhere again.

The only place she belonged was in jail.

At the knock on her door, she let out a long, shaky breath. She knew it would either be Will or Colin, telling her it was time to go. She set down the clothes and called out, "Come in."

The door creaked open and she rolled her shoulders back, mustering one last shred of pride. She wouldn't leave without thanking them first. For giving her a chance. For trying to save her. She understood what they were doing here, now—why they had opened this place. It wasn't their fault she was damaged beyond repair.

But it wasn't Will or Colin.

It was Della.

And the expression on her face didn't quite fit with the message Izzy was expecting.

Della paused in the doorway, her hand on the knob, her gaze dropping to the clothes on the bed. "What are you doing?"

"Packing."

"Why?" Della asked. It was obvious from the tone of her voice that she hadn't put two and two together yet.

Izzy stuffed the rest of the clothes in her bag. She needed to keep moving, to distract herself from the emotions rising up inside her. "They're not going to let me stay after what just happened." She turned, grabbed her laptop, and started to slide it inside the bag, then paused, wondering if she should email herself the spreadsheet first.

Would they allow her to access her email in jail? Or would she have to start her research all over again, from the very beginning?

She flinched at the sudden hand on her shoulder. She hadn't even heard the other woman cross the room. She looked up, into Della's concerned blue eyes. "Do you think they'll call the police," Izzy asked, mortified when her voice cracked, "or let me turn myself in?"

Della pried the laptop gently from her hands. She set it on the desk, led her over to the edge of the bed, and sat. She waited for Izzy to sit down beside her. "No one's going to ask you to turn yourself in."

"But—"

"What happened down there wasn't your fault," Della said. "It was mine—mine and Will's."

Izzy shook her head. "That doesn't make any sense."

"Let me explain." Della drew Izzy's hand into her lap, covered it with both of hers. "Last night, after you cut your therapy appointment short, Will and Colin met with Erin. She told them she was worried about you, that she didn't think you were adjusting well. They asked if there was anything they could do to help...pull you out of your shell. She said she'd heard from one of the other veterans that you didn't cook anymore. She thought, maybe, if you started cooking again, it might help you heal."

Della took a deep breath. "Colin figured they'd put you on kitchen duty this week and see how it went. But Will decided to take it a step further. He thought that if anyone could connect with you on that level, it would be me. So he called this morning and asked me to try to lure you into the kitchen today. I assumed you'd just lost your confidence, that maybe you needed a little encouragement."

She looked away. "I didn't need your help down there today,

Izzy. I've been cooking those dishes all my life. I knew those beans were bland, and I would never have left those biscuits in the oven to burn. I created that situation on purpose. I had no idea you'd..." She lifted her gaze back to Izzy's, her eyes filled with remorse. "I'm so sorry. Can you forgive me?"

Forgive her? "I almost stabbed your nephew."

"I know, honey. And I'm still pretty shaken up about that." She put a hand on her heart, breathed. "But I should have talked to you first, asked you *why* you'd stopped cooking, given you a chance to explain. If you wanted to cook again, I could have eased you into it slowly. Or not. That was your call to make. Not mine. And not Will's."

Izzy was quiet for several long moments as she let Della's words sink in. Was it possible that Will felt the same way? That he wasn't going to ask her to leave? That he would give her another chance?

"Izzy?"

"Yes?" she asked, and her voice sounded different now—hopeful—even to her own ears.

"Did something happen to you...in a kitchen?"

Voices from the yard drifted up, through the open window. The scent of vinegar, grilled corn, and Old Bay seasoning mingled with the salty breezes floating off the water. The faintest rustling of leaves, from the highest branches of the tulip poplars, drew her gaze out, to the edge of the yard. She watched the leaves dance, a playful fluttering of silver and green, before nodding slowly.

"Do you want to talk about it?"

Izzy shook her head. No. She didn't want to talk about it. She wanted to pretend it had never happened. But as the voices beneath her window grew louder, and more people came out of the house, gathering around the tables, preparing to sit down to eat, she realized that wasn't going to be possible anymore. Too many people had seen what had happened in the kitchen.

How many of them would look at her differently now? How many of them would jump to the same conclusion as Della?

How long would it take before they suspected the truth?

"Do you think everyone knows?" Izzy asked, her voice barely above a whisper.

"I don't know, honey," Della said, squeezing her hand. "But what I *do* know is that everyone here is on your side."

When Izzy said nothing, Della shifted slightly on the mattress to face her. "Do you know why Will opened this veterans' center?"

"To help people," Izzy said.

"Well, sure," Della said slowly, "that's one reason. But that's not the only reason."

Izzy waited for her to go on.

"My nephew is a proud man," Della said, "and he doesn't confide in a lot of people, so I hope that you'll keep what I'm about to say between the two of us."

Izzy nodded. "Of course."

"Will left the SEALs because he was suffering from such debilitating flashbacks that he wasn't able to perform his job anymore. He was diagnosed with post-traumatic stress disorder about six months ago and has been receiving treatment ever since." Della looked up, met Izzy's gaze. "He opened this place because he knows, firsthand, what it feels like to need help, and not know how to ask for it."

Izzy's lips parted as, suddenly, everything clicked into place. That was why he'd tried to pull her out of the flashback. That was why there'd been nothing but compassion in his eyes after he'd taken the knife from her. That was why he wasn't up here right now, telling her to pack her bags.

"Everyone here is fighting some kind of battle," Della said

gently. "The sooner you can accept that, and recognize that you're not alone, the sooner you'll begin to heal."

Izzy rose slowly and walked to the window. She looked down at the crowd of people below. They were seated around the tables now, talking and laughing and passing big plates of food around. "I need to apologize to Will," she said. "To everyone."

"Why don't we get you something to eat first," Della suggested, "then we can worry about apologies."

Izzy nodded and, together, they walked back downstairs.

Sprawled across the entrance to the kitchen, Ryan's dog, Zoey, thumped her tail against the floorboards at the sight of them. Ryan and Paul—the only two people left in the kitchen—glanced up when they stepped into the room.

"Hey, Izzy." Paul turned toward her with a bag of seasoning in one hand and a pair of tongs in the other. "I told Ryan about that list you made—of the chefs. He's pumped."

Pumped, Izzy thought as her gaze shifted to Ryan. She doubted that her boss had ever used the word 'pumped' in his life, and she was fairly certain that the list of chefs was the last thing on his mind right now.

He stood at the stove, his hand resting calmly on a sixty-quart steamer pot. He was wearing the same clothes he'd worn out on the boat that day—the gray T-shirt, the faded jeans, the fraying baseball cap—but there were questions in his eyes now, so many questions, in those pale, almost see-through gray eyes.

The timer on the oven binged and he turned slowly back to the stove, lifting the top off the pot. A cloud of steam billowed out, and he reached in with the tongs, pulled the steaming hot crabs out of the pot, and transferred them onto the tray.

Paul slathered them with a few more handfuls of seasoning, then picked them up and looked at Izzy. "Would you grab the door for me?"

Izzy nodded, crossed the room to the door, and held it open for him.

Paul paused in the doorway and lowered his voice. "You all right?"

"Yes," she said, looking away.

"Good," he said, then grinned. "You've got some pretty badass reflexes for a cook."

Izzy blinked, stunned. She lifted her gaze back to his, but he was already walking away. She stared after him, noticing, for the first time, how easily he navigated the steps with two prosthetic legs, how well he hid the slight limp on his right side when he walked. Slowly making her way across the grass, she met the eyes of a few people who glanced up from the picnic tables. There was no judgment on any of their faces, just kindness and compassion and understanding.

Why had she assumed they would all judge her? That, just because her wound was invisible, they couldn't possibly understand?

Hailey scooted over as soon as Izzy got to the first table, making room for her. Izzy sat down, and saw that Hailey's plate was already filled with fried chicken, butter beans, coleslaw, and sliced tomatoes. She was about to offer her a crab from the pile Paul had left in the center of the table, when she remembered that Hailey wouldn't be able to pick it.

She only had one hand.

Was that why Della had made all this extra food? So Hailey wouldn't feel left out?

Wondering if she should offer to pick a crab for her, she saw Kade snag a big crab from the pile, rip all the claws off, and hand them to Hailey.

"Thanks," Hailey said, admiring the big chunks of meat hanging off the end of each claw.

Kade looked over at Izzy. "Yo."

"Yo, yourself," she said, watching him carefully. She couldn't tell from his expression if he'd heard about what happened, if he knew anything at all.

He cracked the body of his crab in half, then nodded to a spot on the table in front of her. "We gave you a mallet instead of a knife."

It took a moment for the words to sink in, for the meaning behind them to register. But when she looked around the table and saw that everyone else had a knife for their claws except for her, she started to laugh. And then Hailey started to laugh. And then Kade started to laugh—a deep, infectious rumbling that had everyone around them laughing, too.

By the time she got a hold of herself, and started to pick her first crab, she had to wipe away a few tears. She looked around the yard, at the people seated at the other two tables, searching for Will so she could apologize as soon as she finished eating. But it didn't take long for her to realize that he wasn't there. And neither was Annie...or Taylor.

And she knew, as her heart sank, that that was a very bad sign.

ANNIE WAITED until Taylor was safely tucked away in her bathroom with the shower running, before turning to face Will. "I'm not okay with this. I'm *not* okay with it."

"I know," Will said calmly. "I understand."

"No," she snapped. "I don't think you do." Sunlight streamed through the skylights, flooding the second-story landing with light. On any other day, she might have taken a moment to admire the way it enriched the warm, golden hue of the walls.

But not today.

Today, all she could think about was that her husband had

almost been attacked by one of the veterans he was trying to help. "This is our *home*, Will. I have boundaries. And she just crossed one of them."

"I understand," he repeated, in that same calm, measured tone that was starting to piss her off. "But I'm okay. Everyone's okay."

"Don't talk to me like I'm a child!"

"Annie." He reached for her, but she took a step back.

This wasn't some lover's spat that he could soothe away with a hug and a few murmured apologies. He could have died down there. She could have lost him. "What if it had been Taylor? What if it had been Della?" Her voice broke, betraying the fear underneath the anger. "She could have sent someone to the hospital today, or worse."

"She could have," Will said evenly. "But she didn't. She stopped. The moment she turned around and saw me, she stopped."

No. Annie shook her head. That wasn't good enough for her. "The woman shot someone, Will."

"Allegedly."

"She pled guilty in court. Under oath."

"To get the deal the prosecution offered," Will said. "I might have done the same thing."

She stared at him. "Accepted a criminal record for life? Even if you didn't commit the crime?"

"If the evidence was stacked against me. Sure."

Annie turned, walked to the window, and laid her hands on the sill. How could he be so calm about this? How could he not understand that this had changed everything?

She took in the crowd of people gathered around the picnic tables. They were picking crabs as if nothing had happened, as if no one had pulled a knife on her husband less than an hour ago.

Violence might be normal to them, but it wasn't to her. And

she wasn't going to pretend, even for a second, that what happened downstairs was okay. "I'm all for helping veterans who want to be helped," Annie said, "but Izzy's had an attitude from the moment she walked through the door. There are plenty of other veterans who would be happy to take her place. We're only one week into the program. It's not too late to open up her spot for someone else. Maybe this isn't the right place for her. Maybe she needs to be somewhere else."

"Where?" Will asked incredulously. "Jail?"

Annie turned back to face him. "Maybe."

"No," Will said, shaking his head. "This is exactly why Colin and I opened this place. To catch the people the system failed. To make sure that no one under our care slips through the cracks. She doesn't belong in jail."

"How do you know?"

Will dragged a hand through his hair. "Because that could have been *me*, Annie."

It was the one thing he could have said to make her pause.

"That *was* me," Will said, lowering his voice. "Six months ago, I was the one having flashbacks. I was the one waking up in a cold sweat every night. I was the one wishing I'd died instead of my friends."

Annie said nothing. Because she knew it was true. She'd been right there beside him through most of it.

But she'd never once thought that she and Taylor were in any kind of physical danger.

Could they have been, if he'd let his PTSD go untreated? If he'd let all that pain and trauma bottle up inside him until it came out in an explosion, like Izzy's had today?

"The thing is," Will said, taking a breath. "I think someone hurt her. And I think it might have been someone on the inside—someone she worked with. It would explain why she's been so isolated from the other veterans. Why she doesn't trust anyone."

Yes, Annie thought. It would. And she could read between the lines of what Will was saying. But she wasn't ready to make that leap yet. Not until she got some answers first. She pulled her phone out, dialed a number, and lifted the device to her ear.

"Who are you calling?"

"Grace," Annie said as the shower in Taylor's bathroom clicked off. "To find out if you're right."

TWELVE

$\mathcal{G}$ race liked it when her friends called her for help. She enjoyed being pulled into the dramas on Heron Island. It made her feel like she was still part of the community, even though she'd left over ten years ago.

Pouring herself a glass of wine in the kitchen of her small Capitol Hill apartment, she couldn't help feeling envious of her brother. Before Ryan had made the decision to move home, she hadn't considered that that would be an option for either of them, at least not at this stage in their careers. But, somehow, in the past year, he had managed to pull it off.

And Ryan wasn't the only one. Will, Becca, Colin, and Annie had all managed to carve out a niche for themselves on the island, causing her to reflect on her own life circumstances.

There was a part of her—a large part—that wished she could join them. But what would she do there? Her job was here, in the city. And she loved her job. She *needed* her job. Not just for the money, but because it was how she made sense of things.

She'd gone into journalism—a truth-seeking career—because her childhood had been shrouded in mystery. Losing a mother had been bad enough, but the fact that they still didn't know what happened to her was what haunted her the most.

She had questions, so many questions, that had never been answered, but the biggest one was why? Why had their mother left them? Why had she walked away from a husband and two children when her life, from everything Grace could remember, had been a happy one?

It didn't make any sense.

She'd gone over the events of the days leading up to her mother's disappearance a hundred times, and nothing had seemed out of the ordinary. For years, she'd been convinced that someone had taken her, that the cops had closed the case too soon. But with no signs of a struggle, or any indication that her mother had been abducted against her will, they'd had nothing to go on.

If only her mother had left a clue, just *one* clue, Grace would have been able to pick up the investigation on her own. But she'd taken nothing. Not her wallet, not her jewelry, not a single piece of clothing except for what she'd been wearing. And neither her brother nor her father would talk about it. Whenever she brought it up, they changed the subject as quickly as possible.

She knew they both secretly blamed themselves, because she blamed herself, too.

How could she not?

She must have done something wrong for her mother to abandon her.

Picking up the glass of wine, she carried it out to the balcony and prepared to spend the rest of the evening funneling all those childhood frustrations into an investigation where she *did* have a lead to follow.

Isabella Rivera.

The woman's name had come up not once, but twice, in the past week. When Annie had called and explained what had happened at the inn earlier, her friend had been understandably panicked. From the moment Annie had set foot on Heron Island, she had made it clear to everyone that Taylor's safety was her number one priority. Now, she and her daughter were sharing their home with a criminal—one who had pulled a knife on her husband less than an hour ago.

The question was...how unhinged was this woman?

Opening her laptop, Grace ran a search on Izzy's name and scanned the first few hits that popped up on the page: "*Army Cook Earns Bronze Star,*" "*Military Chef Awarded Medal for Bravery in Combat,*" "*Sergeant Isabella Rivera Honored for Heroic Actions in Afghanistan.*"

Grace's eyes widened. She hadn't been expecting that. Scrolling through the rest of the links on the page, she paused at the gallery of images. When she saw a picture of Izzy for the first time, her brows shot up.

Whoa.

That was Izzy Rivera?

She clicked on a few of the images, zoomed in. Even in her uniform, with her hair slicked back in a tidy bun, the woman was stunning. Like Penélope Cruz or Salma Hayek stunning.

No wonder her brother hadn't been able to get her off his mind.

She felt a familiar humming sensation, the same one she got whenever she realized that a crucial piece of information had been left out of an earlier conversation. Scrolling through the long list of links regaling Izzy's exemplary military service, she finally found one that connected her to a shooting that had happened in Baltimore earlier that year. She clicked on the story, skimmed through the first few paragraphs, then slowly sat back in her chair.

She remembered this story.

The shooting, which had taken place in the impoverished neighborhood of Sandtown-Winchester on Baltimore's west side, had led to the arrest of one of the biggest drug dealers in Maryland.

Tyree Robinson, the man Izzy had shot, had worked for that drug dealer. When the EMTs had transported him to the hospital for the gunshot wounds, they'd found heroin on him and turned him over to the police. As a third-time offender, Tyree had been facing serious jail time, so the police had offered him a shorter sentence in exchange for his help bringing down his boss. Tyree had taken the deal, and with the information he'd provided, the cops had been able to gather enough evidence to put his boss behind bars.

It had been a huge coup for the Baltimore Police Department.

But what Grace wanted to know was how Izzy fit into all of it? What had she been doing in Sandtown-Winchester that night? And why had she shot Tyree in the first place?

Knowing that she wasn't going to find the answers to any of those questions online, she grabbed her phone and scrolled through her contacts. When she found the name of an old friend who'd transferred from the D.C.P.D. to the Baltimore P.D. a few years ago, she hit 'call' and waited for him to pick up.

"I have a feeling my day's about to get more complicated," Keith Nichols said.

Grace smiled. She'd met Keith over ten years ago, when they'd both been in their early twenties. He'd been a beat cop, fresh out of the Academy, and she'd been a rookie staff writer, covering mostly robberies and assaults. He'd been one of her earliest sources, and they'd built up a mutual respect for each other over the years. If there was anyone who'd be willing to trust her with inside information on a case, it was Keith.

"How much do you know about the Tyree Robinson shooting?" she asked, diving right in.

"A fair amount," he said. "It was a pretty big case."

"Did anything seem off to you about it?"

"Off in what way?"

"I don't know," Grace said. "Any loose strings that never got tied up? Lingering questions that never got answered?"

"Why don't you call the detectives who worked the case and ask them that?"

"Because they'd refer me to your public relations department," Grace said, "and I'm not looking for a scripted response."

"I'm sorry to disappoint you, but I'm going to stick to the script on this one. The Tyree Robinson shooting led to one of the biggest arrests the Baltimore P.D. has made in decades. We put a drug lord behind bars. What else do you want to know?"

"I want to know about the woman who shot Tyree."

There was another pause, longer this time. "What about her?"

"Did they know each other?" Grace asked.

"No," Keith said. "Not that I'm aware of."

"Then why did she shoot him?"

"I don't know."

"What do you mean, you don't know?"

"Nobody knows," Keith said. "After her initial confession, the only person she ever spoke to was her lawyer. By the time her court date came around, she'd already agreed to a plea deal. We don't usually spend too much time asking why after someone pleads guilty."

"But—"

"Look," Keith said, cutting her off. "No one in the department was thrilled with the idea of putting a female vet behind bars, especially one who was a first time offender and who actually did us a service by pumping a few bullets into Tyree. Most of us were relieved to hear that she got off on probation."

"So...you don't think she's a threat?"

"I think," Keith said, "that as cases go, this was one of the few where everything got tied up in a nice, tidy, little bow. So whatever it is that you're looking for, you should let it go."

No, Grace thought, she wasn't going to let it go. Not until she found out the truth. And he was hiding something. She could tell. "Let's just say, hypothetically, that you did want to ask why. Where would you start?"

Keith sighed. "Don't you have anything better to do on a Sunday afternoon than stir up trouble with the cops?"

"I would never dream of stirring up trouble," Grace said innocently, and pictured him rolling his eyes.

"Where's all this coming from anyway?" he asked.

"I'm doing some research for a friend," she said. "It's not even work related."

"You're not writing a story about it?"

"No." At least, not yet, anyway.

"So anything I say would be off the record?"

"Of course."

"Then I'd start with the police report."

Grace reached for her laptop. "The police report from the night of the shooting?"

"Yes," Keith said, "and I'd pay particular attention to the entry points of the three gunshot wounds."

Grace made a note on her screen. "Entry points?"

"That's right," Keith said. "One in the right shoulder. One in the left hip. One just above the right knee."

Grace stopped typing. "Those shots are all over the place."

"They sure are," Keith agreed.

"That's kind of strange, isn't it?" she asked. "I mean, I would have thought that a veteran—"

"—would know how to shoot a gun?" Keith finished. "Yeah, me too."

"So...she's got bad aim?"

"That's one theory."

"Well, if she was a cook," Grace said, searching for a reasonable explanation, "she probably didn't have to fire a weapon very often."

"She might have been a cook, but she served in both Iraq and Afghanistan. She would have known how to handle a weapon, especially at that range."

Grace sat back, her eyes widening. "You don't think she did it."

"I have my doubts," Keith admitted. "A lot of us do."

"Well, if she didn't do it, who did?"

"That's a good question," Keith said. "Unfortunately, the Baltimore P.D. doesn't have the time or the resources to take the investigation any further, not when we already have a confession on file."

Grace lifted her gaze to the telephone wires stretched across the alley behind her apartment, where a mockingbird was imitating the sound of a siren. She could hear the crush of traffic on Pennsylvania Avenue a few blocks away, the pulsing beat of a helicopter in the distance, the swell of voices from the tourists dining at the sidewalk café around the corner. "Were there any witnesses?"

"None that would have held up in court," Keith said. "Most of the people in that neighborhood won't even open their doors for the cops. The only person who would talk to us was an addict who lived across the street. Obviously, we can't trust anything she said, but—according to her—there were two women in the alley that night, not one."

"Two women?" Grace's brows drew together. "If there were two women in the alley, why didn't the other one come forward?"

"I don't know," Keith said. "Maybe she had something to hide."

Grace thought about what Keith had said about the gun, that

it had most likely been fired by an amateur. If Izzy hadn't shot Tyree...

"I know what you're thinking," Keith said. "If she didn't shoot him, why would she take the fall for it?"

She had no idea, Grace thought. But if there *had* been another woman in the alley that night, she was going to find her. The people of Sandtown-Windchester might not be willing to talk to the cops. But she wasn't a cop. She was a journalist. And in her experience, as long as you were willing to listen, almost everybody had a story to tell.

THIRTEEN

*T*he next three weeks passed in a blur of punishing heat and unrelenting humidity. Ryan spent almost every waking hour at the farm, despite the promise he'd made to his sister to try to rein in his workaholic tendencies. He couldn't remember the last time he'd slept through a sunrise or eaten a meal at home. He kept a stash of dog food in the office for Zoey, who spent most of her time, now, stretched across the air conditioning vent under Paul's desk.

Every day, he offered to send his staff home early, knowing that working outside in these temperatures could take a toll, and every day, they refused. Many of them had actually begun to stay longer to finish up whatever projects they were working on before heading back to the inn for the evening.

Ryan respected their work ethic, and he understood their desire to feel valued again, but sometimes he worried that a few of them might be getting *too* attached. This job was only supposed to be a stepping-stone into permanent employment. Realistically, there was only so much they could accomplish in the next two months.

Sitting back on his heels, he wiped the sweat from his brow with his forearm. His hands were covered in dirt from spending the morning planting grasses and shrubs along the shoreline. Ethan and Hailey were inside the environmental center, designing a series of markers that would label each plant. On the other side of the property, Matt and Izzy were stacking cages into a skiff, preparing to transfer the first batch of baby oysters from the nursery to the lease.

As he'd done so many times over the past few weeks, Ryan took a moment to watch her. Ever since the incident in the kitchen, she'd been desperately trying to prove herself. She'd been one of the first to insist on staying late to finish her work. She rarely took a break before looking around to see if anyone else needed help. And she was actually talking to people now. Not long conversations, but enough to show that she wasn't isolating herself anymore.

All of that should make him happy.

Instead, he couldn't stop thinking about what Will had said when they'd finally had a chance to talk about what had happened—that he suspected Izzy might have been raped.

Raped.

In employing a group of wounded warriors, he'd expected to encounter some psychological issues. He'd been prepared to accommodate a wide range of physical disabilities. But this...?

Nothing could have prepared him for this.

And the worst part about it was that it made sense—the way she'd seemed so traumatized when she'd first arrived, the way she'd alienated herself from the rest of the veterans, the way she'd shied away from physical contact with members of the opposite sex.

He wasn't usually the type to jump to conclusions. Years of research had taught him that even the most promising hypotheses could fall apart in the end. It was better to remain skeptical, to temper any emotional reactions until actual proof had been established.

But this wasn't a science experiment.

This was a person.

And the mere *notion* that Izzy might have been sexually assaulted was enough to make his blood boil.

Reaching for the nearest bottle of water, Ryan took a long swallow. He knew that his sister was looking into Izzy's past now. And if anyone could uncover the truth, it was Grace. In the meantime, there was nothing any of them could do but make sure that she, and everyone around her, felt as safe and secure as possible.

"Hey, boss," Jeff said, walking over. "I just finished preparing the financial reports for the board meeting next week."

Forcing all thoughts of Izzy out of his mind—for now, at least —Ryan pushed to his feet. "How do they look?"

"Like we need to do some fundraising."

Ryan nodded. He'd figured as much. With all the extra work he'd taken on to prepare for the arrival of this first group of veterans, he hadn't had time to focus on raising funds for the environmental center. A few of his board members had expressed concern at the last meeting that he might be spreading himself too thin, that in merging the two operations he could get distracted from the overall mission.

It wasn't a concern that he shared. Every move he'd made over the past year had been with the overall mission in mind. His vision for the future had never been clearer. If anything, working alongside these veterans for the past month had solidified it. But he understood that not everyone could picture it as vividly as he could.

He needed to lay it out for them in black and white, make sure he had their full support moving forward. "Did you work up a budget for the rest of the year?"

Jeff nodded and handed him a copy of the report.

Ryan took it, already scanning the charts and columns as he made his way over to the picnic area.

"Most of your income is made up of grants," Jeff said, taking a seat at one of the tables in the shade. "Grant money's great and all, but I think you need to diversify, tap into some different income streams."

Ryan lowered himself to the seat across from Jeff. He'd been thinking the same thing. He'd relied pretty heavily on grants to cover most of his start-up costs. With his credentials and his ability to sell himself on paper, he won most of the ones he applied for anyway. But, from everything he'd read, the success of most nonprofits after the first year depended on individual donations.

He was going to have to step up his game—and fast.

"How'd you come up with these numbers?" Ryan asked, zeroing in on the fundraising projections.

"Paul figured you'd want to throw at least one big event in the fall, to line up with oyster season. And I factored in the expenses of hosting a few smaller functions between now and the end of the year to start building up your roster of individual donors." Jeff pointed to a number on the page. "This is how much we think you should spend on each of the events. And this," he said, pointing to another number, "is how much you should be able to make back from them."

"You don't think that estimate's a little high?"

Jeff raised a brow. "Not if you do a good job with the events."

Ryan managed a half-smile in return, then continued to scan the rest of the report. The truth was, throwing parties and courting individual donors was his least favorite part of the job. It was one thing to appeal to private foundations and government agencies that had publicly announced that they had funds to invest and were actively seeking worthy causes to support. But asking individuals to open their personal checkbooks, especially face to face, made him extremely uncomfortable.

He had underestimated how much that would be a part of this job. It was one of the reasons he'd wanted to combine his nonprofit with his father's oyster farm. The business would naturally provide a wider platform to reach people who might be interested in supporting the environmental center. But he needed to be careful in putting too much emphasis on the farm as a potential source of income for the nonprofit.

He had no idea how many actual donors it would attract this year. And without a solid base of supporters, he'd have nothing to fall back on if the farm hit a rough patch.

He glanced up as Ethan and Hailey walked out of the environmental center. "Do either of you have any experience with event planning?"

Ethan shook his head.

"No," Hailey said. "What do we need to plan an event for?"

Ryan set the report down on the table. "We need to raise some money for the environmental center."

Hailey grabbed a bottle of water from the cooler and walked over to sit beside him. "What kind of event do you want to throw?"

"I'm not sure yet," he said, taking the bottle from her, opening it, and handing it back. "I'm open to ideas."

She took a drink. "Have you asked Paul? I bet he'd have some ideas."

Ryan looked over at Jeff.

"I asked him about it this morning," Jeff said. "He thinks Ryan should host a big event in October, when oyster season opens. Maybe get a local brewery involved, hire a band, charge tickets to get in."

"I guess that makes sense," Hailey said. "It's kind of a bummer that we won't get to be here for it."

It was, Ryan thought. If they were going to help him plan an event that big, they ought to be able to be part of it, see it through to the end. If there was one thing he'd learned about these vets, it was that they liked to see a project through to the end.

"Maybe we could host a crab feast," Ethan suggested. "Then we wouldn't have to wait until the fall."

Ryan looked up as Izzy rounded the corner of the shed. She walked over to the cooler, fished out a handful of ice and pressed it to the back of her neck.

"Got any experience with fundraising, Izzy?" Jeff asked.

"No," she said, turning to face them. "What do we need to raise money for?"

We, Ryan thought, not *you*. They were definitely making progress. "The environmental center," he answered. "I need some help coming up with ideas for events—at least one big one and maybe a few smaller ones before the end of the year."

Izzy sat down on the cooler, moved the ice to another spot on her neck. "What have you come up with so far?"

"Either a crab feast in August, or a big oyster event in October," he said, noticing that she still kept her distance physically, even if she was slowly opening up in other ways.

Izzy leaned back against the shed, slipping a little farther into the shade. "I think you should focus on smaller, more intimate gatherings. Maybe start by hosting an open house once a month. Invite everyone on the island. Tell them you want to show off the progress we've made. Invite your current donors and ask them each to bring a friend. Let word spread about this place organically."

He liked the idea of an open house, Ryan thought. It was definitely more his style than a big, splashy event. But it would be harder to estimate how effective it would be if they didn't know how many people would come each month.

"If we offered the open houses in the evening," Hailey said, picking up on Izzy's idea, "from, say, five to seven o'clock, we could serve beer and wine. Oh!" Her eyes widened. "We could even hire a sommelier to come out and do a wine tasting to match up with the oysters. That would be fun, right?"

"It would," Jeff said, nodding. "It could be good for other businesses on the island, too. People could come here for a drink and a tour, then go out to dinner afterwards, make a night of it."

"I like it," Ryan said as the phone in his pocket started to ring. "Why don't you three flesh it out, put some ideas down on paper, and help me pitch it to the board next Thursday?" He stood and pulled out his phone. It was one of the distributors he'd been emailing back and forth with all week about shipping prices. He should probably take this.

"Actually," Izzy said, leaning forward, "I think we should show them."

Ryan paused, his finger hovering over the 'accept' button. "What?"

She looked up at him, and there was a gleam in her eyes he'd never seen before. "Where do you usually meet?"

"Here," he said. "In the office."

"What time?"

"Six o'clock."

"Perfect," she said, smiling. "Let's host our first open house next Thursday. Tell your board members to come an hour early. Ask them each to invite a friend who could be a potential donor and we'll serve drinks, oysters, maybe a few other finger foods. We can make a small toast to each of your board members to thank them for everything they've done to make this place a reality. Then, while you hold your meeting, we"—she swept her arm out to include Hailey, Ethan, and Jeff—"will give everyone else a private tour."

Jeff looked out at the water thoughtfully. "Do you think we have enough time between now and then to pull it off?"

"Absolutely," Izzy said.

"I think it would be fun to show off what we've been working on," Hailey said. "We only have two months left. We might as well get a jump on things."

Ethan looked at Izzy. "I'm in, as long as we can have something to eat besides oysters."

"We'll have something to eat besides oysters," Izzy assured him, then looked back at Ryan expectantly.

Ryan lowered the phone to his side as the call went to voicemail. How could he say no when she was looking at him like that?

"Trust me," Izzy said. "I've got this."

There was an edge to her voice now, an intensity that he'd never heard before. She needed this, he realized. She needed to prove herself to him and the rest of the veterans.

But was she ready? What if the stress of it triggered another flashback? What if her plan backfired?

It was a risk, he thought, but, hey, so was everything else he'd done over the past year. What was one more? "All right," he said. "I'll tell my board members to arrive an hour early next week and bring a friend."

SHE WAS GOING to need help, Izzy thought as she traded in her waterproof boots for a pair of flip-flops at the end of the day. And not just from Ethan and Hailey. If she was going to pull this off, she was going to need a chef. And she knew exactly who she wanted to ask.

Grabbing one of the secondhand beach cruisers Will and Colin had left around the island for them to use, she waved goodbye to the rest of the veterans as they pulled away in the van. She waited just long enough for the cloud of dust to settle behind them before pedaling toward the village.

She hadn't been inside the Wind Chime Café yet. It was usually closed by the time she got off work. But she'd tasted enough of Della's cooking to know that the woman was a natural. She was the kind of chef Izzy most admired—the kind who cooked from the heart and whose dishes were so deeply rooted in a sense of place that you could feel her love for this island coming through in every bite.

It was the same feeling Izzy was hoping to convey at Ryan's first open house.

She had no doubt that, with the right presentation, the environmental center would sell itself. All they had to do was get people there.

Riding down Main Street, she moved over to the shoulder to let a lone truck rumble past. It was a quiet evening in the village. The heat had chased most people indoors. The only business that seemed to be attracting anyone was the ice cream shop, where a line of people had formed behind the counter—mostly tourists, but a few locals, too. After a month on the island, she was starting to recognize the difference.

It was hard to believe she had been here that long, and how much had changed since she'd first arrived. She was beginning to understand what the locals saw in this place. Even her job at the farm was beginning to grow on her. There was something about the repetitive nature of the work, of being able to tend to something and watch it grow, that calmed her. Caring for the baby oysters was a dirty, smelly job, but it was *her* job. And she was actually starting to feel strangely protective of the little filter feeders.

When she spotted the white building with the purple shutters and the wide wrap-around front porch decorated in wind chimes, she slowed to a stop. Hoping to catch Della before she left for the day, Izzy hopped off her bike, wheeled it onto the grass, and propped it against the trunk of an oak tree. A warm breeze blew through the village, teasing the chimes into a gentle dance.

The sound was so inviting, she couldn't help taking a moment to admire them. She hadn't seen them close up before, and hadn't realized how different they all were—each one a unique piece of art, lovingly crafted by hand. She remembered what Ryan had told her that day at the harbor, that Annie and Taylor made wind chimes from things they collected around the island.

Had they made *all* of these?

Walking slowly up the porch steps, she spotted Taylor sitting with another child about her age at one of the tables inside the café. A moment later, Riley appeared behind the glass door, barking and wagging her tail enthusiastically. Izzy smiled at the dog and waited for Taylor to open the door, since the CLOSED sign was turned toward the street.

"Hi," Taylor said brightly, letting her in.

Riley circled around Izzy, wiggling her furry body in unrestrained joy. Izzy reached down, rewarding her with a scratch behind the ears. "Hey, Taylor," she said, looking up at the child. "I haven't seen you around the inn much lately. Are you enjoying your summer vacation?"

She nodded. "Jess and I are helping my mom decorate the new menus. Want to see?"

"Sure." Izzy followed her over to the table where Jess was stenciling a purple dragonfly border around a piece of white card stock. "That's beautiful," Izzy said, noticing how the colors matched the outside of the building.

"Thanks," Jess said, smiling up at her.

Izzy took in the silver café tables and black and white checkered floor. A glass display case, which she imagined would be filled with pastries and desserts during normal business hours, took up most of the counter space beside the register. From a quick glance at the number of specials crossed off the chalkboard menu above the bar, it looked like it had been a busy day.

"Well, hello there," Della said, walking out of a room in the back and smiling warmly at Izzy.

"Hi," Izzy said, returning her smile. "It smells amazing in here."

"I just put a batch of caramel pecan rolls in the oven," Della said, wiping her hands on her apron. "I wanted to get a jump start on a few things for the morning."

"Is that the kitchen?" Izzy asked, peering at the room Della had just walked out of.

"It sure is. Would you like to see it?"

Izzy hesitated, but her curiosity outweighed her fear and she nodded.

Della led her through the swinging, shutter-style half-doors, into a cozy corner kitchen barely big enough to hold two people. She could smell the sticky buns rising in the oven. A batch of skillet brownies was cooling on the stove. Pots and pans covered every flat surface, grouped into a kind of organized chaos that only another chef could understand.

Standing in the doorway, Izzy waited for the memories to creep in, but there was something about the size of the kitchen, and the cluttered chaos of it, that made her feel safe—like nothing bad could ever happen here. "It suits you," she said finally.

"I like to think so." Della smiled and transferred four brownies from the cast-iron skillet to a serving plate. "Here," she said, handing the plate to Izzy. "Carry these out to the girls and take one for yourself. I'm going to pour us each a glass of milk."

Izzy walked out to the dining room and set the plate between Taylor and Jess. For a moment—just for a moment—she remembered how much pleasure the simple act of making a dish and serving it to someone had once brought her. It had been so long since she'd allowed herself to think about that, she wasn't prepared for the sharp stab of longing that came along with it.

"I'm about to start on the caramel glaze for the sweet rolls," Della said lightly, walking up behind her, "if you care to give me a hand."

It was an invitation, Izzy thought, without any strings attached or hidden agendas this time. And while she couldn't deny that a part of her wanted to say yes, she knew better than to risk it. At some point, the memories would catch up with her, and then she'd be right back where she'd started.

Right now, all that mattered was getting through the next two months without any more incidents. If she could finish this program with a good enough reference from Ryan to land a job in Baltimore, she might actually be able to support herself and live a semblance of a normal life again.

"Actually," Izzy said, taking the glass of milk Della handed her. "I wanted to talk to you about catering an event."

"Oh?" Della asked as she settled into the chair beside Taylor.

"We're hosting an open house at the environmental center next Thursday, and I was hoping that you and Annie might..." The sound of footsteps on the stairs had her trailing off. She glanced over at the stairwell that led to the second-story apartment and spotted Annie making her way down to the café. "Oh, good, I'm glad you're here. I was hoping to talk to both of you."

Annie's steps slowed the moment she laid eyes on Izzy, her expression shifting from distracted to wary. "Hello."

"Hi," Izzy said, noticing that her tone wasn't nearly as friendly as Della's or Taylor's had been. Hmm. She hadn't been expecting that.

"Izzy wants us to cater an event for her," Della said, a little too cheerfully. "She was just about to tell us what she had in mind."

"I see," Annie said, pausing at the foot of the stairs, making no moves to come any closer.

Izzy looked back and forth between the two women, wondering what was going on. She hadn't seen much of Annie lately—Annie *or* Taylor—which, now that she thought about it, seemed kind of strange. Surely, they would have crossed paths at the inn.

Unless...

A sinking feeling formed in the pit of her stomach. Was it possible that Annie and Taylor were avoiding her? For the same reason that Ryan had hesitated before agreeing to let her plan the open house—because he thought she was going to flip out again?

"Go on, then," Della said encouragingly. "Tell us about this event you want us to cater."

Izzy swallowed. Her throat felt dry all of a sudden, parched. She'd apologized to both Annie and Taylor after the incident. She'd thought they'd forgiven her, that—like Della and Will— they understood that it had all been a mistake. That she had never intended to hurt anyone.

But maybe she'd been wrong. Maybe they hadn't forgiven her. Maybe they were keeping their distance because they were afraid she was some kind of ticking time bomb, ready to explode at any moment.

Izzy took a sip of the drink in her hand, trying to calm her nerves, then glanced down at Taylor, whose mouth was rimmed in chocolate from the brownie she'd just devoured. The child smiled up at her, offering her the last brownie off the plate. Okay, Izzy thought, taking it. Maybe Taylor had forgiven her. But Annie obviously hadn't.

"We're hosting an open house at the farm next Thursday to raise money for the environmental center," Izzy began. "Ryan's board members will be there, along with some of their friends who we're hoping to convert into donors. We're going to issue a general invitation to the islanders and ask everyone to come around five o'clock. Anyone who's curious about what we've been up to for the past month is welcome to stop by."

She looked at Della. "We'll serve oysters, obviously, and have some drinks on hand, but we wanted to offer a few other options as well. I was thinking maybe some rockfish, a big bowl of crab dip, and some kind of salad in case anyone's a vegetarian. Nothing fancy. We want to keep it simple and low-key, but classy. It's a fine line, but I think you know how to walk it."

She turned to face Annie again. "We don't have much to offer in terms of a budget. We're trying to *raise* money, not spend it, but I was going to talk to Zach tonight. He's one of the other veterans—"

"I know who Zach is," Annie said.

Right, Izzy thought, taking a breath. God, she used to be better at this. "I was going to see if he'd talk to Bob Hargrove about giving us a discount on a couple of rockfish that day, since it's for a good cause. And I've already talked to Jake Haddaway about the crab meat. He said he could get us a better price than what they're selling it for at the market if we give him a heads-up the night before." She paused, took another breath. "Lastly, if you agree to cater it, I'll personally make sure that every person who attends the event knows who's responsible for the food and leaves with one of your business cards."

"I think it's a lovely idea," Della said, as soon as Izzy had finished.

"I think it's awfully short notice," Annie said. "And we don't really do much catering."

Della narrowed her eyes at Annie. "We've been *talking* about getting into catering a lot lately."

"In the winter months," Annie said, correcting her. "When business slows."

"This could be an opportunity for us to get our name out

there for the future," Della argued. "If Ryan's board members are inviting their friends, and they're people he's hoping to tap as potential donors, then we can probably assume that they're fairly wealthy." Della angled her head. "You know how those people like to throw parties."

Izzy nodded, grateful for Della's support. "Not only will it be a good opportunity for you to get your name out there, but it'll give us a chance to start pitching the café as *the* place to stop before visiting the farm. As soon as Ryan's operation is up and running and he starts offering tours on a regular basis, he's going to attract a fair amount of tourists to this island. I've been talking to Paul about possibly adding a link to the café on the website, suggesting that visitors stop here and pick up lunch before heading to the farm."

Sensing from the expression on Annie's face that she'd begun to catch her attention, Izzy took it a step further. "Depending on the time of day and the type of tourists the farm ends up attracting, you could even offer a few pre-designed picnic baskets—one for a couple on a date, one for a group of friends, one for a family with young children."

"You know," Della said thoughtfully, "we've talked about the possibility of Ryan's farm bringing more tourists to the island. But we hadn't thought about offering picnic baskets. I love that idea." She looked at Annie, her eyes lighting up. "We could even partner with some of the other businesses on the island, see if they'd like to add something to each of the baskets."

Yes, Izzy thought, that was exactly along the lines of what she'd been thinking. And she had her own ideas for what could go in each of the baskets, but she didn't want to overstep her bounds. She looked back at the woman standing at the foot of the steps.

"Have you talked to Ryan about this?" Annie asked. "He hasn't said anything to me."

"No," Izzy admitted. She wanted him to experience it first-hand, the same way his guests would. She knew that, as soon as he saw it, everything else would fall into place. "He doesn't have time to think about this right now. He's swamped with getting the farm ready for the launch. He trusted me to plan this event. I know I can do a good job. But I can't do it without you."

"Mom," Taylor said, exasperated. "It's Ryan. You have to say yes."

"We'd be honored to cater Ryan's first open house," Della said, giving Annie a pointed look. "Wouldn't we?"

"All right," Annie said, sighing. "Fine. We'll do it. For *Ryan*."

"Thank you," Izzy said, letting out a breath of relief. "Thank you so much."

"You're welcome," Della said as she stood. "Now, could you please eat that brownie? I've been waiting for over five minutes to see your reaction."

Izzy smiled and took a bite of the brownie. It was perfectly cooked with a gooey, dark chocolate center and a thin crackly crust that released the faintest hint of peppermint when it broke. She suppressed the urge to groan. "These are amazing, Della. Where's the mint flavor coming from? It's so subtle, I can barely taste it."

"I laid a few mint leaves on the top while they were cooking," Della said, pleased with Izzy's reaction. "Not so many that they'd overwhelm the flavor, just enough to leave a trace of it. I thought it would be a nice cooling touch for the summer."

Brilliant, Izzy thought, taking another bite. She looked over at Annie—wondering if she had any idea what a gift she had in Della—and saw that the redhead was watching her. Her body language wasn't quite as standoffish as it had been when she'd first walked down the steps, but her expression was still guarded, and Izzy could sense a lingering discomfort.

She had a feeling she was going to have to work twice as hard to get Annie to warm up to her.

"The wind chimes are beautiful," Izzy said after she'd finished the brownie. "Did you really make all of them by hand?"

"We did," Annie said.

"How long does it usually take you to make one?" Izzy asked.

"It depends," Annie said, and received another long look from Della when she didn't elaborate.

"We're working on two more right now," Taylor said, glancing up from the menu she was decorating. "Want to see?"

"Taylor," Annie warned, with a quick shake of her head. "I'm sure she doesn't—"

"Come on," Taylor said, standing and taking Izzy's hand. "I'll show you."

Izzy hesitated, looking at Annie.

Annie's gaze shifted to her daughter. "Why don't you go get them and bring them downstairs?"

"We'll just be a second," Taylor protested, already tugging Izzy toward the steps.

Annie took a deep breath, then stepped aside to let them pass. "Okay," she said, resigned. "I'm right behind you."

"I'll be right back, Jess," Taylor said over her shoulder as she led Izzy up the stairs.

Jess nodded and waved her away, absorbed in her stenciling.

Izzy climbed the last few steps, pausing at the top of the landing when Taylor ran into one of the bedrooms to retrieve the chimes. The first thing that struck her was how bright and homey the apartment was. It had the same comforting, inviting feel that the inn and the café had, which made sense if Annie had decorated all three of them.

Through the windows on the far side of the room, she spied a ribbon of water cutting through the marshes. Two Adirondack chairs sat at the end of a rickety pier, overlooking a sheltered cove where marshmallow flowers bloomed along the shoreline. Wanting to see more of the view, she took another step into the room, and noticed, for the first time, the empty mugs on the coffee table, the dirty dishes piled in the sink, and the unmade beds in both of the bedrooms.

Confused, she turned to face the woman who'd walked up the steps behind her. "Are you sleeping here?"

"Yes," Annie said.

"But...I thought you lived at the inn?"

"We do," Annie said, looking away. "It's temporary."

"Here they are," Taylor exclaimed, walking out of her bedroom and holding up the two chimes. Oblivious to the conversation that was taking place in the room, she lifted the chime made of eagle feathers and arrowheads. "This is the one I was telling you about on the boat."

Izzy nodded, swallowing a sudden lump in her throat. Annie and Taylor had moved back into the apartment above the café because they didn't feel safe staying in the same house with *her*.

She had known shame before. She'd become well acquainted with the emotion over the past nine months. But she couldn't remember ever feeling quite like this.

"And this is the one we're making for Ryan," Taylor said, lifting a spiral of oyster shells suspended from a piece of driftwood. She gave the chime a little shake, and the sound of clinking seashells—the same sound Izzy had woken up to three weeks ago —filled the room.

"He'll love it," Izzy said, forcing the words out.

"I know," Taylor said, "but it won't balance." She climbed up onto the coffee table and twisted the loop around one of the blades of the ceiling fan. "See? There's something wrong."

Sure enough, the whole chime tilted, causing the piece of driftwood to sag down on one side and the strings to tangle together.

"I've pulled it apart and started over three times," Taylor said. "Mom can't get it to balance either. We can't figure out what's wrong with it."

Izzy's heart sank. Because she knew what was wrong with it.

It was her.

She was creating so much instability in Annie and Taylor's lives that they couldn't even make their wind chimes anymore.

She had thought that she'd gotten control of her personal issues, that she'd contained them—at least temporarily. But she hadn't considered the ripple effect of her actions, and how they might still be impacting other people.

She'd been working so hard over the past few weeks to prove that she was worthy of the second chance Will had given her. But in driving herself to distraction at work, she'd only succeeded in numbing the pain. No matter how well she hid it, the pain was still there. And it was spilling over now, hurting other people, too.

She needed to find a way to be free of it.

But how?

FOURTEEN

Grace stepped out of her car, eyeing the boarded up row houses and trash-littered sidewalks of Sandtown-Winchester. She'd spent most of the past three weeks driving back and forth to this neighborhood, talking to as many people as she could during her off hours. She hadn't found any leads on Izzy yet, but she'd heard plenty of other stories. And those stories had reminded her of how much she'd once loved this grittier, grassroots style of reporting—talking to people out in the streets, knocking on doors and getting strangers to open up to her, piecing together clues from each conversation to slowly reel in the truth.

She hadn't realized how much she'd missed it until now.

Locking the door to her car, she ignored the massive dog that barked at her from behind a chain link fence and headed south toward an intersection she'd driven through earlier. For the past several years, she'd been covering politics for *The Washington Tribune*. The editors had steered her in that direction because of her ability to get to the heart of a story and expose the truth. They'd said they needed someone like her on the inside to keep the politicians in check. But there was something so insular and incestuous about Capitol Hill. The more time she spent there, the more jaded she felt about the people she was interviewing.

She was tired of writing stories about schmoozy politicians who cared more about their polling numbers and reelection campaigns than getting any real work done.

She passed a homeless man asleep on the sidewalk, his fingers wrapped around a crumpled paper bag that held a fifth of some kind of hard alcohol. She smelled urine, heard a baby crying somewhere down the street, and felt the ground shake from the bass pumping through the stereo system of a car in the distance.

At the next intersection, she spotted the two women she'd seen when she'd driven by earlier. They were leaning against a cement wall, sharing a cigarette and looking bored. It was still light out, and would be for another couple of hours, but they were already dressed for the night. One wore white platform heels, a red mini skirt and a body-hugging tank top. The other was in tall leather boots, silver hot pants, and a baby tee that molded to her breasts.

As soon as she was within earshot, Grace called out, "Good evening, ladies."

They turned, looked her up and down, then pushed off the wall and sauntered toward her.

The woman in the boots smiled. "Good evening to *you*, sugar."

Grace breathed in the scent of cheap perfume, cigarette smoke, and sex as the woman in the mini-skirt lifted a lock of her hair and twirled it around her finger. "You looking for a little fun?"

Grace smiled. "Not tonight."

A black Mercedes with tinted windows turned onto the street. The woman in the boots headed toward it, putting a little extra sway in her hips until it slowed. The window rolled down and she leaned into the car to flirt with the man behind the wheel.

The woman in the mini-skirt turned her attention back to Grace. She looked her up and down again, slower this time, still playing with her hair. "You looking for a different kind of fun?" she asked, lowering her voice. "Cause we can get it for you, whatever you want."

Grace didn't doubt it. She knew most prostitutes were hooked into drug dealers, whether they were buying it for themselves or passing it along to a client. "I'm looking for information."

"What kind of information?"

Grace pulled out a picture of Izzy, showed it to her. "Do you recognize this woman?"

The woman studied the picture, frowning. "Ain't that the girl who shot Tyree?"

"Yes," Grace said. "Her name's Isabella Rivera. I'm trying to fill in a few blanks from that night."

The woman stepped back. "You a cop, or something?"

"No," Grace said, catching the eye of the man behind the wheel. He stared at her, hard.

"'Cause I ain't talking to no cop," the woman said.

"I'm not a cop," Grace said, still holding the man's gaze. When he rolled his window up, cranked the volume on the stereo, and sped away, she looked back at the woman in the mini-skirt. "I'm a reporter."

"A reporter?" she said doubtfully.

"That's right," Grace said.

"Violet," the woman in the mini-skirt called over to her friend, "this girl says she's a reporter."

Violet lifted a brow, sashaying over to them with a new gleam in her eye. "You writing a story about us?"

Grace smiled. "No."

"I bet we could give you something to write about," Violet purred as she rubbed up against Grace. "Couldn't we Lana?"

Taking the cue from her friend, Lana walked over and threaded her arm through Grace's. "I bet we could give you *all kinds* of things to write about."

Grace rolled her eyes, pulled a pack of cigarettes out of her pocket, and offered them each one. "How long have you been working this corner?"

"A while," Lana answered, eventually dropping the act.

Violet followed suit, lighting up and blowing out a stream of smoke. "At least a year, maybe more."

"So you see who comes and goes in this neighborhood?" Grace asked.

They both nodded.

Grace showed the picture to Violet. "This is Isabella Rivera, the woman who shot Tyree Robinson. Do you know what she was doing in this neighborhood that night?"

"No," they both said immediately, exchanging a look.

Violet took a pull off her cigarette. "We ain't gonna talk about that night."

"Fair enough," Grace said, backing down. Keith had warned her that most people would refuse to talk about that night, for fear of retaliation from the gang who ruled these streets. Before he'd snitched, Tyree had been one of them. "Forget about the night of the shooting. What about before that?"

Lana was quiet for a long time, studying the picture over Grace's shoulder. When she glanced up, she looked at her friend. Violet gave her a small nod. "Mmm-hmm," Lana finally admitted. "I seen her around before."

"You have?"

"I think she's got a friend who lives around here."

"A friend?" Grace asked. This was news to her.

"Yeah." Lana nodded. "Another Mexican girl, like her." She

took another drag, blew the smoke in the other direction. "Your girl used to drive over here and pick her up, give her rides back and forth to work. Sometimes she'd come with bags of groceries and clothes and stuff."

Interesting, Grace thought. "Did you tell this to the cops?"

Lana and Violet both laughed.

She'd take that as a no, Grace thought as a gust of cooler air blew down the street, causing an empty paper cup to skitter across the pavement. She looked up at the sky, at the storm clouds brewing in the distance, and heard the first low roll of thunder. "Do you have a name?"

"Nah," Lana said.

"Any idea what street she lives on?" Grace asked.

Lana angled her head. "You got another one of those cigarettes?"

Grace handed her the whole pack.

Lana smiled. "Calhoun, I think. On the east side, toward Fremont."

ALONE IN HER ROOM, Izzy sat at the desk under the window, watching the clouds gather along the horizon. She could feel the pressure in the air, hear the rumble of thunder in the distance. After three weeks of mind-numbing heat, they were finally going to get a reprieve, but it would take a storm to tip the balance back into their favor.

Was that what it was going to take with her—some kind of seismic reckoning to make her face the trauma she'd experienced? The last thing she wanted was to dredge the memories up, to relive the horror of the rape all over again, but what if that was the only way to release the pain?

The screen of her laptop blinked, going into sleep mode, and she nudged the track pad to wake it up. Staring blankly down at the spreadsheet of women who'd served under Bradley Welker, she tried to focus on her research, but her thoughts kept straying back to Annie and Taylor.

And the fact that she'd essentially kicked them out of their home.

She was the one who should have been kicked out. She was the one who didn't deserve to be here.

Why had Will let her stay if Annie was against it? Shouldn't they have made that decision together, as husband and wife?

Was she creating a wedge between them now, too?

Another rumble of thunder rolled over the water as she typed the next name into the search bar and hit 'enter'. She clicked on the link to Alicia Booker's Facebook page, expecting the typical stream of family photos, cat memes, and news articles. After five months of tracking these women, she still hadn't found anything that would raise a red flag. She was starting to wonder if she was wasting her time.

Resting her fingers on the track pad, she was about to scroll down when she noticed that Alicia's most recent photo had been posted over three weeks ago.

Three weeks ago?

She frowned, reminding herself that not everyone posted every day, or even every week. Some people only posted sporadically. Alicia could be one of those people who used social media more as a way to keep in touch with old friends than share information about herself.

She moved on to the next photo, a picture of Alicia's son, and saw that it had been posted only a few hours before the first one. The next one had been posted less than twenty-four hours before that. She felt a tightening, deep in her chest, as she continued to scroll down the page, through several months' worth of photos. Up until her most recent post, Alicia had been active on Facebook almost every day, sometimes two and three times a day.

Trying not to panic, Izzy pulled up the rest of Alicia's social media pages, just to be sure, and found the same thing on all of them. Three weeks ago, Alicia Booker had gone off the grid. And she was currently stationed at the same base in North Carolina where Izzy's career had ended, serving under the command of Bradley Welker.

Izzy's hands shook as she toggled back to Alicia's Facebook page, as she clicked on the button to send a private message. A small box popped up in the corner, and a blinking cursor stared back at her. What was she supposed to say? How was she supposed to start a conversation like this?

Her fingers curled back from the keyboard, squeezing into fists. There were a dozen alternative explanations for why Alicia could have gone dark. Someone in her family could have fallen ill. Someone could have passed away. There was no reason to jump to conclusions. Not yet. Not until she heard back from her.

"Alicia," Izzy typed out quickly. "Hi. You don't know me, but we served on the same base last year. I need to speak with you about something. It's urgent. Please call me as soon as possible." She added her cell phone number and hit send before she could overthink it.

Please let me be wrong. Please let me be wrong.

She reached for her phone to make sure the ringer was on, then jumped when someone knocked on the door. "Yes?"

The door opened and Erin poked her head in. "Did you forget about me?"

Shit. Izzy checked the time on her phone, realized that she was ten minutes late for her therapy appointment. "Sorry," she said, knocking her knees on the underside of the desk when she tried to stand. "I lost track of time."

Erin studied her from across the room. "Is everything okay?"

"It's fine," Izzy said quickly. "I'm fine. Everything's fine."

A gust of cold air blew into the room and Izzy turned to close the window. She saw the birds flying away from the darkening sky, the boats heading for shore, the tops of the trees beginning to bend under the force of the wind.

She remembered the storm that had ushered her onto this island three weeks ago—the pounding rain, the flooding roads, the suffocating darkness. She glanced over her shoulder at Erin. "Are you sure you still want to meet? The roads can flood out here when it storms."

Erin held her gaze, continuing to study her. "Yes. I still want to meet."

Izzy closed the window and snagged a sweatshirt from the closet, trying to act like it didn't matter one way or another.

But it did matter. It mattered a lot. Because, at any moment, she could get a call from Alicia.

She pocketed her phone, increased the volume on the ringer as high as it would go, then turned to face Erin. "Ready when you are."

Erin led her downstairs, grabbed two umbrellas from the stand by the door, and handed one to Izzy. "We might need these for the walk back."

Izzy nodded, took the umbrella, and followed Erin across the yard to the cottage where she held her counseling sessions. It was still her least favorite part of the program, but she'd managed to make it through her last three sessions without having a full-blown panic attack. Part of that probably had to do with the fact that Erin hadn't brought up Bradley again. The social worker had avoided the subject entirely, letting Izzy talk, instead, about her work at the farm, her ideas for how to help Ryan grow his business, and what kind of jobs she might be interested in applying for at the end of the summer.

She hoped Erin would stick to the surface-level questions tonight.

She wasn't sure what would happen if she tried to get her to open up about her past. She might just start talking, and not know how to stop.

"I made some chamomile tea," Erin said. "Would you like a cup?"

Izzy nodded, her hand still firmly wrapped around the phone in her pocket. There was a eucalyptus candle burning on the coffee table in the sunroom. The pillows on the sofa looked like they'd recently been fluffed. And a crocheted blanket was draped loosely over one side, the same milky green as the sea glass mobiles that spun softly overhead.

She took a seat in her usual spot, perched on the edge of the middle cushion, not wanting to get too comfortable.

"I love watching a storm roll in over the water," Erin said from the kitchen. "Don't you?"

Izzy looked out at the water, at the white caps knifing over the surface. The clouds had swallowed up what was left of the sunset and the air felt like it was charged with electricity...or maybe that was just her nerves.

She couldn't tell anymore.

"Sure," she said, slipping the phone out of her pocket and setting it on the cushion beside her. Face up. On any other night, she might have enjoyed watching the storm. But she wished this particular storm could have held off for another hour or two. It was only making her more anxious.

"Are you expecting a call from someone?" Erin asked, noticing the way Izzy was still clutching the device when she walked into the room a few moments later.

"Yes. I'm expecting a call from...a friend. If it rings, I might have to answer it."

"All right." Erin placed both mugs on the coffee table and

then settled into the chair across from her. "Anything you want to talk about?"

"No," Izzy said quickly. "It's nothing. I just...have to answer it if it rings."

Erin opened her notebook, made a few notes, then looked up again. "How's everything been going since the last time I saw you?"

"Good."

"Good?" Erin asked, surprised.

Izzy nodded, seizing on the first positive thing she could think of. "Work's been really good."

Erin made another note in her book. "How so?"

"Ryan agreed to let me plan an event for him—a fundraiser for the environmental center." Izzy let go of the phone and folded her hands in her lap. "It's our first event at the farm, so it's kind of a big deal."

Erin smiled, obviously pleased. "That's wonderful. When's the event?"

"Next week," Izzy said, and ate up at least ten minutes of the clock by explaining how she'd enlisted Della's help, and some of the other veterans, too. She'd already spoken to Zach at dinner tonight, and he'd agreed to ask his boss about supplying the rockfish. Kade had volunteered to donate some flowers, with Gladys' permission. And Megan had offered to help spread the word about the event to the islanders.

"Do you have any experience planning events?" Erin asked once Izzy had finished.

"I do," Izzy said, nodding. "I helped plan tons of events when I worked for General Walters and his wife. It's probably my next favorite thing after..."

Erin glanced up. "After what?"

After cooking.

The candle between them flickered, releasing a curl of smoke, the same color as the charcoal gray sky bearing down on them. Erin reached up to switch on the floor lamp, filling another small corner of the room with light, but not before Izzy caught sight of the wall of rain offshore.

Any minute now, they were going to get slammed.

A streak of lightning snaked down, electrifying the sky, and the clap of thunder that followed it, only a few seconds later, was loud enough to make her flinch. Izzy glanced down at her phone, checking to make sure she still had a signal. The connection was faint, but it was still there. Relieved, she looked back up.

Erin continued to watch her for several moments in silence. "Are you sure you don't want to talk about that call you're expecting?"

Izzy nodded. "I'm sure."

"You seem awfully distracted by it."

"It's nothing," Izzy said as the first slap of rain smacked against the windows of the sunroom.

Leaning back in her chair, Erin set her mug on the table beside her. "Izzy?"

"Yes?"

"This is our fourth session together. We only have eight sessions left. And while I'd be happy to continue meeting with you after this program ends, I have a feeling I'm not going to be high on your list of people to call when you return to Baltimore."

"That's probably true," Izzy said slowly.

"Then, given that, I think it's time to stop dancing around the elephant in the room."

Another streak of lightning. A crack of thunder.

Izzy looked away. No. She couldn't do this. Not now. Not tonight. Not until she heard from Alicia.

"Izzy." Erin's voice was softer, now, gentler. "I need to tell you something."

No. Izzy shook her head. Whatever it was, she didn't want to hear it.

More rain slammed into the cottage, streaking down the glass. Somewhere, in the yard, a branch fell.

Erin waited until Izzy's gaze lifted again, met hers. "I never spoke to Bradley Welker."

Izzy blinked. "What?"

"I never spoke to him," Erin repeated. "That would have been a huge breach of client confidentiality. The only reason I brought him up was to see if he was a trigger for you."

A trigger? Izzy's heart began to pound. "I don't understand."

Erin slowly closed her notebook and set it aside. "I looked you up before I came here. I looked all of you up. I wanted to find out as much as I could about each of your backgrounds, so we didn't have to waste too much time getting to know each other. I knew that, with some of you, I'd only get three months to make a difference."

She'd looked them up?

"You're not the first female veteran I've worked with, Izzy. I've seen plenty of cases of post-traumatic stress disorder, and only a small percentage of them are related to combat. When I heard that you'd left the Army less than a year ago, and found out that you hadn't been deployed to a war-zone since 2009, it didn't take me long to put two and two together."

Izzy's heart beat faster. What was she saying? That she knew? That she'd known all along?

"I understand why you don't want to talk about it. I don't blame you," Erin said. "But you didn't do anything wrong. You have nothing to be ashamed of. And the only one you're hurting, now, by not speaking up, is you."

The blood rushed in Izzy's ears, drowning out the sound of the rain. *Speak up?* She wanted her to *speak up?*

As if saying the words out loud would make any difference.

She'd already tried that once, and it had been a mistake. Besides, what was the point in speaking up when she had no proof? No one would believe her anyway. Hadn't Bradley said as much?

She was a cook. He was an officer—a highly regarded one, and one who'd praised her publicly. He'd been quoted in over a dozen articles saying how brave he thought she was, how grateful he was that she'd been there that day to save his life.

No one would believe that he'd raped her. Not in a million years.

"Izzy," Erin said softly, "as long as you stay silent, he wins."

Izzy's whole body vibrated, not just from shock, but from anger, now, too. "How dare you?"

"Izzy—"

"No!" Izzy snapped, cutting her off. "How dare you let me sit here and babble on about oysters when you *knew*? You *knew* I was raped, and you brought up the name of my attacker in our first session together. What the hell kind of a therapist are you?"

"I know that you're hurting," Erin said calmly. "And I know that you're angry. You have every right to be. But, by not speaking up, you're allowing him to control you. Don't give him that power, Izzy. Don't let him win."

"He *already* won!"

"No," Erin said. "You're wrong. There's no statute of limitations on rape in the military. The law changed a few years ago. You can still report it. It's not too late."

Izzy looked back at her, at this woman who thought she knew so much, but who didn't know anything. She didn't know anything at all. "I *did* report it!"

Confusion flashed across Erin's face. "You did?"

"Yes!" Izzy shouted. "I went to the hospital. I got a rape kit. I filed a report. I did *everything* I was supposed to do."

"I don't understand," Erin said. "What happened?"

Izzy pushed to her feet, strode to the window overlooking the water. She could see the waves crashing against the shoreline, splashing up into the yard. "I had to take some time off afterwards to recover. There was some damage...internally."

She pressed a hand to the glass, squeezed her eyes shut. She could feel the rain lashing against her palm, hear the wind howling through the tops of the trees. "I went to work the next week and made an appointment with my commanding officer to explain what had happened. He said there was no record of a report, or a rape kit, or a hospital visit."

The memories swam back and Izzy struggled not to choke on them. "He said...I must have imagined it. That the stress of war must have caused a...condition. That I needed to see a psychiatrist and have an evaluation to find out if I was still fit to serve." The rain whipped against the glass, drummed against the roof. "I didn't *imagine* it."

"I believe you."

It was only three words, but something inside Izzy cracked open the moment Erin said them. Because no one had ever said them before.

She hadn't realized how badly she'd needed to hear them.

How badly she'd needed just one person to be on her side.

But it didn't change the fact that she still had no proof.

"Without the rape kit, it's his word against mine," Izzy said. "And who's going to believe me? I'm a cook. He's a colonel. A jury would take one look at me"—she waved a hand up and down her body, gesturing to the curves she hid so carefully beneath baggy clothes now—"and think that I asked for it."

"You didn't ask for it."

Izzy shook her head. She must have done something wrong. She must have done something to make him believe that she'd wanted it.

"Izzy," Erin said quietly, walking up behind her. "Look at me."

Izzy turned, lifted her gaze to Erin's.

"You didn't ask for it. You didn't deserve it. And it wasn't your fault."

Izzy felt her body constricting, coiling in on itself as the pain she'd been holding inside for so long fought to get out. Burying her face in her hands, she started to weep. Erin helped her back to the sofa. She continued to say the words—*You didn't ask for it. You didn't deserve it. It wasn't your fault*—over and over again, until Izzy slowly began to hear them, until they slowly began to register.

Until she slowly began to realize what she should have known all along, that the only thing she'd done wrong was let Bradley get away with it.

When she could finally see again without a wall of tears blurring her vision, she noticed that the clouds had passed, the wind had died, and there was only the softest pattering of raindrops against the roof. She looked back at Erin, who was sitting beside her now. There was nothing but kindness and compassion in her eyes.

Why had it taken her so long to realize that this woman only wanted to help her?

"I was late today because I've been tracking all the women who've served under...my attacker," Izzy said, not wanting to speak his name out loud anymore. Not wanting to grant him even that smallest of courtesies. "I've been trying to figure out if he's done this to anyone else, or if I'm the only one."

Erin took a deep breath. "Most rapists are repeat offenders. The chances that you're his only victim are extremely slim."

Izzy nodded, because she'd read the same thing online. The fact that she hadn't found anything until today didn't mean that nothing had happened. "I saw something on one of the women's

Facebook pages today, right before our appointment. I sent her a message and asked her to call me. I'm waiting to hear back," she said, then added, with a touch of desperation. "It could be nothing."

"It *could* be nothing," Erin said slowly, "or it could be exactly what you think it is."

Izzy looked down at her phone, saw that the screen was still blank. No missed calls. No missed messages.

"What are you going to do if she says he assaulted her, Izzy?"

Izzy continued to stare down at her phone, willing it to ring. "I don't know."

FIFTEEN

One week later, Annie drove up the gravel lane to the farm. Taylor sat in the passenger seat, holding a pepper grinder and a pair of grilling utensils in her lap. Della had called a little while ago and said she'd forgotten them. It was fortunate that the farm was less than a half a mile from the café. They were going to have to get better at this if they were going to accept any more catering gigs in the future.

As far as Annie was concerned, they weren't ready. Business at the café was ticking along comfortably now, but she still had a lot of loans to repay. She had planned to start crunching numbers after the tourist season slowed to see if an expansion would be feasible.

At this point, they didn't have the workforce to support it. She and Della were the only two people who worked at the café. If they decided to give it a shot later this year, she would have to hire someone to manage the events and maybe another part-time person to staff them.

She wasn't sure she could afford that yet.

Besides, there'd been enough changes in both her and

Taylor's lives over the past year. She just wanted everything to stay calm and stable for a while.

Pulling into an empty parking spot outside the two-story house that served as the farm's office, she checked the clock on the dashboard. It was 4:45PM, which meant they had at least fifteen minutes until Ryan's first guests would arrive.

"Do you want to run those things over to Della?" Annie asked, helping Taylor out of her seatbelt.

Taylor nodded, hopped out of the car, and went to the back seat to let Riley out. The dog scrambled out of the car and raced toward the water with Taylor close on her heels.

Annie stepped out of the driver's side more slowly, pausing for a moment to take in the view. She was secretly glad to have an excuse to swing by early. Della was in charge of the food, so she wasn't worried about that, but Izzy had insisted on taking care of the presentation.

And she wasn't sure what to expect from the female veteran.

The few times they'd crossed paths over the past week, Izzy had seemed edgy and distracted. Will had even commented that he'd noticed her obsessively checking her phone. Della had waved all of it off and told Annie that she worried too much. And maybe she did. But until Grace found out if the woman was dangerous or not, she was going to continue to err on the side of caution.

For Taylor's sake.

Closing the door to her car, she headed across the lawn to the picnic area. She could smell the lemon and thyme rub Della had put on the rockfish, the smoke from the charcoal grill, and the salty scent of freshly shucked oysters. As summer evenings went, they couldn't have asked for a better one. The skies were clear. The surface of the water shimmered with drops of reflected sunlight. And there was a soft wind blowing in from the south—

strong enough to keep the bugs away but not strong enough to blow anything over.

"Hey, Annie," Matt said, from behind a table where he and Wesley were shucking oysters.

"Hey," Annie said, noticing the matching T-shirts they were wearing. The material was an earthy, sage green in a thin, washed-out cotton that looked like it had been worn a hundred times right out of the box. The name Pearl Cove Oysters was printed across the front in bold white font above an illustrated graphic of two halves of an oyster shell, partially open, but still connected at the hinge. "Love the T-shirts."

"Thanks." Matt smiled, popped another oyster open, and carefully set it on the bed of crushed ice between them. "The shipment came in this afternoon. Perfect timing."

"Did Paul design them?" Annie asked.

Matt nodded. "He rocked it, right?"

Yes, Annie thought. He had. She looked down at the table, taking in the artful display of oysters on ice, the buckets of chilled champagne and polished flutes inviting guests to grab a glass and help themselves, and wondered if Paul had had a hand in that, too.

She was about to move on to the next table, when an assortment of colorful toppings and sauces caught her eye. She'd never seen Della make anything like them before. They looked more like something she would have served at Citron Bleu—the upscale D.C. restaurant where she'd worked before moving to the island last year. "Did Della make these?"

"No." Matt shook his head. "Izzy did."

Annie glanced up, surprised. "I thought Izzy didn't cook."

"She doesn't," Matt said. "She said it wasn't technically cooking since she didn't have to go in the kitchen. Della brought the ingredients out and Izzy mixed them up at one of the picnic tables. Here." He handed her the oyster he'd just shucked. "Try one. They're off the hook."

Puzzled, and more than a little curious, Annie added a spoonful of the first sauce to her oyster, then tipped the whole thing back and let it slide into her mouth. The combination of flavors was so unexpected, she didn't even know what to make of it at first. She tasted salt, citrus, mint, and something spicy. And, then, all at once, the flavors rolled together, complementing each other and, somehow, balancing perfectly with the buttery base of the oyster.

Off the hook didn't even come close to describing this sauce. "What is this?"

"Blood orange juice with mint leaves and chilies." Wesley grinned and handed her another oyster. "Try the next one. It's a cucumber lime granita."

Cucumber lime granita? Since when does an Army cook know how to make a cucumber lime granita?

Annie tipped the oyster back, swallowed, and then slowly lowered the empty shell to her side.

"Insane, right?" Matt asked, grinning now, too.

Annie nodded, blown away. "I've never tasted anything like that before."

"Me neither," Wesley said, laughing. "I didn't even know what a granita was before tonight." He handed her a third oyster. "The last one's a Prosecco mignonette."

Annie tasted the final sauce, savoring the sharp, sensual tang of the vinegar against the creamy sweetness of the oyster. The hint of Prosecco added a fun, flirty touch to what would have otherwise been a typical mignonette sauce. But there was nothing typical about any of these sauces.

Looking back up at Wesley, she felt something stir, deep inside her, in response to the decadent blend of flavors and textures. If these sauces were any indication of Izzy's overall cooking style, then she had greatly underestimated the woman's talent.

"Check out what's on the next table," Wesley said, holding his hand out for her empty shells. "She put that together, too."

Admiration, Annie thought. There was admiration in his voice when he talked about Izzy now. She handed him the shells, walked over to the next table, and immediately saw why.

At first glance, it was a simple display of books and pictures, but something about the way they'd been arranged made you want to walk closer, reach down, pick one up. Some of the photos were old, so old they were yellowing at the edges, and Annie's eyes widened when she realized that they were pictures of Coop Callahan as a young man.

Coop couldn't have been more than seventeen or eighteen years old in some of the shots. Propped up on stacks of books about wetlands and watermen and the history of the Chesapeake Bay, there were pictures of Coop out on his workboat—hauling up bushels of crabs in the summer and dredging for oysters in the winter. There were pictures of him loading crab pots into the bed of his truck, mending a trotline on the steps of his porch, and shucking oysters at a local seafood festival.

There were pictures of Ryan, too, at different stages in his life. There was one of him holding up a ribbon from the first science award that he'd won in grade school, one of him jumping off the back of a research ship in his scuba diving gear in graduate school, and one of him gracing the cover of *Science* magazine, from only a few years ago.

But it was the ones of them together—father and son—that had Annie reaching down, brushing her fingers over the wooden frames. Every picture on this table told a story of a father and son, who'd lived two very different lives, but who'd ended up back here together—as if every step they'd taken had led them to this moment.

"Mom!"

Annie turned and saw Taylor waving her over excitedly from the other side of the picnic area.

"Mom, come here! You have to see this!"

There was more?

Dazed, Annie made her way over to where her daughter stood beside another longer table. Halfway across the picnic area, her jaw simply dropped. Nasturtiums trailed through more beds of raw shucked oysters. Daisies, zinnias, and dahlias surrounded platters of rockfish and crab cakes, which had been garnished with paper-thin lemon slices and sprigs of fresh thyme.

There was a salad she didn't recognize—some exotic combination of black beans, mangoes, cilantro, and citrus that had Izzy written all over it—and a plate of jalapeño cornbread so temptingly moist, she had to stop herself from taking a slice.

"Look," Taylor said, pointing to Annie's business cards, which were artfully displayed in a premier spot in the middle of the table, exactly the way Izzy had promised they would be.

Jesus, Annie thought. They'd hardly done anything. They'd barely even supplied the food.

Glancing over her shoulder, she caught the 'I told you so' look in Della's eye, and felt the first sharp tug of guilt.

All around them, Ryan's employees were busy putting the finishing touches on each of their parts of the operation. There was a nervous energy in the air, but there was also excitement. And pride. She could see it in their faces.

"Oh, hi," Izzy said as she came around the corner and stopped abruptly at the sight of them. "I didn't know you were here."

She was wearing a Pearl Cove Oysters T-shirt—as all Ryan's employees were—and her hair was pulled away from her face. But instead of her usual knot of messy curls that barely required a mirror, she'd braided it into a single sleek strand. She'd taken her time with the rest of her appearance, too, donning a clean pair of khaki shorts and a pair of sneakers that looked like they'd recently had a tumble through the washing machine.

"Did *you* do all this?" Taylor asked, gazing up at Izzy in awe.

Izzy nodded, glancing at Annie nervously before reaching down to adjust a few nasturtium leaves so the vibrant blooms were more visible.

"Where did you get all these flowers?" Taylor asked.

"The Flower Shoppe," Izzy said. "Gladys donated them. She said they were mostly day-old flowers that she'd have to throw out anyway."

They didn't look like day-old flowers, Annie thought. And she'd bet a month's worth of income that Gladys had sent a fresh supply over with Kade earlier, and told him to keep that tidbit of information to himself.

Izzy stepped back, surveying the table. "Is it too much?"

Too much?

Izzy reached for one of the platters. "Because I could—"

"No." Annie put a hand on her arm to stop her. "It's...perfect."

Izzy looked up. "You like it?"

There was so much hope and vulnerability in the other woman's expression, Annie felt another wave of guilt roll through her. Where was the angry, closed-off woman who'd driven onto this island five weeks ago? Who was this woman standing before her now?

Was it possible that Annie had been so consumed with protecting Taylor that she hadn't noticed the transformation?

Annie thought back to when she and Taylor had first arrived on the island last fall—how defensive and prickly she'd been during those first few weeks, how guilty she'd felt at not being able to protect her daughter from the school-shooter, how terrified she'd been that it could ever happen again.

But she hadn't shown that fear to anyone, had she? No, she'd lashed out at anyone who'd tried to get too close.

She thought about what Will suspected had happened to Izzy—that someone had sexually assaulted her. For the first time since hearing those words, she let them sink in. Really sink in. And tried to imagine how angry *she* would have been if that had happened to her.

About as angry as Izzy had been when she'd first arrived on the island.

"Mom," Taylor said, tugging on her hand. "Can we go find Ryan? I want to ask him where he hung the oyster shells we painted in summer school."

"Ryan's not here," Izzy said. "He had to run an errand."

Annie looked at Izzy. "Ryan's not here?"

Izzy shook her head. "He left a couple hours ago, but he should be back any minute."

"You mean...he hasn't seen any of this?" Annie asked.

"No." Izzy's gaze shifted to the driveway. "Not yet."

A slow smile spread across Annie's face. Now she was glad she'd come early for an entirely different reason. Ryan was going to flip when he saw this.

RYAN'S TRUCK rattled over the steel plates of the drawbridge as he crossed over the narrow strip of water that separated Heron Island from the rest of Maryland's Eastern Shore. He hadn't meant to be gone for so long. He hadn't wanted to leave the island at all today. But he'd gotten a call that morning from another oyster farmer who'd needed to offload a piece of equipment—one of the few pieces of equipment Ryan hadn't bought yet. When he'd heard that the guy was selling it for less than half the original price, he'd figured it was worth the drive to check it out. And when he'd seen that it was in even better condition than the guy had said it was over the phone, he'd decided to go for it.

It was an investment, he told himself as he turned onto the gravel lane that led up to the farm. An investment that would allow them to buy more seed, move more oysters through the upwelling process, and plant more cages in the Bay, which would ultimately improve both the quality of the water *and* their bottom line. Despite that, he suspected his father would take one look at the mechanical seed-sorter in the bed of his truck when he unloaded it tomorrow and shake his head.

Pulling onto the grass behind the office to keep the parking spots in the front open for guests, Ryan wondered if his father would even bother to stick around for the open house tonight. He'd made it clear, from the very beginning, that he wanted no part in promoting the business. And while tonight's event was supposed to be more about the environmental center, both operations were going to be on full display.

It was a decision that, in hindsight, Ryan wished he'd taken a little more time to consider. The response to the invitations they'd sent out had been overwhelmingly positive. Most, if not all, of his board members' friends had said yes, and when those friends had heard that it was an open house, they'd invited a few friends of their own. Now, if you added in the number of islanders who'd promised to stop by, they were expecting around eighty people.

Eighty people.

That was twice the amount they'd planned for.

Reaching over to the passenger seat, he put an arm around Zoey, drawing comfort from the fact that no matter what happened tonight—even if their first event turned out to be a total disaster—his dog would still love him. She rewarded him with a sloppy kiss on the cheek before jumping out of the truck. Ryan stepped out after her, saw Riley streak across the lawn to greet them, and caught the first whiff of grilled seafood.

"Hey, boss," Paul said, walking out of the office. "Welcome back."

"Thanks," Ryan said. "Any fires I need to put out before our first guests arrive?"

"None that I know of," Paul said, tossing him a ball of rolled-up cotton.

Ryan caught it. "What's this?"

Paul pointed to the T-shirt he was wearing.

Ryan's gaze dropped to the front of Paul's shirt, taking in the Pearl Cove Oysters logo for the first time. "No way."

"Way," Paul said, grinning. "They came right after you left."

Ryan held up the shirt in his own hands, shaking it out so he could get a closer look, and felt a surge of pride as he studied the design. "I love it."

"Yeah?"

"Yeah." Ryan nodded. "This is exactly what I was looking for."

"Good," Paul said, laughing, "because everybody's already wearing theirs."

"They are?" Ryan asked, following Paul around the side of the office to the picnic area. He hadn't expected...

Halfway across the parking lot, he stopped. He didn't even notice when Riley nipped at the shirt in his hand, trying to play tug-of-war. He was too busy staring at the scene in front of him—the beds of ice filled with freshly shucked oysters, the exotic flowers trailing through platters of crab cakes and whole grilled rockfish, the antique oyster tins that had been turned into center-pieces on every table, each holding a bottle of chilled champagne.

From behind the shucking station, Matt and Wesley tipped their heads at him. He walked slowly over to them, taking in the plump, meaty oysters resting in each shell. The sharp scent of potting soil drew his gaze down to a pair of bushel basket planters that someone had filled with a variety of colorful flowers—the first of many that had been placed strategically around the property to soften the edges of the utilitarian buildings.

He looked down at the dock, saw that every hose had been rolled up, every line had been neatly coiled, every empty cage had been carefully stashed out of sight. He could tell that the upwellers had been scrubbed recently, could hear the water flowing easily through the pipes. He felt someone slip a cold beer into his hand, and was about to turn to see who it was, when he spotted the table of photographs.

Were those pictures of...*him*?

He walked over, reached down, picked one up. It was a picture of him as a seven-year-old child in his father's workboat, holding up the first rockfish he'd ever caught. He remembered that day, but he couldn't remember ever seeing this picture before. Still holding the frame, he looked at the next one—a black and white shot of him as a teenager in the same workboat, culling wild oysters while his father manned the dredge.

There were more, several more, he realized as he made his way down the table. He was almost at the end when he spotted a picture of him as a child wearing a pair of his father's white oyster boots. He was young, maybe around five-years-old at the time. The boots were several sizes too big and came up over his knees, but he looked so happy to be following his father around the docks that it didn't matter if he could hardly walk in them.

He paused, staring down at the picture for a long time. "Who did this?"

"Izzy," Matt said. "Izzy did all of it."

Ryan turned, saw that a crowd had gathered around him, and found her standing on the edge of it, off to one side. Even now— even after all this—she still seemed unsure of herself, as if she were worried about how he might react. "Where did you find these?"

"I got a few of them from Jake," Izzy answered. "He had a box of old photos that his wife had taken from when you and Becca were kids. The rest I got from your father."

"My father?"

Izzy nodded.

"He's seen this?"

"Of course," Izzy said. "He helped me put it together."

Ryan looked down at the photograph again. He didn't even know his father *had* these photos. "Is he...here?"

"I think he's in the shed with Jeff," Hailey said from the door of the environmental center. "Do you want me to get him?"

Ryan continued to stare down at the photograph. If his father was still here, did that mean he was staying? Was he actually going to stick around for the event? He heard voices coming from inside the shed and glanced up just as the two men walked out, carrying a cooler of beer down to the dock. His father's back was to him, but Ryan could see that he was wearing the Pearl Cove Oysters T-shirt.

Ryan's gaze shifted back to Izzy. There were so many things he wanted to say to her, so many questions he wanted to ask. But everyone was still gathered around him, waiting for a reaction. All of that would have to wait until later. "Thank you," he said, holding her gaze for a long time before looking around at the rest of his staff. "All of you."

"Hey, boss," Paul said, nodding toward the road. "I think someone's here."

Sure enough, a car was just beginning to make its way up the lane. Ryan set the picture down on the table. With one hand, he dragged the shirt he was wearing over his head and tossed it to Matt to stash under the shucking station. He pulled on the Pearl

Cove Oysters T-shirt that Paul had given him, and walked out to meet their first guest.

The pop of a champagne cork behind him was the first of many he would hear over the next two hours. By six o'clock there was a line of cars parked on both sides of the driveway stretching all the way down to the road. All thoughts of having a formal board meeting had been thrown out the window, and each of his board members had come up to him individually to toast the success of his first event.

"Hey, man," Colin said, walking up to him and grinning. "Congratulations."

"Thanks." Ryan accepted the beer his friend handed him and tossed the one he'd been holding into the can for recycling. "I think I've been nursing that last one for over an hour."

"I figured," Colin said. "You've been swarmed since I got here."

Ryan tipped the bottle back, taking advantage of the momentary reprieve to survey the scene around them. Everywhere he looked, people were chatting, laughing, sipping champagne, and eating oysters. A crowd had formed around the shucking table, where Matt and Wesley were entertaining guests with stories of working on the boat with Ryan's father. Several people were seated around the tables in the picnic area, devouring the food Izzy and Della had prepared.

Hailey and Ethan were giving tours of the environmental center—explaining the reefs that were being built in the Bay to help rehabilitate the wild oyster species, signing up volunteers to assist with the next planting, and encouraging everyone to bring their children and grandchildren back for a visit. Taylor had taken it upon herself to show off the turtles, seahorses, and fish in the tanks to the few kids who'd come with their parents. And Paul was wandering around taking pictures of everything to upload to social media.

On his way through the picnic area, Paul paused in front of Ryan and Colin, snapped a quick shot with his phone, and gave them a thumbs up before heading down to the dock.

"I had an interesting meeting with Paul earlier this week," Colin said once he was out of earshot.

"Yeah?" Ryan asked, taking another sip of his beer.

"He didn't mention anything to you about it?"

"No," Ryan said. "What's up?"

Colin leaned a shoulder against the shed. "I've been floating his résumé out to a bunch of potential employers. I've shown them the website he designed for you, explained how he's helping you launch this business, and told them that you'd give him a glowing recommendation."

Ryan nodded. "Absolutely."

"I've gotten a lot of interest. I actually have three interviews set up for him next week." Colin turned his beer bottle around, showed Ryan the label of a local brewery. "This is one of the companies. I thought it'd be a good fit 'cause they're relatively small, they've only been in business for a couple years, and they still have room to grow."

"That's great news," Ryan said.

"It would be," Colin agreed, "except that he doesn't want the job."

"Why not?"

"He wants to work for you."

"Me?" Ryan's brows shot up. "Permanently?"

Colin nodded.

"Shit."

"I know," Colin said.

Ryan looked down at the dock, where Paul was showing his most recent pictures to Megan, who was laughing and helping him pick out which ones to post. "What did you tell him?"

"I told him, no. We've got to keep his position open for the next group of vets. If we hired everyone who wanted to stay, we wouldn't have a program anymore."

That was true, Ryan thought, but he hadn't considered that some of his employees might want to stay. When he thought about everything Paul had done for him, it was hard to imagine anyone else ever being able to fill his shoes.

"Anyway," Colin said. "I wanted to give you a heads-up in case he hadn't talked to you yet. The fact that he hasn't makes me wonder if he's planning to try a different approach with you. When he proposed the idea to me, he already had a plan mapped out for the rest of the year with graphs and projections to support his argument. He's obviously given it a lot of thought. But you understand why we have to say no, right?"

"Yeah," Ryan said slowly. He understood. But it didn't mean that he had to like it. "Have you made any progress with any of the others?"

Colin nodded. "I've got a few leads on almost everyone now. Well, everyone except for Izzy. She's going to be a little harder to place. Her criminal record is causing a lot of employers to balk." He lifted his beer, took a long swallow. "That said, if any of them could see what she's done here tonight, I think they'd reconsider."

Ryan shifted slightly so that he could see her. He'd known she was behind him. He'd been aware of her all night—what she was doing, who she was talking to. He wasn't the only one who'd been swarmed from the moment their first guests had arrived. Everyone wanted to meet the woman behind the artistic displays of shellfish and mouthwatering mignonette sauces.

Every member of his staff had gone above and beyond, but it was Izzy who'd stolen the show. Over the past two hours, he'd watched her transform into a totally different person. Gone was the detached, guarded veteran who'd first arrived on the island five weeks ago. In her place was a warm, welcoming, approachable woman who seemed completely comfortable in her own skin.

She was a natural host, adept at forging connections and making people feel at ease. She made sure that everyone knew who had catered the event, introducing them to Annie and Della and telling them all about the café. If someone asked her about the oysters, she steered them toward Ryan or Coop. And whenever anyone complimented the rockfish or crab cakes, she walked them straight over to Jake Haddaway and Bob Hargrove so they could meet the men who'd pulled the seafood out of the water that day.

From his spot at the edge of the shed, Ryan watched her walk toward them with a middle-aged man wearing a pink button-down shirt and pressed khakis. The man had a cultured New England accent that screamed Ivy League education and old money. And, like every other person at this party, he was enamored with Izzy.

"I respect what you're doing," the man said. "I do. It's just that—come on, let's be honest—this is the Chesapeake Bay. You're never going to able to grow a quality oyster here. The waters aren't salty enough."

Izzy smiled, taking the glass of champagne he was drinking and replacing it with a glass of buttery white wine. "It's not just about the oyster," she said smoothly, "it's about what you pair it with. Our oysters might not be as salty as the ones you're used to in Boston, but they have their own unique flavor profile that's completely distinct to this area." She waited for him to take a sip of the new wine before handing him an oyster. "I think if you'd open your mind a little bit, you might be able to taste it."

The man smiled back at her, taking the oyster and accepting the challenge. Ryan had to stifle the urge to roll his eyes when the man took another sip of his wine, making a big show of swishing it around, before lifting the shell to his mouth and tipping it back.

"No one's going to compare a Pearl Cove oyster to a Wellfleet oyster," Izzy said as the man chewed. "They're the gold standard of the salty, cold-water oysters. Everybody knows that. But we're not trying to *be* Wellfleet."

The man swallowed and Izzy motioned for him to take another sip of his wine.

"As long as an oyster represents the place where it comes from, it matters," Izzy said. "The Chesapeake Bay has a history and a culture that can be tasted in its seafood. It's what makes this place so special. And I might even argue that because of that history—because of the struggle our oysters have gone through—it's an even deeper, richer experience."

Izzy held out her hand for his shell and the man laughed, clearly delighted with both the attention and the debate.

"All right," he said, giving her his empty shell. "Let me have another one and I'll see if I can taste the soul of the Chesapeake Bay this time."

Izzy smiled and handed him another oyster, but she wasn't ready to let him off the hook yet. "Have you ever been out to Wellfleet, seen how those guys grow their oysters?"

The man shook his head, his expression turning thoughtful.

"Wellfleet's run by a father and son team, like our farm is, but their process is a lot different," Izzy said. "They grow most of their oysters in bags instead of cages. They stake them out in the tidal flats off one of the beaches in Wellfleet Harbor. And because the tides there are so extreme, part of their field is actually exposed twice a day. As soon as the tide goes out, they drive their trucks onto the beach, set up their culling stations, and harvest their oysters without even having to get in a boat."

Izzy topped off his wine. "We don't have that option, because our shorelines are too muddy. We have to grow our oysters in deeper water and use heavier cages. And since most of our fields are only accessible by boat, we have to work twice as hard." She

motioned for him to follow her down to the dock. "Let me introduce you to Coop Callahan. He's been working these waters
since he was seventeen, and though I've never heard him
complain, he'll be the first to admit that farming oysters in the
Chesapeake Bay is not for the faint of heart."

Ryan stared at her, speechless. How did she know so much
about Wellfleet? And when had she become such an advocate for
Chesapeake Bay oysters? He thought back to the day, five weeks
ago, when he'd given her one to try for the first time. *'It's an
oyster,'* she'd said. *'They all taste the same.'*

Had she been lying then? Not wanting to admit that she'd
felt anything? Because it had been easier to pretend she couldn't
feel anything at all?

Izzy's gaze lifted, locked on his, as she walked by. The truth
was right there, written all over her face. She *had* felt something,
Ryan realized. She'd felt it from the very first day.

Beside her, the man in the pink shirt said something, and Izzy
looked away, turning her attention back to their guest. But Ryan
couldn't take his eyes off her. He continued to watch her as she
made her way down to the dock, as she introduced the man to his
father. When she laughed at something one of them said, the
sound rolled all the way through him.

Ryan drained the rest of his beer in one long swallow.

When he finally looked at his friend again, Colin lifted a
brow. "Anything going on there that I should know about?"

Ryan said nothing as he set the empty bottle down on the
table beside him, as his friend continued to study him.

"Look," Colin said. "I know I don't have to say this, but Izzy's
off-limits—at least until the end of this program. We're all happy
she's starting to come out of her shell, but she still has a long way
to go. The last thing she needs right now is a complication."

A complication? Is that what Becca had been for him? What
Annie had been for Will?

Izzy wasn't the first person who'd come to this island to heal. And Ryan had absolutely no intention of messing with that process. But he sure as hell wasn't going to take a warning from someone who wouldn't even be here right now if he hadn't fallen in love with *his* complication.

Reaching into the bucket of ice at his feet, Ryan snagged another beer. Maybe it was the sheer hypocrisy of his friend's warning, maybe it was the overwhelming success of this first event, or maybe it was the fact that—from the very first moment he'd laid eyes on Izzy—he hadn't been able to stop thinking about her, but whatever it was, it all led in the same direction.

Ryan raised his bottle to Colin before taking a sip. "Roger that," he said. Then he clapped his friend on the shoulder and headed down to the dock to talk to Izzy.

$\mathcal{B}$y the time the last car pulled out of the driveway, the sun was only two fingers away from the horizon. It was that shimmering golden hour right before sunset where everything seemed to glow. Alone, Izzy propped her trusty beach cruiser against the shed, and walked out to the pier to check on the upwellers one last time before leaving.

Their newest crop of baby oysters had gotten plenty of attention tonight, and after all the hands that had been on them, she wanted to make sure the systems were still functioning properly. Carefully inspecting each of the tanks, she adjusted the tilt of a few buckets, checked the water pressure in each of the pipes, and spread a few of the babies around that had gotten clumped up.

Satisfied they were safe for the night, she wiped her wet hands on her shorts and looked out at the water. She could still feel the endorphins pumping through her—that same natural high she always felt after a successful event. But the buzz seemed stronger this time, fueled by a deeper emotion she hadn't experienced in several months.

Pride.

She'd forgotten how good it felt, how badly she'd needed it. Wanting to hold onto it—to let the emotion wrap itself all the way around her—she lingered on the pier, listening to the water lapping against the pilings and watching the colors in the sky shift from blue to gold.

When she'd replayed the entire evening in her mind, soaking up all the memories, she thought back to all the places she'd lived in her life—the farms of her childhood, the military bases during her years of service, the brief stint in Baltimore after she'd left the Army—and tried to remember if any of them had been this beautiful.

Or this peaceful.

For the first time since crossing the drawbridge five weeks ago, she wondered what it would be like to stay here. She'd been on the move her whole life. Every location had been chosen for her. Even the house in Baltimore that she'd bought for her grandmother had been tied to a job; the only reason they'd moved there was because her grandmother had secured a position as a domestic worker with a family in that city.

Now that her grandmother was gone, did she even want to live in Baltimore anymore?

She guessed, when it came down to it, she didn't have much choice. From what she'd heard from Colin, employers weren't exactly lining up to call her in for an interview. She'd go wherever she could find work. The same way she'd done in the military. The same way she'd done with her mother and grandmother as a child.

A faint jingling of dog tags drew her gaze over her shoulder. Surprised to find Zoey lumbering toward her, she reached down to pet the chocolate lab as soon as she was close enough. "What are you still doing here? I thought your dad..." She trailed off as Ryan walked out of the shed. "Hi," she said, straightening. "I didn't see your truck. I thought you'd left."

"I parked behind the office," he said. "I was unloading some boxes on the second floor and saw you out here."

"I wanted to check on the nursery," she said, a little embarrassed at having been caught out here so long after the party had ended, "make sure all the pipes were still running after so many people had touched them."

"I always check everything before I leave," Ryan said, but he didn't seem to mind that she was still here. If anything, he seemed glad to have the company. Stopping a few feet away from her, he leaned his arms on the edge of the tank and looked out at the water.

The last rays of sunlight warmed his profile. There were more blond streaks in his hair now than when she'd first met him. His skin was several shades darker, and the muscles in his arms were more defined than they'd been at the beginning of the summer. A vision of him shirtless—when he'd changed into his Pearl Cove Oysters T-shirt earlier—swam into her mind.

Her body responded instantly, the same way it had then. She felt the sharp tug of attraction, the tightening deep in her belly, and braced herself for the memories of the last time a man had touched her.

But they never came.

Instead, Zoey leaned against her, nuzzling her hand for a chin-scratch.

Izzy let out a breath, marveling at the fact that she was alone with a man she was attracted to and she wasn't freaking out. Determined to face her fears a little longer, she followed Ryan's gaze out to the water. "What kind of boat is that?" she asked, eyeing the graceful sailing vessel that had caught his attention.

"It's a skipjack," he said, "one of the Bay's earliest oystering boats. They've been used to dredge oysters for over a hundred years, but they're unique to this area. You won't find them anywhere else."

"Do people still use them to...dredge for oysters," she asked, testing out the new verb.

"Very few," Ryan answered. "Their heyday was in the late 1800's, when our oyster harvests were at their peak. The decline of the oyster population hit them hard. There are only about twenty skipjacks left in the Bay now, and only about five or six of those are still dredging commercially." He nodded toward the one in front of them. "That's Billy Sadler's boat. He takes tourists out on sunset cruises to bring in some extra cash in the summer. It's what a lot of skipjack captains are doing now."

Izzy wondered how they felt about that—being the first generation to witness their livelihood fall into history. It couldn't be easy. But, then again, what was the alternative? If they didn't want to do what Ryan was doing, at least they still got to go out on their boats, talk about the good old days, share their favorite stories with people who were interested enough to pay money to hear them.

"Speaking of random oyster facts," Ryan said, turning to face her, "how did you know all that stuff about Wellfleet?"

Izzy smiled, remembering the conversation she'd had with the man in the pink shirt earlier and how much she'd enjoyed chipping away at his pretentions. "Paul asked me to help him come up with a plan for how to launch your two brands at the end of the summer. I figured I should start by looking at what some of the most successful farms are doing to market their oysters first—see if there was anything we could learn from them. Once I started digging into their websites, I guess I got a little excited."

"Clearly," he said, with a note of laughter in his voice.

"You went to graduate school up there, right?" Izzy asked. "In Massachusetts?"

Ryan nodded. "I lived in Woods Hole for six years."

"Did you ever consider staying up there?" she asked, wanting to satisfy a curiosity that had been nagging her ever since learning about those other farms. "If you'd opened a farm in New England —where the waters are saltier and the oysters already have a great reputation—you wouldn't have had so many battles to fight."

"I prefer to make things difficult for myself," Ryan joked.

He was making light of it, Izzy thought, shifting slightly so she could get a better view of his face. But there was nothing lightweight about any of the decisions he'd made. She knew, now, why he'd come back here. He'd come back because this was his home, because these waters were suffering, and because this was where he could make the most difference.

In opening a farm on the Chesapeake Bay, Ryan had known exactly what he was getting into. He'd known he would face resistance, not only from future consumers, but from some of the islanders—people he'd grown up with. And, somehow, despite the risk, he'd managed to convince his father to join him as well.

Remembering how strangely he'd reacted to the photographs of the two of them earlier, she asked, "Do you think your father had a good time tonight?"

"I'm amazed he stayed as long as he did. Cocktail parties aren't really his thing."

Izzy smiled. "Yeah, I picked up on that."

Ryan's gaze drifted out to the water again. A pair of kayakers had paused at the edge of the marshes to watch the sun sink into the horizon. All around them, the surface of the water shimmered, reflecting the shifting colors of the sky. "That table you set up—the one with the pictures of my father and me. It almost made it seem like we were close."

"Aren't you?" Izzy asked, surprised.

Ryan shook his head. "He wishes I were teaching on a research ship or working in a lab somewhere."

Izzy's brows drew together. "What do you mean?"

"He thinks I made a mistake in moving back here—that I'm

wasting my degree and wrecking my chances of ever having a career in academia again."

"Do you want to have a career in academia again?"

"No."

"Then...I'm not sure what the problem is."

Ryan looked at her. "He doesn't want me here."

"Of course he does," Izzy said, rolling her eyes. Coop Callahan might be a man of few words, but there was no doubt in her mind that he loved his son. "He believes in you."

Ryan laughed. "Yeah, sure."

Izzy paused in the middle of petting Zoey. "You're kidding, right?"

He shook his head slowly.

Izzy stared at him. She couldn't believe this was how he saw his relationship with his father. How could he be so intelligent about so many things, and so dense about this? "Your father gave up his *livelihood* for you, Ryan. He turned his back on the only world he'd ever known to work on this farm—because you asked him to. And when you decided to team up with Will and Colin, and hire a bunch of veterans you'd never even met, he went along with it. He might not know how to say it to your face, but he believes in you."

Ryan continued to regard her skeptically, but at least he wasn't laughing anymore. Izzy wondered how long it would take him to recognize the truth. Shaking her head, she looked back at the sunset, at the shots of pink streaking through the sky.

"What about you?" Ryan asked. "Are you close with your parents?"

"My parents are gone."

"Both of them?"

Izzy nodded, tracking the path of a blackbird over the marshes. "I never knew my father. He died before I was born in the village where my family lived in Mexico. I was raised by my mother and grandmother."

"Did you grow up in Mexico?"

"No." Izzy shook her head. "I was born here. My mother was pregnant when she and my grandmother...made the crossing."

Ryan was quiet for a few moments, processing what she'd just said. "What happened to your mother?"

"My mother died in the fields when I was thirteen."

"What fields?" Ryan asked, confused.

Izzy said nothing, waiting for him to put two and two together.

"Wait..." Ryan said, his eyes widening. "You don't mean...?"

Izzy looked down at her hands, which would forever bear the scars of her childhood, no matter how hard she tried to forget that time in her life. "We were working on a farm in Arizona," she said. "It was apricot season." She looked up, saw the moment the realization dawned on his face. "To this day, I still haven't eaten one. I doubt I ever will."

"Izzy," Ryan said, his voice filled with compassion. "Why didn't you say something before?"

"What was I supposed to say?" she asked. "That I grew up in a family of migrant workers? That I spent all my free time as a child picking fruits and vegetables? That, when I was thirteen, my mother passed out from heat stroke and by the time my grandmother and I found her body, it was too late?"

"If we had known—"

"—you wouldn't have asked me to work here," Izzy finished. "I know. I get that. And it's why I wanted to switch with someone initially. But I guess, in a way, I'm glad that Colin didn't honor that request, because I know, now, that this farm is nothing like the ones I grew up working on as a child—and you're nothing like the farmers I knew then either."

She offered him a small smile, but he didn't smile back. His expression was filled with such care and concern that it caught her off guard. She rarely talked about her childhood. She'd learned, years ago, that it wasn't a topic most people were comfortable with. Most people in this country preferred to pretend that the immigrants in the fields were invisible, that they didn't even exist.

She should have known that Ryan wouldn't feel that way, that he wouldn't be able to look away from this.

"Is that why you joined the Army?" he asked.

Izzy nodded. "I enlisted the day I turned eighteen. The military gave me stability, a steady paycheck, and respect—three things I'd never had before then. Strangers would stop me in the street and thank me for my service." Shaking her head, she thought about the first time that had happened, how proud she had been. "My grandmother and I spent almost two decades chasing harvests, never knowing where the next job would be or how long it would last. We lived in so many different states and I went to so many different schools, it's a miracle I even graduated high school."

"How did you?" Ryan asked.

Izzy rested her hands on the edge of the tank, letting the tips of her fingers dip into the cool water. "We used to do my homework assignments together. The three of us—my mother, my grandmother, and I—would gather around the kitchen table after dinner each night and I would teach them everything I'd learned in school that day. Then, we'd make our way through each assignment, no matter how long it took, so that they got an education, too."

She lifted her gaze to the sky, to the brushstrokes of lavender bleeding through the blue. "I worked in the fields with them after school, on the weekends, and all summer long, but my education was always their number one priority. It was the reason they came to this country, the reason they sacrificed everything—so that *I* could have a better life."

Taking a deep breath, she turned to face him again. "I think, if your father is anything like my mother or my grandmother, he just wants you to take advantage of all the opportunities that weren't available to him. It's not that he doesn't want you here. It's just that he wants *more* for you—more than he had. It might be hard for him to accept that after everything you've accomplished, after all the paths you could have chosen, you chose this."

Ryan held her gaze for several long moments. There were emotions in his eyes—emotions she couldn't read and didn't understand. The wind had quieted to barely more than a whisper and the sun had slipped below the line of trees to the west. In the distance, she could hear the faint clanging of drawbridge bells as the operator prepared to let one of the last boats through for the night.

"It's getting late," she said. "I should head back."

She started to turn, but he caught her hand. "Stay," he said quietly.

Izzy froze at the unexpected contact. She looked down at their joined hands, then back up at his face—all sharp angles and shadowy plains in the fading light. Her pulse jumped, skipping a beat. They were all alone, she realized. His closest neighbor was more than a quarter mile away. No one would be able to hear her if...

No, she thought. *Don't go there. Don't let yourself go there.*

Ryan's grip was gentle, but steady. And somehow she knew, instinctively, that he would let go the moment she showed even the slightest hint of discomfort. Maybe it was the fact that she didn't want him to let go that rattled her more than anything. "It'll be dark soon."

"I'll drive you back," he said, nodding toward the sunset. "The show's not even over yet."

It was such a simple request, one that, from the outside, seemed perfectly innocent, but she knew that his wanting her to stay had nothing to do with the sunset. "I don't think—"

"Stay," he said again. And there was something about the way he said it—the way his voice rippled over the water, pulling her toward him—that had her fingers curling, closing around his.

Ryan's eyes never left hers as he took a step toward her. "I know I'm not supposed to say this." He reached up, brushed the hair back from her face. "But watching you come alive tonight was one of the most beautiful things I've ever seen."

Before she had a chance to react, to even consider what was happening, his mouth was on hers. And all the passion, all the heat, all the frustration he hid so carefully beneath that calm, easygoing cover shattered the last of her resolve. She felt something snap, break open inside her, and then she was kissing him back, like a woman who was starving.

"Izzy," he breathed, pulling her against him.

Their bodies locked together, and the taste of him—salty, minty, masculine—shot into her like a drug. She could feel the warmth of his skin through his shirt, the beat of his heart against her palm as she ran her hands up the hard muscles of his chest. She'd forgotten what it felt like to kiss without fear, to touch without fear.

To *live* without fear.

Ryan's teeth scraped over her bottom lip and a small sound escaped from somewhere deep in her throat. His fingers threaded into her hair, tugging it free from the braid, and with every curl that slipped loose, she felt another piece of herself unravel. Her hands twisted into his shirt, pulling him closer. She wanted more of him, all of him.

She wanted...

The drawbridge bells began to clang again, signaling that the last boat had passed through for the night. Something about the noise—the subtle warning of it—had her easing back. Dazed, she looked up, into eyes the color of liquid smoke. She could see the longing in them—the same longing that was pulsing through every inch of her body.

"Izzy, I..."

A flash of light drew her gaze over his left shoulder. The first fireflies were beginning to come out for the night. The moon was a glimmer of pale white overhead. And all that was left of the sunset was a wash of dusky blues.

Somewhere, in the back of her mind, it occurred to her that they should probably talk about this. But she didn't want to let go of this feeling yet. She wanted to hold onto it for a little while longer.

"It's almost dark," she said softly. "The others will start to worry if I'm not back soon."

Ryan lowered his mouth to hers again, making it clear he was in no hurry for her to leave. She gave in to the kiss, just for a moment, before pressing a hand to his chest and pushing lightly against him.

He drew back instantly.

Izzy stared at him, stunned, when she realized that was all it had taken for him to stop. All the heat, all the passion was still there, but he'd pulled back the moment she'd asked him to.

She wondered if he had any idea how much that meant to her.

Ryan reached up, tucking a lock of her hair behind her ear so tenderly it made her heart ache. "I'll drive you back."

A part of her wanted to say yes, just so she could spend a little more time with him. But she knew that she couldn't walk into the inn like this. She needed some time to think first, to process what had happened, and she needed to do that alone. "No," she said. "I'll bike."

Ryan nodded, even though she could tell that he didn't want her to go. He kept her hand securely in his as they walked over to the beach cruiser. He waited for her to get settled, then leaned down and left her with one last bone-melting kiss before stepping back and watching her pedal away.

It took about ten minutes for the feeling in her legs to return, for the fog in her mind to clear. Halfway through the marshes, she let go of the handlebars, running her fingers through the spray of wildflowers lining the side of the road. When the phone in her basket began to ring, she thought nothing of it. Figuring it was probably someone from the inn calling to find out where she was, she pulled it out and glanced down at the screen.

It wasn't the inn.

It was a number she didn't recognize.

Izzy stopped pedaling. There was only one person she was expecting a call from right now. Forcing herself to remain calm, she hit the 'accept,' button and lifted the phone to her ear. "Hello?"

"Is this Izzy Rivera?" a female voiced asked.

"Yes."

"This is Alicia Booker."

Izzy let the toes of her sneakers drag over the pavement as she rolled to a stop.

"I'm sorry I didn't call you back sooner," Alicia said. "I just checked my Facebook account and saw your message."

"That's okay," Izzy said, amazed at how steady her voice sounded to her own ears. "Thank you for getting back to me." She climbed off the bike, still gripping one handlebar with her free hand. "I think I mentioned that we served on the same base in North Carolina."

"You did."

Izzy took a deep breath. "I know this is going to sound strange, but I've been keeping track of some of the women who are still serving on that base, mostly through social media, and I noticed that you went off the grid a few weeks ago."

The line went quiet on the other end.

Izzy's hand tightened around the phone. "I don't want to pry into your personal life. I just want to know if...you're okay."

Alicia said nothing for a long time, and when she finally spoke, her voice was hollow. "He did it to you, too, didn't he?"

Izzy closed her eyes. She wasn't the only one. Bradley had raped someone else. And she could have prevented it. "Yes."

"Did he...?" Alicia paused and sounded uncomfortable all of a sudden. "Was he able to go through with it?"

"Go through with it?" Izzy asked, confused. "What do you mean?"

"He didn't actually rape me," Alicia said. "He just tried to."

Izzy's eyes widened. "He...didn't?"

"I fought him off."

Izzy flashed back to how fast it had happened with her, how quickly he'd rendered her completely defenseless. "How?"

"I was accepted into Ranger School last month," Alicia explained. "I've been taking classes in hand-to-hand combat for over a year now, so I can prove to the men that I belong there. I'm not just after the tab. I want to join an actual unit afterwards."

Izzy lowered the bike to the middle of the road, and slowly sank down to the pavement beside it. He hadn't raped her? He'd tried, but he hadn't gone through with it? "Did you tell anyone?"

"No. I took pictures of the bruises, just in case. But I'm black and blue from my combat classes all the time. It wouldn't have been enough to hold up in court. And I don't have any other evidence."

"Neither do I," Izzy said. "But if it happened to both of us, there have to be others."

"I agree. And I want to do something about it. But I'm in the middle of a custody battle over my son right now. I can't afford to have my name dragged through the mud. You know what happens to women who cry rape in the military. My ex's lawyers would have a field day with this."

Izzy's gaze dropped to the bike, lying awkwardly on its side beside her. Yes, she thought. She knew exactly what happened to women who cried rape in the military. They were accused of trying to get attention. They were branded as sluts and liars. They were turned into outcasts from the very people they'd served alongside for years.

"Do you think you can find more?" Alicia asked suddenly.

"I don't know," Izzy admitted. She'd been doing this research for months, and, so far, she'd only turned up one name.

"If you can find more, I'll go public with you," Alicia said. "I don't think two is enough."

How many more? Izzy wondered. How many more would it take for people to believe them?

"I'll start asking around on my end," Alicia said. "It could take a while, since I'll need to be discreet about it, but I'll let you know if I find anything."

"Thanks," Izzy said dully.

"And, hey," Alicia said, her voice softening. "I'm sorry...about what happened to you."

Izzy nodded, even though Alicia couldn't see her. Too numb to speak, she ended the call and slowly lowered the phone to the pavement. She didn't know how long she sat there, but when she finally looked up again, all the color had drained from the sky. There was nothing but darkness, the croak of a bullfrog, and the rustle of marsh grasses against a fallen tree.

SEVENTEEN

Something was wrong, Ryan thought as he watched Izzy pull away from the dock with his father the next day. It was around ten o'clock and the boat had already been out to the lease once that morning. Matt and Wesley were in the shed, sorting through the oysters they'd harvested, and Izzy had taken their place on the boat—a request she'd made as soon as she'd finished her tasks in the nursery.

Ryan had a feeling that request had a lot more to do with *him* than her wanting to spend the rest of the day on the boat with his father.

Since the moment she'd arrived with the others that morning, she'd barely spoken two words to him. She had circles under her eyes, like she hadn't slept. And he could tell, from the haunted expression on her face, that she was sliding back into that dark place she'd worked so hard to claw her way out of over the past five weeks.

What had he been thinking by kissing her the night before? He'd only joined her out on the pier because he'd wanted to spend some time with her, to get to know her a little better. Yes, he was attracted to her. Yes, he'd planned on kissing her eventually. But he hadn't meant for it to happen so soon.

He'd figured it would take at least a few more weeks to lay the groundwork. He'd wanted to test out the waters first, make sure she was a hundred percent comfortable around him before trying anything physical. If what Will suspected was true—that she'd been sexually assaulted—he'd figured it would take a while for her to warm up to someone in that way again.

So, instead of giving her the time and the space that she'd needed, he'd kissed her.

And probably ruined everything.

Stripping off the gloves he'd been wearing to help Matt and Wesley unload the cages from the boat, he made his way over to the picnic table where Jeff had left a hard copy of a document he wanted him to review. It was a thank you note to everyone who had made a donation to the environmental center the night before. He picked it up and tried to focus on the paragraphs Jeff had written, but the words blurred on the page.

He couldn't stop thinking about Izzy.

Hell, he hadn't been able to stop thinking about her for weeks now. She was the first thing he thought about in the morning when he woke up, and the last thing he thought about before he fell asleep at night.

He'd never met a woman who'd invaded his thoughts the way Izzy did. It made him feel strung out—twisted up inside—like he was being pulled in a thousand different directions.

He'd always been able to compartmentalize his emotions at work, to detach himself from any issues related to his personal life.

Not that there'd been very many.

Women had come and gone in his life as naturally as the tides. Most of his relationships had only lasted three or four months. They were usually with women he worked with, or had some kind of interest in his field. And he hardly ever had to make the first move.

He couldn't remember the last time he'd actively pursued a woman—or imagined a future with one of them.

Looking back out at the water, he watched Izzy lean over the side of the boat to hook one of the lines. For the first time in his life, he'd met a woman he didn't want to let go of. He didn't want to keep her at arm's length like he had with the others. He didn't want any space between them at all.

Setting the unread letter on the table, he pulled out his phone and dialed his sister's number. He didn't know what was taking Grace so long, but if he was going to convince Izzy to give him a chance, he needed to know what had happened to her. He needed to know the truth.

And he needed to know it now, before he screwed things up any further.

Izzy's head was pounding. It felt like someone had wedged a shucking knife in the base of her skull and just kept twisting...and twisting...and twisting. Clenching her teeth against the pain, she caught the dripping oyster cage as it rose out of the water and guided it into the boat. As soon as it was safely onboard, she unhooked it from the hoist, and started to spray it down with the hose.

A river of mud flowed back toward Coop, where he stood at the helm with one hand resting casually on the wheel and a half-smoked cigarette dangling from his lips.

She'd been out on the boat with him enough times over the past few weeks to know that he preferred to work in silence. Which was fine with her. She was too freaked out to talk to anyone anyway. She knew, now, that her rapist had attacked someone else—that what happened to her hadn't been an isolated incident, motivated by revenge. In the space of one year, he'd targeted both her and Alicia.

And if there were two of them, there had to be more.

She'd been up all night trying to find them. She'd scoured the social media pages of every female soldier on her list, searching for something—anything—that would raise a red flag. But there were too many names now. She'd expanded her list to include any woman who'd ever served on the same base as Bradley Welker, not just the ones who'd served under his command. And she didn't know if she was even looking in the right places anymore.

What if she'd missed something? What if she'd accidentally skipped a name? What if she'd been scrolling too fast?

Coop walked up to the other side of the platform when she set down the hose. He helped her empty the oysters into bushel baskets, and without another word, returned to the helm. Izzy dragged the baskets to the front of the boat, then headed back to her own station, her rubber boots tracking mud all over the deck, her waterproof bibs squeaking with every step.

She knew, now, that she couldn't do this alone. It was only a matter of time before Bradley attacked someone else. She needed to find the rest of his victims. And she needed to find them fast.

But who could she ask for help?

Leaning over the side of the boat, she hooked the next cage, attached the line to the hoist, and then straightened to let the hydraulics do the rest of the work. She'd almost called Erin a half dozen times last night. She'd wanted to tell her therapist, if only to have someone to talk to. But she knew what Erin would say as soon as she found out—that Izzy and Alicia needed to come forward. And as much as Izzy agreed with that, she had to honor Alicia's request.

She'd considered telling Will and Colin, just to get the whole thing out in the open. Maybe they'd know someone who could help her track down the rest of the victims. But the thought of having to relive the incident again, of actually having to say the words out loud in front of them, made her feel physically ill.

And then there was Ryan.

What was she supposed to do about Ryan?

The way they'd left things last night, she could only assume that he thought she liked him as much as he liked her—which was true. But if anyone found out that she was carrying on with her new boss, it would kill her credibility when she finally came forward to accuse her attacker. Anyone who believed that this was how she behaved at work could conclude that she must have been doing the same thing with Bradley.

That she must have led him on in some way.

That she must have *asked* for it.

"You gonna pull that cage in, or just leave it hanging there?" Coop asked.

"Sorry," Izzy said, grabbing the cage and guiding it onto the platform. She sprayed it off quickly, then looked back up at Coop. He was watching her closely now, with a look on his face she'd never seen before. He had the same perceptive gray eyes as his son. And despite the fact that he kept most of his thoughts to himself, she had a feeling he didn't miss much.

Determined not to make another mistake, Izzy set the hose down, got a good grip on the cage, and waited for him to walk over and help her empty it. Instead he stayed where he was.

"I'm not used to working with someone who's quieter than I am," Coop said.

A wake from another boat hit them, and Izzy tightened her grip on the cage to keep from losing her balance.

Unfazed by the swaying deck, Coop flicked ashes from his cigarette over the side of the boat. "You got something on your mind?"

"Not really."

Coop continued to watch her as he finished the rest of his cigarette. When he finally stuffed the butt into a soda can and walked over to help her, Izzy let out a breath. They went back to work, and Izzy focused all her attention on the task at hand. They'd already planted all the oysters she'd graduated from the nursery that morning. They'd checked a few of the older lines for signs of mortality and over-silting. And now they were pulling up cages to take into the shed for Matt and Wesley to run through a piece of equipment that would wash, sort, and tumble the oysters.

It was hard, sweaty, backbreaking labor, but it was keeping her mind in check and she was grateful for the distraction. When another workboat cruised by twenty minutes later, Coop lifted a hand to wave to the man behind the wheel. The man waved back and Izzy caught the nostalgic expression that passed over Coop's face.

It was gone as quickly as it came, but there was no mistaking it.

"I heard you went out on Jake's boat a few weeks ago," Coop said, breaking the silence.

Izzy nodded.

"Had you ever been out crabbing before?"

"No," she said, shaking her head.

"What'd you think?"

"I liked being out on the water," she said, peeling the top off one of the cages and extracting a tiny seahorse that had gotten trapped inside. "It's a lot of work, but I can imagine worse ways to make a living."

Coop nodded, his gaze shifting to the next workboat that was coming in for the day.

Izzy released the seahorse back into the Bay. When she straightened and looked at Coop again, she saw that he was still watching the workboat. There was a man about his age behind the wheel. He had a teenage boy and a black lab on board with him. The boy was playing tug-of-war with the dog over a piece of rope.

Coop continued to watch them until they passed under the drawbridge and disappeared out of sight.

"Do you miss it?" she asked.

Coop slid another cigarette out of his pack. He took his time lighting it before turning around to face her. "Sometimes," he admitted, blowing out a stream of smoke. "But I don't miss not knowing if I'll make enough to provide for my family each week."

The word 'family' triggered something inside Izzy, and she remembered suddenly that she hadn't seen any pictures of Coop's wife in any of the albums she'd gone through before the event. She was fairly certain Ryan hadn't ever mentioned anything about a mother either. That was kind of strange, wasn't it?

"I've never heard Ryan talk about his mother," Izzy said. "What happened to her?"

Coop's expression darkened. "Ryan's mother took off when he was ten."

"Took off?"

Coop nodded.

"Where did she go?"

He lifted a shoulder. "Don't know."

"You don't...know?" Izzy asked, confused.

Coop shook his head, looked away. "She didn't leave a note."

Izzy's eyes widened. "You mean...she just left? Without saying anything?"

"That's right."

"She never called afterwards?"

"Nope."

"Did you look for her?"

"Yep."

"What happened?"

"Nothing." Coop took another drag. "Police couldn't find anything. We couldn't find anything. She just...disappeared."

Izzy flashed back to the day Ryan had told them the story about the selkie—about the seal woman who'd abandoned her family, who'd vanished without a trace. Was that why he'd been so sad afterwards? Because that fairy tale mirrored his own childhood?

She'd lost her own mother when she was thirteen, but at least she knew what had happened to her. What if her mother had walked away, without offering a single explanation?

What kind of a scar would that leave?

"It wasn't easy on any of us," Coop said, looking back at the farm, where Ryan was testing out the piece of equipment he'd bought the day before, "but it was harder on the kids than it was on me, because they didn't understand why she left."

"Why did she leave?"

"She wanted more than this," Coop said simply.

"More than what?" Izzy asked.

"This life," Coop said, gesturing to the boat. "This island. Me. That's why I wanted Ryan to leave. That's why I wanted both my children to do more with their lives—so they'd never know what it felt like to not be enough for someone."

EIGHTEEN

*G*race heard her phone buzz and saw her brother's name flash up on the screen for the third time that day. She hit the decline button—the same way she had the first two times—and slipped the phone in her pocket. She didn't have time to talk to him right now.

She'd been stuck on Capitol Hill all week, waiting for Congress to vote on a new health care bill. Lawmakers from both sides of the aisle had been meeting around the clock, trying to rally their supporters. In the end, instead of actually holding a vote, they'd decided to pass a seven-day extension so they could do the same thing all over again next week.

She could scream.

Not only because Congress could barely fulfill its most basic functions anymore, but because she hadn't been able to make it back to Baltimore since the day she'd met Lana and Violet. It hadn't taken her long, after Lana had pointed her in the right direction, to track down the name and address of Izzy's friend.

All she needed to do now was pay her a visit.

Stepping out of her car in Sandtown-Winchester, Grace eyed

the six-unit apartment building on the south side of Calhoun Street. Every window on the first floor was barred. A sheet fluttered from one of the second-story windows, and she could smell cheap beer and cigarettes as she crossed the street to the building. She opened the front door and strode into a lobby that, from the looks of it, had seen better days.

Crumpled fast food wrappers and empty pizza boxes littered the stairwell. The grimy, yellowish-white paint on the walls was peeling. Rap music blared from an apartment down the hall. And outside the back door, which was propped open by a cinderblock, two men in their early-twenties stood smoking a joint.

They didn't even bother to try to hide it when they saw her.

Grace climbed the steps to the third floor. She knocked on the door to Izzy's friend's apartment, then stepped back so she was fully visible through the peephole. She kept her facial expression friendly and her body language relaxed until the door opened just enough to catch on the chain lock.

A Latina woman in her late-twenties eyed her warily through the gap.

"Carolina Flores?" Grace asked.

The woman hesitated. "Yes."

"Hi. I'm Grace Callahan. You don't know me, but I'd like to talk to you about a mutual friend."

"Who?"

"Izzy Rivera."

"Izzy?" Carolina unhooked the chain and opened the door. "Why? What's wrong? Is she okay?"

"She's fine," Grace said. "She's staying with some friends of mine on Heron Island—in a rehab program for vets. My brother, Ryan Callahan, is one of the employers for the program. And the man who owns the inn where she's staying is one of my best friends."

Carolina nodded and let out a breath. "Please," she said, moving back from the door. "Come in."

"Thank you," Grace said, stepping into the apartment. The first thing she noticed was that it looked nothing like the rest of the building. In lieu of the peeling, yellowish-white paint, Carolina's walls were a bright, cheerful turquoise. A colorful Mexican tapestry hung over the sofa and several similar pieces—smaller, but just as vibrant—were scattered throughout the living room. The radio was tuned to a local Hispanic station, and two small children were sitting on the floor making finger puppets.

They stopped what they were doing as soon as Grace walked into the room. From the looks on their faces, it was obvious they weren't used to visitors.

"Rosa," Carolina said, holding out her hand to her eldest child.

Rosa stood and went to her mother's side immediately. "Yes, Mamá?"

"This is Ms. Callahan," Carolina said. "She's a...friend of Izzy's, but I need to speak with her alone for a little while."

Rosa looked up at Grace apprehensively.

The younger child—a boy, probably only three or four years old—didn't appear quite as concerned as his sister. As soon as he caught his mother's eye, he held up both hands, wiggling his fingers to show off his puppets.

Carolina's face softened. "They're beautiful, Miguel. I love them."

"Puppets!" Miguel said excitedly.

"Would you like to make up a story to go with them?" Carolina suggested. "You could tell me about it at dinner."

Miguel nodded.

"I bet your sister would be willing to help you." Carolina looked back at Rosa, lowering her voice. "Why don't you two go into my room? I'll call you as soon as dinner's ready."

"Okay," Rosa said, but she didn't let go of her mother's hand.

Carolina leaned down, whispered something in her ear, and gave her a brief, reassuring hug. When Carolina pulled back, Rosa nodded and let go of her hand. She helped her brother gather their things and led him into the bedroom. But Grace noticed that she left the door open a crack instead of closing it all the way—probably so she could keep an eye on them.

"She's protective of you," Grace said.

Carolina nodded, gesturing for Grace to follow her into the kitchen. "She has been ever since her father passed away last year."

"I'm sorry," Grace said. She knew what it felt like to lose a parent, how scary it was to imagine anything bad happening to the one who was left. "Do you have any other family in the area?"

"No." Carolina went to the fridge and pulled out a bag of coffee grounds. "Unless you count Izzy. She's practically family."

Grace noticed that the refrigerator door was covered in graded homework assignments from Rosa's previous school year —all As. "When was the last time you spoke to Izzy?"

"A couple weeks ago," Carolina said, carrying the coffee pot over to the sink.

"How did she seem to you?"

"Good." Carolina started to fill the pot with water. "Why?"

"Something happened between her and another veteran a few weeks ago. There was an incident in the kitchen at the inn where she's staying. Did she mention anything to you about it?"

"I don't think so," Carolina said, glancing over her shoulder. "What kind of incident?"

"One involving a knife."

"*What?*" Carolina bobbled the coffee pot. "What happened? Did someone try to hurt her?"

"No," Grace said, surprised at how quickly she'd jumped to that conclusion. "She almost hurt someone else."

"That's impossible. Izzy would never hurt anyone."

"She...wouldn't?"

"No," Carolina said emphatically.

"How do you know that?"

"Because..." Carolina trailed off. A flicker of fear, deep in her eyes, betrayed the fact that she was hiding something.

Grace walked over to the sink and shut the water off when the pot started to overflow. "I wasn't there. But, from what I understand, Izzy was having a flashback at the time. When the other veteran tried to pull her out of it, she went after him with a knife."

Carolina wrapped her arms around her midsection. "I can't believe she would do that."

"My friend—the one who owns the inn—he's the veteran she went after. He understands that she was probably just reacting to whatever was in her mind. And he's willing to give her another chance. But his wife isn't. She and their daughter moved out of the inn a few weeks ago because they're afraid Izzy might be dangerous."

Carolina looked away, clearly distressed.

"Do you have any idea why she might have reacted that way?"

"Have you asked her that?"

"No. But a lot of other people have. And she won't talk about it."

Carolina continued to study a spot on the opposite wall.

"If you could think of anything—anything at all—it would really help us. My friends are taking on a huge risk in letting Izzy stay. She's already on thin ice. If she makes another mistake, she could lose her place in the program."

"What?" Carolina's gaze snapped back up, and it wasn't just a flicker of fear in her eyes now, it was full-fledged panic. "If Izzy doesn't finish the program, she'll go to jail."

"I know."

Carolina paled. "She's *not* dangerous. I promise. You have to believe me."

"I want to believe you. I do. But the only reason she's even in that program is because she shot someone."

"Izzy never *shot* anyone!" As soon as the words left her mouth, Carolina took a step back. Then another. "I... I didn't mean... What I meant was..."

"What?" Grace pressed. "What did you mean?"

Carolina took another step back and her whole body started to shake.

"You were there, weren't you?" Grace said, her voice softening. "You were there the night Tyree Robinson got shot."

"I...I don't know what you're talking about."

"I know there were two women in the alley that night," Grace said, her eyes never leaving Carolina's face. "What I don't understand is why Izzy would take the blame for something she didn't do."

The thrum of the bass from the music on the first floor pulsed through the floorboards. Outside, a basketball cracked against the backboard of the lone hoop set up between the two buildings, rattling the chain net.

"Carolina," Grace said gently. "I'm not going to go to the police. I *am* a reporter, but I'm not writing a story about this. I'm not going to print anything you say. I'm only here for my friends. And for Izzy. If you tell me what happened, I might be able to help you—both of you."

"You can't help me."

"How do you know?"

"Because I know," Carolina said, her dark eyes filling with tears. "But if I tell you what happened, will you promise that Izzy can keep her place in the program? That she won't have to go to jail?"

"I promise."

Carolina drew in a shaky breath. She took a moment to collect herself, then looked at the door leading into her bedroom, which was still cracked. "Please," she said. "Just...give me a moment."

Grace finished making the coffee while Carolina went to check on her children. When she came out of the bedroom, she closed the door all the way behind her. "On the night of March 27th," Carolina said, walking into the kitchen, "Izzy was supposed to give me a ride home from work. I usually work late on Thursdays, and she insisted on driving me so I wouldn't have to walk home from the bus stop after dark. I work for a family in Guilford —the same family Izzy's grandmother worked for before she got sick. That's how we met."

Carolina went to the oven and adjusted the heat on the casserole that was baking inside before turning to face Grace again. "Izzy hated that I lived in this neighborhood. Every time she came over, she said it wasn't safe. After my husband died, she begged me to move in with her. But I was too proud to accept her offer. I wanted to pay my own way—even if this was all I could afford. I'd been living here for a few years by then anyway. I figured if something bad were going to happen, it would have already happened."

Carolina took a deep breath and Grace could tell she regretted that now. "When I finished up work an hour early that night, I sent Izzy a message, telling her I didn't need a ride. I thought it would be faster to take the bus than wait for her to pick me up. But traffic was terrible that night. There'd been some kind of accident and we sat on the road forever. By the time we finally got to my bus stop, it was almost dark. I hadn't been able to call the woman who watches my children to tell her I was running late. I was on my way to her house when I ran into Tyree."

Grace stood up a little straighter. "Tyree Robinson?"

"Yes."

"You knew him?"

Carolina nodded. "He lives—well, he *lived*—in the neigh-borhood."

"Right," Grace said slowly.

"He was interested in me," Carolina said. "He'd *been* inter-ested in me for months. I always told him no, but he'd been more aggressive about it lately. I tried to be polite—you don't want to make enemies in this neighborhood, especially with someone like Tyree—but that night, I was in a hurry." Behind her, the coffee maker started to gurgle. "He got angry when I brushed him off. He started to follow me. I told him to go away. I tried to ignore him. But he wouldn't stop."

Grace said nothing, waiting for her to go on.

"When he grabbed my arm the first time, I was able to get away, but he caught the strap of my purse. He took it, held it away from me, and said he could buy me a better purse—a fancier purse. I asked him to give it back. He said, no, not until I gave him something in return."

Grace felt a slow roll in the pit of her stomach.

"I didn't really think he was going to hurt me at that point," Carolina said. "I was more worried about my kids. I didn't want them to think something had happened to me." She looked back at the bedroom, where her children were playing quietly on the other side of the door. "I didn't have anything valuable in my purse. I never carried more than twenty dollars in cash. And my keys were in my pocket. So I decided to walk away." She took a breath. "The next time he grabbed me, he wouldn't let go."

"Carolina," Grace said quietly. "Do you want to sit down?"

"No." Carolina shook her head. "He didn't... He wasn't able to... Izzy found me in time."

"She...found you?"

"The woman who was watching my children had called her.

She was worried because I'd never been late before. I'd given her Izzy's number as a backup, in case anything ever happened. Izzy knew I'd taken the bus home, but she couldn't reach me by phone either. So she drove over and started looking for me. She found my purse lying on the sidewalk outside the alley."

Grace let out a breath.

"She came into the alley right when he was...about to..."

Grace nodded.

"I think she caught him off guard, because when she pushed him off me, he almost fell. He got angry, really angry. He started yelling at her, calling her a crazy bitch. But she wouldn't stop... pushing him. She just kept pushing him toward the back of the alley, and telling me to run. There was a pay phone across the street. I was about to run over to it and call for help, when he... pulled out a gun."

The coffee maker hissed, letting out a puff of steam. "Somehow, Izzy knocked it out of his hand. It landed on the ground, only a few feet away from me. She kept telling me to run. But I couldn't just leave her there. I was afraid he was going to do the same thing to her that he'd tried to do to me."

"So you picked it up."

Carolina nodded. "He had her by the neck. He was...strangling her. I thought he was going to kill her. I didn't know what else to do." She squeezed her eyes shut, trying to block out the memories. "The next thing I knew, Izzy was taking the gun from me and rubbing it down with her shirt. I didn't understand what she was doing. I couldn't hear anything she was saying, except for the word, 'run.' I tried to get her to come with me, but she wouldn't. So...I ran."

"I don't understand," Grace said. "Why didn't you just come forward, tell the truth? It was self-defense."

Carolina looked back down at her hands.

The sound of a child's laughter drifted toward them and, all at once, everything clicked into place—the neighborhood, the secrecy, the fear in Carolina's eyes when she'd first answered the door. "You're living here illegally."

Carolina didn't move. She didn't say anything. But the truth was written all over her face.

"She did it to protect you," Grace breathed, "so your name wouldn't go into the system."

"No," Carolina said brokenly. "She didn't do it for me. I would never have allowed that."

Grace's eyes widened. "Your children...?"

"They're citizens. They were born here." Carolina looked back up at Grace, pleading with her to understand. "I could have been separated from them."

Grace took a step back as the full impact of what Carolina was saying began to sink in. "Izzy took the fall so your children wouldn't have to grow up without their mother?"

"Yes," Carolina whispered, bowing her head. "She's a hero. She's *my* hero."

NINETEEN

Three hours later, Grace sat at a table in the café with Ryan, Annie, Will, Becca, and Colin. Overhead, a lone ceiling fan whirred. The only other sound was the click, click, click of a tangled pull cord knocking against one of the light fixtures.

No one made a move to fix it.

"So...she's innocent," Becca said, the first one to speak after Grace finished telling them the story.

Grace nodded.

"But"—Becca looked around at the rest of her friends' faces, each registering a different stage of shock—"she pled guilty."

"In exchange for the deal the prosecution offered," Grace said.

"Right," Becca said. "I get that. But why did she have to take a deal at all? Even if she *had* been the only one in the alley that night, it was still self-defense. Tyree pulled a gun on her."

"I know," Grace said. "I asked myself that same question. My best guess is that she did it to prevent any further investigation. A self-defense argument would have required a trial. It would have strung things out. The detectives working the case would have spent more time in that neighborhood, asked more questions. They might have been able to piece things together, the same way I did."

Across the table from Grace, Will shook his head. "She shot him with his own gun."

"Exactly," Grace said. "The fact that she was able to disarm him would have actually worked against her in court. The prosecution could have argued that she'd had the upper hand at that point, that it hadn't been necessary to shoot him at all."

"She wiped the gun down before the police got there?" Colin asked.

Grace nodded. "She wiped all the prints off the gun, but there could have been more in the alley. If the investigation had continued, the police could have found them. They might not have been able to identify a match right away, since her friend is living here illegally. But that, alone, might have raised more questions. Eventually, someone could have pointed them in the right direction. The only way Izzy could be sure to prevent that from happening was to confess as quickly as possible."

"What about Tyree?" Colin asked. "Wouldn't his story have conflicted with hers?"

"I wondered about that, too," Grace said. "But remember, he tried to rape Izzy's friend. And he wouldn't have wanted the police to know that. This guy is a seasoned criminal. He'd already served two years in prison before this. And he knew he was going to jail again. It wasn't like this was his first time dealing with the police. When they started questioning him, he probably waited to see how much they knew first. As soon as he found out that Izzy had admitted to shooting him, and no one was accusing him of sexual assault, he probably just went along with it."

"I don't understand how the police missed all this," Becca said. "It doesn't make me feel very safe."

"Baltimore has one of the highest crime rates in the country. Every cop in that city is overworked. The detectives are stretching themselves to the limits, just trying to keep up. They don't have the time or the resources to turn someone away who's willing to make a confession." Grace sat back in her chair. "Tyree's shooting led to the arrest of a major drug dealer. A lot of cops think Izzy did them a favor. They were relieved when she got off on probation. Even if some of them still have their doubts about whether or not she actually did it, the last thing they want is to start poking holes in a case that's already closed."

Becca frowned.

"I know it doesn't seem fair," Grace said, "but think of the alternative. Izzy's friend could have come forward and told the truth. A jury might have cleared her of any criminal charges. But, afterwards, she could have been deported to Mexico—a country she left when she was four years old. She has no family there, no friends, no job. She would have been separated from her children and forced to decide between bringing them to Mexico to live with her, or letting them stay here, in someone else's care, where —as citizens—they would have access to the best education and job opportunities in the world."

Outside, the air had grown still. The wind chimes hung silently from the beams of the porch. "So...what do we do now?" Becca asked.

"I told Izzy's friend I'd get back to her with the names of a few immigration attorneys," Grace said. "The last one she hired charged her two thousand dollars before telling her she didn't have a case. I'll need to do some research first—make sure whoever I refer her to is legit. It's possible, with the right attorney, and a *very* sympathetic judge, she could obtain some kind of legal status in this country. If she were ever able to accomplish that, she could potentially reopen the case and try to get the charges against Izzy dropped. But that would be up to them."

Colin shook his head. "That criminal record is going to follow Izzy around for the rest of her life."

"That may be," Grace said. "But she's not dangerous. Every single person at this table knows that now. And every single one of us can vouch for her to a potential employer." She turned to face Annie, who was sitting in the chair beside her. "I think it's safe to say that you and Taylor can move back to the inn."

Annie looked away, her expression filled with remorse. "I feel terrible. I should never have treated her so badly."

"Then make it up to her," Will said simply.

"How?"

He took one of her hands, threaded their fingers together. "You'll think of something."

Grace checked the clock on her phone. "I'd like to try and get to the inn before Izzy goes to bed. I want to tell her what I know, see if she'll tell me the rest." She looked up at Ryan. "Will you give me a ride? My car's almost out of gas."

Ryan nodded.

"Are you going to tell us what she says?" Will asked.

"I don't know," Grace said, pocketing her phone. "The only reason I told you this much was so Izzy could keep her place in the program and Annie could move back to the inn."

And she'd been careful not to reveal Izzy's friend's name, Ryan thought. Or where she lived. Or what she looked like. Even though she could trust every person in this room with her life, and she'd sworn them all to secrecy beforehand, she still hadn't revealed her source.

"If I'm right about what happened," Will said, "will you at least tell me if the guy who assaulted her is still out there?" He exchanged a look with Colin. "You don't have to tell me his name. I just want to know if he's still out there."

"I'm not making any promises," Grace said, stepping through the door that Ryan held open for her.

Ryan followed her outside and they crossed the yard to his truck. As soon as they were both inside, safely out of earshot from the others, she turned to him. "I'm not almost out of gas."

"I didn't think you were." Ryan let the keys dangle in the ignition without starting the truck. They sat in silence, parked under the oak tree, listening to the chorus of chirps and trills from the night-singing insects. "How are you holding up?"

"I'm having some trouble...detaching myself."

Ryan nodded. He'd lost his ability to detach himself from anything related to Izzy weeks ago. And that was *before* he'd heard about what she'd done for her friend.

"I don't usually have that problem," Grace said, picking at a few pieces of dog hair stuck to the seat. "When I talk to people on the job, I'm just looking for information—clues that will lead me to the truth. Emotion doesn't really factor into it. But this... I don't even..."

"I know," he said quietly.

Grace looked back up at him. "She could have gone to jail, Ryan."

"I know."

"Her friend said she wouldn't have let that happen—that she would have turned herself in if it had come to that—but Izzy couldn't have known that."

No, Ryan thought, she couldn't have.

Izzy had been willing to go to jail for a crime she didn't commit in order to keep a young mother with her children, when his mother—his and Grace's own mother—had left them as if they hadn't mattered at all.

Izzy stood in the hallway connecting the foyer to the kitchen at the inn, clutching her laptop in both hands. It had taken her most of the evening to work up the courage to come down here. She'd exhausted every other option first. She'd even considered the possibility of hiring a private investigator. But who was she kidding? She couldn't afford that. She didn't even know if she was going to have a job at the end of the summer.

What she did have were ten people, in the next room, who might be willing to help her.

If she told them the truth.

Tightening her grip on the laptop, she took a step forward. Then another. There was a chance that some of them might not believe her. Which was why she'd changed her mind at least a dozen times before coming down here. But this wasn't just about her anymore. It was about finding the rest of the women Bradley had assaulted before he hurt anyone else.

That was all that mattered.

"Yo," Kade said, glancing up from the baseball game he was watching with Jeff and Troy. "Where've you been all night?"

"Upstairs."

"In your room?"

She nodded.

"I knocked on your door a couple times."

"I know," she said, pausing at the edge of the couch. "I didn't answer."

Kade's brows drew together.

"I need to talk to you."

He started to stand.

"No," she said. "All of you."

On the other side of Kade, Troy picked up the remote and switched off the TV. "What's up?"

Izzy waited for the rest of the people in the room to stop what they were doing. Sitting at the table by the window, Zach, Wesley, and Matt slowly laid down their playing cards. From her chair by the fireplace, Megan looked up from the book she was reading. Hailey and Paul each set down their phones. And Ethan paused in the middle of raiding the fridge for a late-night snack.

"I owe you an explanation," Izzy began.

"About what?" Jeff asked, his expression reflecting the same confusion that was on most of their faces.

"About what happened in the kitchen a few weeks ago," Izzy said, "with Will."

"You had a flashback," Zach said, lifting a shoulder. "It's not a big deal."

"It *is* a big deal," Izzy said. "I could have hurt him. And I want you to understand why."

A few of the others exchanged glances.

Looking around the room, Izzy realized, suddenly, that she knew why everyone else was here. She knew why they'd left the military, why they'd applied to this program, and what traumas—physical or mental—they were working to overcome. She was the only one who hadn't shared her story.

Just do it, she thought. Just rip the bandage off and get it over with. "Last year, on August 30th, I was sexually assaulted by a man named Bradley Welker." Out of the corner of her eye, she saw Kade stiffen. "He attacked me in the kitchen on the base where I was working in North Carolina, which is why I can't cook anymore—because every time I do, it triggers a flashback."

Behind her, the refrigerator door closed. She heard footsteps coming toward her as Ethan walked into the room.

"It wasn't a random assault as we'd served on the same base in Afghanistan several years before. He was a lieutenant colonel at the time, and under normal circumstances we probably wouldn't have had many interactions other than me putting food on his plate. But on that deployment, our dining facility was attacked. Several soldiers were killed, and dozens more were wounded—including Bradley. I managed to pull him and two other officers to safety before the next bomb hit, and I was later awarded a Bronze Star for saving their lives."

Izzy took another breath, trying not to focus on the stunned expressions on the faces all around her. "Afterwards, all three officers thanked me. Bradley was particularly outspoken in his gratitude. He gave dozens of interviews to the press, praising the cook who'd saved his life. He even came to my awards ceremony. So, when he raped me, and I tried to report it, no one believed me. When my commanding officer ordered a psychiatric evaluation to determine if I was still fit to serve, I decided not to reenlist."

"Oh my God," Hailey breathed. "Izzy—"

Izzy held up a hand. She needed to finish. She needed to get it all out—all at once. "I thought I was the only woman Bradley had raped. I thought he was trying to get back at me because I'd emasculated him in some way by saving his life. And I thought, if it was just me, I could deal with it. I could find a way to move on. But it wasn't just me."

Taking a step toward the coffee table, she set her laptop down in front of Kade, Jeff, and Troy. "Last night, I found out that he attacked someone else. She was able to fight him off. But he still has something over her. And she'll only go public with me if I can find *more* women to back up our claims." She opened the top of the laptop to reveal her spreadsheet. "I've been tracking the social media accounts of every female soldier who might have come into contact with him for months now. I know there are others. There have to be. But I can't do this alone anymore. I need help."

Jeff looked up from the screen incredulously. "Is that what you've been doing up there, all those nights when you wouldn't hang out with us?"

"Yes."

Kade stood abruptly and crossed the room to the wall of windows. Pressing a hand to the glass, he stared out at the darkness, too emotional to speak.

"How long did you say you've been working on this?" Troy asked, looking down at the screen again.

"Five months."

Troy scrolled down the page, his eyes widening. "How many names do you have?"

"About three hundred."

"Holy shit," Matt said, making his way over to the sofa with Wesley and Zach in tow.

"Does anyone else know about this?" Hailey asked as she helped Paul to his feet.

"Erin knows," Izzy said.

Hailey looked relieved. "What about Will and Colin?"

"No."

A few people glanced up, surprised.

"I've already tried going to the top before," Izzy said. "The next time I report this to a superior, I want to know that I have a case."

Beside her, Ethan put a hand on her shoulder. "Will's staying at the café with Annie and Taylor tonight, so we should have the place to ourselves. What exactly do you want us to do?"

It took a moment for his words to register, for the full weight of them to sink in. They believed her? All of them? Just like that? "Well," Izzy said, letting out a long breath, "there are eleven of us. If we split up, and we each take thirty names, we could make it through the list pretty fast."

"Got it," Paul said, already reaching for his laptop. "Kade, are you in?"

From his spot by the windows, Kade finally turned. His expression was murderous. "A *spreadsheet?*" he asked. "You think you're going to stop that guy with a *spreadsheet?*"

"Uh-oh," Ethan said, his hand sliding off Izzy's shoulder.

"Where is he?" Kade asked, his eyes flashing.

Izzy took a step toward him. "Kade—"

"No!" he shouted, his deep voice booming through the room. "I'm not going to sit here and scroll through social media accounts when that guy is still out there! Do you even remember what you were like when you first got here? You were shattered, Izzy! He almost *destroyed* you!"

"But he didn't," Izzy said quietly. He hadn't, had he? In the end, he hadn't destroyed her at all.

Matt and Wesley came to stand beside her. "I think Izzy's right," Wesley said. "If we go after him now, she's got nothing. If we build a case against him, we might actually be able to put him away."

Kade clenched, unclenched his fists. "He *raped* her. Isn't that enough?"

"Not unless I can prove it," Izzy said. "And the only way I can do that is either with evidence—which I don't have—or with enough women saying the same thing that people start to believe us. Bradley's reputation is rock solid. It's going to take more than one or two of us making accusations to crack through it."

"This is bullshit," Kade said.

"You're damn right it's bullshit," Matt said. "None of us are going to argue with that."

"I need you *here*, Kade," Izzy said, when he still wouldn't move from his spot by the windows. "Your wife and children need you here."

Kade stared back at her, unblinking, as his warrior instincts challenged his ability to see this situation in anything other than black and white. But everyone had an Achilles heel and Izzy knew that the only reason he'd enrolled in this program was to get his wife and kids back.

He'd taken her advice after their first run together and sent his wife flowers. His wife had rejected the first delivery, and the second, but she'd accepted the third, along with the letter he'd written. So he'd sent more—a new delivery every day—along with a letter. And just this week, they'd started talking on the phone again.

He wasn't going to risk having all that progress wiped out overnight.

"I think we should start," Izzy said, still holding Kade's gaze, "by having everyone scan the list to see if they recognize any names. Some of you might already be friends with one or two of these women online. If so, we'd have access to more information."

"What, exactly, are we looking for?" Troy asked.

"Anything unusual," Izzy said. "Posts that seem out of character. Large gaps between posts if they usually post a lot. That sort of thing."

"What if we can't see anything?" Hailey asked. "Don't a lot of people have private accounts?"

"Yes," Izzy said. "And that's the biggest flaw in my system. At least a third of their accounts are private." When she saw a few of them deflate, she added, "I know it's not perfect. I've known that from the beginning. But, up until recently I thought I was the only one. I didn't think I was actually going to find anything."

"Is this how you found the other woman?" Megan asked.

"Yes."

"Then it's worth a try," she said, looking around at the rest of the veterans. "We can at least start there, right? Maybe one of us will see something Izzy missed."

"I'll get my laptop," Zach said, pushing to his feet.

"Me, too," Matt said, then glanced at Ethan and Wesley. "Want me to grab both of yours while I'm up there?"

They nodded.

"Can I print this out?" Troy asked, gesturing to the list on the screen. "Make copies for everyone?"

Izzy nodded.

Wesley headed into the kitchen to make a pot of coffee and Ethan cracked open a soda.

When Kade held out his hand for one, Izzy let out a breath. "Thank you," she said quietly.

From across the room, Kade continued to study her. "Did you think we wouldn't believe you?"

"Yes," she admitted.

Kade shook his head. "Just because one asshole didn't believe you, doesn't mean no one will."

Izzy looked around at the others. She could tell from their expressions that they agreed with him. A few of them actually looked a little hurt that she hadn't told them sooner.

Was it possible that she'd been going about this the wrong way from the beginning? That she should have pressed charges regardless of whether or not she'd had any evidence? That, in speaking out, she could have prompted other women to do the same?

She'd been holding onto so much pain for so long, blindly assuming that everyone would react the same way as her commanding officer, she'd never considered that some people might take her side.

And wasn't that exactly what Bradley was counting on? That she wouldn't have the courage to speak out against him? That she wouldn't dare accuse him without any evidence and risk the public backlash?

Sure, some people might have called her a liar. Some might have called her a whore.

But she wasn't a whore.

She knew that.

And that was all that mattered.

Even if her word hadn't been enough to convict him in court, it might have been enough to plant some doubt in a few people's minds. It might have been enough to poke a few holes in Bradley's Teflon reputation. It might have made it a little easier for the next woman to come forward.

Because there *would* be another woman. There would always be another one. As long as the previous victim stayed silent, bound by her own debilitating shame, the abuser could act again and again and again.

The only way to stop him, and to be free of that shame, was to give it a voice.

By the time Troy returned with copies of the spreadsheet, Izzy knew what she needed to do. She didn't know how she was going to do it, but she was going to do it, whether they found the rest of the women or not.

She helped Troy pass out the copies and once everyone had a chance to look at the list, they divvied up the names and spread out throughout the two adjoining rooms. She was about to take a seat on the empty barstool beside Hailey when the front door opened.

Everyone froze.

A moment later, Ryan walked into the room, followed by a woman Izzy didn't recognize. Halfway to the bar, he stopped walking. He took in the gurgling coffee maker, the laptops on every table, the muted expressions on all their faces. "What's going on?"

The rest of the veterans looked at Izzy.

When Izzy didn't say anything right away, Ryan's gaze dropped to the spreadsheet in front of Hailey. "What is this?" he asked, reaching for it.

Hailey put her hand on it, spreading her fingers to cover as many names as she could. "It's nothing."

Ryan frowned, tugging it free. "It's obviously *not* nothing."

No, Izzy thought. It wasn't. And if there was anyone who deserved to know the truth, it was Ryan. Will and Colin might have accepted her into this program, but Ryan was the one who'd given her a job. Ryan was the one who'd taken on all the risk in employing her. Ryan was the one who'd convinced her to believe in something again, when she'd tried so hard not to care.

"You're right," Izzy said. "It's not nothing."

Ryan slowly lowered the sheet back to the bar.

Izzy glanced at the woman beside him. She was probably the same age as Ryan. She had the same sun-streaked blond hair and pale gray eyes. And she was as tall and slender as he was lanky.

"I'm Grace," she said, introducing herself. "Ryan's sister."

His sister, Izzy thought. Of course. Ryan had a twin sister who lived in D.C.

"You're the journalist, right?" Hailey said from beside her. "The one who works for the *Tribune*?"

Grace nodded.

Izzy paused. A journalist? She remembered Ryan talking about having a sister, but not what she did for a living. "What kind of journalist?"

"Investigative."

Izzy slowly set her laptop down on the bar. Ryan's sister was an investigative journalist for *The Washington Tribune*—one of the most widely read newspapers in the country?

Hailey's eyes met hers, and Izzy could tell she was thinking the exact same thing.

Izzy looked back at Grace. "I need your help."

∼

It wasn't like he hadn't been prepared for this, Ryan thought. Will had warned him about the possibility weeks ago. But hearing Izzy say it—hearing her say the words out loud—had shaken him to the core.

He understood, now, why she'd been so closed off when she first came to this island. It wasn't just that she'd been raped. Her best friend had almost been raped, too. And she must have assumed, since the system had failed her, that it would fail her friend as well. So she'd taken matters into her own hands to protect her.

She'd been willing to sacrifice her future—her entire future—for another woman and her two children. As if her own life hadn't mattered. As if she'd had nothing left to live for. She'd already lost her career, her ability to cook, her trust in other people. Everything she'd ever believed in had been shattered.

All because of what one man had done.

Ryan wasn't a violent person. He could count, on one hand, the number of times he'd lost his temper. But he could feel the anger building up inside him now—the need to do something about it, to respond in some way, physically.

Intellectually, he knew that responding to violence with violence rarely solved anything. It often made things worse. But he would love nothing more than to drive down to North Carolina right now and smash his fist into Bradley Welker's face —over and over and over again—until the man was unconscious.

Instead, he stayed where he was, biding his time. He waited for Izzy to finish answering all of Grace's questions. He waited for Will, Colin, Becca, and Annie to arrive. He waited for Izzy to tell the story all over again. And, then—once everyone had turned their attention to searching for more victims—he went to her.

Resting a hand on the back of her chair, he lowered his voice. "Can I talk to you for a second?"

She looked up. "Sure."

He nodded toward the front of the house, where they could have a little more privacy. She slid off the bar stool and followed him out to the porch. As soon as they were both outside, he turned to her.

In the muted glow of the porch light, the circles under her eyes appeared even darker. He could tell she was exhausted. Not just physically, but emotionally. He had to slip his hands in his pockets to keep from reaching for her. To keep from pulling her into his arms.

All he wanted was to hold her. To tell her that everything was going to be all right. But she'd made it clear today that she didn't want that kind of comfort from him. That she regretted what had happened between them the night before. And he needed to address that. "I need to apologize."

Izzy's brows drew together. "For what?"

"For kissing you," he said. "I don't want things to be awkward between us. I got...caught up in the moment last night. It won't happen again."

"I don't want things to be awkward between us either," Izzy said slowly. "But I'm not sorry that you kissed me."

That wasn't exactly the reaction he'd been expecting. "You're not?"

"No."

"But...you could hardly look at me today."

"That's because I heard from Alicia right after I left you last night. I didn't know what to do about it. I was afraid if anyone found out about you and me, they would think I'd been doing the same thing with Bradley. That, if I ever tried to come forward and accuse him publicly, they could point to this as a pattern and say it was consensual, that I must have asked for it."

"You *didn't* ask for it," Ryan said, the anger building inside him again at the mere mention of her rapist's name.

"I know," she said. "Or, at least, I know that *now*. I didn't before." She took a step toward him, hesitantly. "I was also afraid that I'd never be able to kiss anyone again without thinking about Bradley, and I was wrong about that, too. The only person I was thinking about last night was you."

When she took another step toward him, Ryan's heart began a slow, dull thud in his chest. What was she saying? That she *wanted* him to kiss her again?

"I'm not sure if it was a fluke," Izzy said, "or if there's something about kissing you that keeps me from going there, but maybe we should try it again, just to be sure."

She didn't need to say anything else, because Ryan was already pulling her into his arms. When she pressed up on her toes, meeting him halfway, he laid his lips on hers. He heard her sigh, right before she melted into him. And all the anger that had been building inside him dissolved instantly.

He kissed her slowly, wanting to savor it, wanting to remember what it felt like—the moment he realized he was falling in love.

By the time they pulled apart, he knew there was no going back, but they needed to talk about how to navigate the next seven weeks. "I'm still your boss."

"I know," she said.

"Do you want me to talk to Will and Colin—see if we could find you another job for the rest of the summer?"

"No." she said. "I don't want that."

"Neither do I."

Izzy took a deep breath. "But I don't want to keep any more secrets either."

"Then we won't," he said, brushing a thumb over her cheek. "You focus on finishing the rest of this program. I'll focus on the farm and the environmental center. When we want to spend time together, we'll spend time together. It's as simple as that."

She smiled softly. "That sounds nice."

He bent down, touched his lips to hers one last time, because he didn't know how long it would be until he got her alone again. Then he took her hand, and started to lead her back inside.

Two steps into the foyer, Jeff rounded the corner from the kitchen, a somber expression on his face. "We found something."

TWENTY

*B*radley Welker scrawled his signature across the bottom of a form his assistant had left for him to sign, then reached for the next one, paying no attention to the words on the page. His thoughts, as they had been for weeks now, remained fixed on Alicia—and the fact that she'd gotten away.

No one had ever gotten away before.

It was bad enough that he'd had to live with the humiliation of being *saved* by a woman for seven years. Now, he had to accept the fact that he'd been beaten by one in a fight?

Scraping his pen across the next signature line, he thought about going after her again. He'd gotten his hands on some pills recently—pills that would ensure her submission. It would be easy enough to slip one into her drink, to finish what they'd started several weeks ago.

But if he asked her into his office again, even under the guise of an apology, she would probably suspect something. It might be better to lay low for a while, at least where she was concerned. In the meantime, he needed to find another target, an easier one—one who wouldn't expect anything.

Turning the page, he spotted the next 'sign here' sticker, perfectly aligned with the blank above the signature line, and wondered why all women couldn't be more like his assistant. Judy had a clear understanding of her role in society. She had no interest in advancing past an administrative support position at work.

It was her home life that mattered most.

She was a dutiful wife, married to her high school sweetheart for over thirteen years, and a devoted mother of three children. She was perpetually cheerful, impeccable in her appearance, and every morning she had a fresh cup of coffee waiting for him on his desk.

It was so obvious that this was the way the world was supposed to function. Why were so many women trying to change that? Why were they fighting for jobs that didn't belong to them? Why couldn't they see how happy everyone would be if things just stayed the same—or, better yet, went back to the way they'd been before?

At the sound of footsteps in the hallway, Bradley glanced up. He was surprised there was anyone else in the building. His assistant, and the rest of his colleagues, had left over two hours ago. He was planning to leave soon, too, once he got through this pile of paperwork.

When the footsteps turned toward him and a woman in fatigues appeared in his doorway, he frowned. Enlisted soldiers were expected to make a formal appointment to see him through his assistant, not stop by his office unannounced.

"Sergeant Rhee, sir," the female soldier said, standing at attention. "Lieutenant Woods said you wanted to see me."

Ah, yes. Sergeant Rhee. He *had* wanted to see her. They'd only been introduced once before, so he wasn't surprised he hadn't recognized her. "You're here late, Sergeant."

"Yes, sir," she said. "I'm trying to get everything in order before I leave. Would you like me to come back tomorrow?"

Bradley sat back, assessing the petite Asian-American female in his doorway. It was a shame he couldn't make out the shape of her body through her uniform. Her curves were clearly smaller than he preferred, but she had an appealing face. High cheekbones, full lips, exotic almond-shaped eyes that were so dark they were almost black. "No. This is fine."

"Thank you, sir."

He stood, gesturing toward the comfortable seating area in the corner. "I heard your orders came earlier this week."

"They did, sir."

"When do you leave?"

"Two weeks," she said, taking a seat on the sofa.

Bradley settled into the chair beside her. "You think you're ready to go back to school full time? It'll be a big change from what you've been doing."

"I am, sir," she said. "I never thought I'd get the opportunity to go to medical school. This is a dream come true for me."

Bradley nodded. In an effort to strengthen a shrinking workforce of doctors in the armed services, the military had launched a program to assist highly qualified enlisted service members in applying for medical school. The two-year program would give them a chance to complete all their pre-med courses and prepare for the MCATs. If they passed, they would be admitted to the Uniformed Services University of Health Sciences Medical School, where they would earn a fully funded graduate degree while maintaining their active duty status.

The program only admitted a handful of service members each year and it was a huge honor to be chosen.

"The program's still fairly new," Bradley said. "As one of the first female candidates, a lot of people will be watching to see how well you do. I hope you're up for that kind of pressure."

"I am, sir," she said. "I won't let you down."

Bradley smiled. "I'm happy to hear that." Especially since her name was connected to his now. As a favor to her platoon commander, Lieutenant Woods, he'd written a letter of recommendation to include with her application. Lieutenant Woods could have written it himself, but Bradley had a friend in the admissions department so it carried more weight coming from him.

Lieutenant Woods had filled him in on all of the particulars—her years of service as a combat medic, her two tours in Afghanistan, the medals she'd won for her bravery overseas. Whether or not that background had prepared her for a career as a doctor remained to be seen, but he hadn't minded writing the letter. It had only added to his reputation as a champion of women's advancement in the military. Plus, it meant that he had something over her.

"Do you have any idea what kind of doctor you want to be?" he asked.

"Yes, sir," she said, sitting up even taller than she had been before. "A neurosurgeon."

"A neurosurgeon?" he asked, lifting a brow.

"That's right, sir. Traumatic Brain Injury is one of the most common afflictions among service members now. I've seen the damage that IED explosions can do firsthand. I want to be able to do more to help my fellow soldiers."

"I see," he said. How noble of her.

And if she were a man, he might be impressed. But she wasn't a man. She was a woman. And women did *not* become neurosurgeons.

He had assumed, when he'd written the letter, that Sergeant Rhee had planned to become a general practitioner, an emergency room doctor, or a pediatrician—specialties commonly occupied by women. He knew the Army needed doctors. He understood they would have to fill some of those positions with women, simply to meet their diversity quotas.

But this...?

This was taking it too far.

Everywhere he looked, the systems, the order, the structure; they were breaking down. He felt like a one-man Army, trying to make things right again.

What was wrong with everyone?

Why couldn't they understand that the world needed order? That it depended on it? That these roles had been established for a reason?

He stood abruptly and walked to the table where he kept his decanter of scotch. "I didn't realize how late it had gotten," he said. "You don't mind if I have a drink, do you?"

"No, sir. Of course not."

"Would you like one?" he asked.

"Oh...no, thank you. My husband's expecting me. I should probably be going soon."

"It's very good scotch," he said, glancing over his shoulder. "A friend of mine brought it back from Scotland. Maybe just a taste?" He smiled. "You know what they say about drinking alone."

She laughed. "Okay. You twisted my arm."

He dropped a few ice cubes into each of their glasses. "Would you mind grabbing the door for me? The cleaning crew usually comes through here around this time. It can get noisy when they run the vacuum."

"Of course, sir."

He heard her get up, walk to the door, and made a split-second decision to slip one of the pills into her drink. It wouldn't carry quite the same level of satisfaction as physically overpowering her. But he might as well practice first—see how the pills worked before he used one on Alicia.

Carrying both glasses over to the seating area, he flicked his gaze over her body again. It really was a shame that those uniforms were so unflattering. "How does your husband feel about the move?"

Sergeant Rhee took the glass he handed her, sat down on the sofa again. "He's a consultant for a defense contractor in Northern Virginia. He's been working remotely for the past several years, following me from base to base. It'll be good for both our careers to be in the D.C. area for a while."

Interesting, Bradley thought, settling back into his chair. He wondered how her husband felt about being a trailing spouse, letting his wife's career dictate where they lived. "Has he been supportive of your decision to go back to school? To become a neurosurgeon?"

She smiled. "He has. He's been very supportive."

Bradley smiled back, lifted his glass. "To your success."

"Thank you, sir," she said, taking a sip.

Bradley wondered how much of her husband's support was an act, how much he secretly resented her decision. He would probably be doing them *both* a favor by putting her in her place.

"This *is* good scotch, isn't it?" Sergeant Rhee asked, holding up her glass and studying the amber-colored liquor.

"It is," he said, wondering how long it would take for the pill to kick in. When she took another sip—bigger this time—it occurred to him that he hadn't really thought through what he was going to do with her afterwards. He had no interest in finding a way to transport a temporarily unconscious woman. And she couldn't stay in his office all night.

"You said your friend brought it back from Scotland?" she asked, still looking at the glass.

Bradley nodded. "He and his wife took a vacation to the Highlands recently. It was an anniversary trip. They'd been planning it for years."

"I hear it's beautiful there," she said. "Are you married?"

"No," he said, forcing a note of wistfulness into his voice. "I came close a couple of times, but my career always got in the way."

"I understand," she said. "The military lifestyle can be tough on families. And you've done very well for yourself."

Yes, Bradley thought. He had.

He watched her take another sip and decided that he probably shouldn't wait for her to finish the entire drink. It might be better to send her on her way while she was still conscious, make sure she'd at least made it to her car first. Whatever happened afterwards wasn't his problem.

"Have you found a place to live in D.C. yet?" he asked, making conversation to fill the time.

"We put an offer on a house in Falls Church yesterday," she said. "I've been told the public school systems in Fairfax County are excellent."

"Do you have children?"

"I do," she said, smiling. "I have a son."

"How old?"

"Six."

"Have you told him about the move?"

"I have." She took another sip, swayed a little in her seat. "I know he'll be sad to leave his friends behind, but he's still young. Kids are pretty resilient at that age—at least that's what everyone tells me."

Bradley nodded, watching her closely.

"It'll be harder when he gets older, though," she said, slurring her words. "I have friends whose children mope around for months after they move."

If she were a good mother, Bradley thought, she'd stay home, help her children adjust to the moves.

Sergeant Rhee looked back down at her drink, blinked a few times, as if she were having trouble focusing. "Is this scotch... stronger than normal?"

Bradley's lips curved. "Are you having trouble holding your liquor, Sergeant?"

She squeezed her eyes shut, opened them. Disoriented, she tried to set the glass down on the table in front of her, but her perception was off. The bottom cracked against the edge of the table, causing some of the liquor to slosh out.

She knelt, immediately, and began to mop up the spill on the floor with the sleeve of her uniform. "I'm sorry, sir," she slurred. "I'm afraid I'm a bit of a lightweight."

"Here," Bradley said, handing her a cloth.

She took it, finished wiping up the mess, then tried to stand, but she couldn't quite make it to her feet.

Bradley rose slowly, offered her a hand.

She let him help her to her feet, since her own legs wouldn't cooperate. "Thank you," she said, offering him a wobbly smile. "I should probably go before I make a fool of myself."

"You don't need to go yet," he said, drawing her down to the sofa beside him.

Confused, she looked down at their joined hands. "Sir?"

"Relax," he murmured, letting his gaze drop to her mouth.

She stiffened and tried to move away from him. "I don't think I should be here anymore."

He tightened his grip on her hand. "You haven't thanked me properly yet."

"Th-thanked you...?" she stammered. "For what?"

"For writing the letter." He caught the flash of fear in her eyes and fed off it, started to feel things shifting back into place again. "You didn't honestly think I'd write you a letter of recommendation and not expect anything in return?"

"Sir," she said more firmly, struggling to pull her hand free. "I'm going to have to ask you to stop."

"Stop what?" He reached for the zipper of her uniform jacket with his free hand and slid it down. "This?"

She tried to twist away from him. He shoved her down to the cushions so she was pinned beneath him. "Please," she said, writhing against him. "Stop. I don't understand what's happening."

"You're not very bright, are you?" he asked, stripping her jacket off. "Most women aren't." His eyes raked over her breasts, the shape of them finally visible beneath the sand-colored T-shirt. "But sometimes you forget that, don't you? You think you can do anything." He jerked the hem of her shirt out of her belted fatigue pants. "That's why I need to put you in your place sometimes. Make sure you know exactly where you belong."

"Stop!" she shouted, struggling against him. "Get off me!"

He yanked her shirt up, over her breasts, and froze when he caught sight of the thin wire taped to her skin. "What the hell?"

Sergeant Rhee drove her knee up, hard, into his groin as three men wearing military police uniforms stormed into the office. "Hands on your head, where I can see them," the closest officer shouted. "Now!"

Wheezing in pain, Bradley covered himself, his eyes darting back to the woman on the sofa. "What the hell is this?"

The woman stood, readjusted her shirt. "I'm not Jackie Rhee. I'm Special Agent Elena Kwan with CID."

CID? The Army's Criminal Investigation Division?

One of the officers grabbed Bradley, hauled him to his feet. Another seized his hands, cuffed them behind his back.

"Colonel Bradley Welker," Elena said, looking straight at him, with clear eyes and perfectly clear speech, "pursuant to Article 120 of the Uniform Code you're hereby apprehended to face charges for the attempted rape of Jackie Rhee and Alicia

Booker. At this time, you are also facing charges for the rape of Isabella Rivera, Lisa Khan, Kendra Williams, Alexa Martinez, Chelsea Howe, Leslie Wright, Talia Turner, Renee Yi, Petra Capoor, Celia Jackson, Karen Hayes, Abigail Ruiz, and Laura Cole."

TWENTY-ONE

*T*hirteen.

There'd been thirteen of them.

Fifteen if you counted Jackie and Alicia.

Alone in her room, Izzy read the last paragraph of the article Grace had released in the online version of *The Washington Tribune* as soon as they'd received confirmation from CID that Bradley had been apprehended. Most of the story had been pieced together beforehand. She'd known what it was going to say. But it was different seeing it in black and white—seeing all their names together in one place.

It had been three weeks since she'd told the rest of the veterans the truth. During that first night alone, they'd found two more potential victims. Grace had insisted on taking over after that. With the full support of her editor, she'd armed herself with a team of research assistants, thrown money in a hundred different directions, and personally flown to interview three of the women who'd been reluctant to speak over the phone.

As soon as they discovered that all the women Bradley had assaulted were minorities and that each of them had done something, or were attempting to do something, that was traditionally done by a man, they were able to narrow down the pool of women he might potentially target next to only a handful of women currently stationed on the base in North Carolina.

At that point, Colin had put in a call to the highest-ranking officer in the Army's Criminal Investigation Division. CID had agreed to prioritize the investigation, and they'd called each of the women in to explain the situation. Following any direct or indirect communications from Bradley, the women were to report to them immediately.

When Jackie Rhee had reported that Bradley had wanted to see her, CID had set up a sting operation with one of their own agents, banking on the fact that Bradley wouldn't be able to tell the difference between two similar looking Asian-American women. Elena had only taken a few small sips of the drink, knowing there was a chance it could have been spiked. Her behavior had all been an act.

Now, between the recording, the date-rape drug they'd found in her drink, and the DNA samples they'd collected from the sofa —which Izzy had no doubt would match at least one of the women who'd been assaulted there—they had enough evidence to guarantee a conviction.

All fifteen women had agreed to press charges. All fifteen had agreed to come forward publicly. All fifteen had agreed to put their names out there, and accept the stigma of 'rape victim' or 'attempted rape victim,' because—despite whatever backlash they might receive—*they* knew that they had nothing to be ashamed of.

None of them had asked for this. None of them had done anything to deserve it. And it sure as hell hadn't been any of their faults.

The only thing they'd done wrong was try to keep the truth to themselves and carry the burden alone. In coming together, and speaking out, they had ensured that Bradley Welker would never hurt anyone ever again.

At the knock on her door, Izzy glanced up.

Kade stood in the hallway, holding a tablet displaying the same article she'd been reading on her laptop. "Hey."

"Hey," she said back.

"Did you read it?" he asked, gesturing to the computer on the bed in front of her.

She nodded. "I just finished."

"Me too." He studied her face. "You okay?"

"Yeah," she said. "I am." For the first time in a long time, she was one hundred percent okay.

"Paul turned on the TV downstairs," Kade said. "All the major news networks have picked it up. It's everywhere."

Izzy smiled. "Good."

She wanted it to be everywhere. She wanted everyone to know the truth. And by the end of the day, they probably would. In addition to telling the stories of all fifteen women, Grace had managed to include quotes from three senators and two members of congress—all of whom had been pushing for years to pass legislation that would make it safer for women to report sexual assaults in the military.

Bradley's court-martial was sure to become a highly politicized event. The media attention wasn't going to die down anytime soon.

"I forwarded the article to my wife," Kade said. "I told her that I knew you. That you were here, in this program. That you were the one who convinced me to send the flowers—and keep sending them, even after she rejected the first few."

Izzy closed the top of her computer, pushed it away from her. "You would have figured it out for yourself eventually."

"I'm not sure I would have," Kade said. "She's going to want to meet you."

Letting her feet drop to the floor, Izzy stood. "I'd like to meet her, too."

Kade held out his hand. "Maybe we should take her to that old house, show her the punching bag where it all started."

Izzy laughed. "I think we definitely should. She might want to take a few swings at it herself—pretend that it's you."

Kade smiled, but his expression sobered when she put her hand in his. "You know who you are now, right? You're never going to let anyone take that away from you again?"

Izzy nodded. Yeah, she knew who she was. She'd just forgotten for a little while.

"Good," he said, giving her hand a squeeze before tugging her out of her room for the last time. "Let's go celebrate."

Hailey met them at the bottom of the steps. "They got him," she said, drawing Izzy into a fierce one-armed hug. "Thank God."

"I hope he spends the rest of his life behind bars," Paul said when Hailey pulled back.

The four of them walked into the living room, where a small crowd had gathered in front of the TV.

"This is wild," Zach said, his eyes glued to the screen.

"I can't believe how fast they picked it up," Jeff said, widening the circle to make room for her.

Izzy took a step closer, saw a picture of Bradley's face flash up on the screen, and stopped walking.

Paul put a hand on her shoulder. "Do you want us to turn it off?"

A few others glanced back and Wesley even picked up the remote, expecting her to say yes, but Izzy could tell from their expressions that they didn't want her to. This was a big story. Everyone here had played a part in it. They probably felt like heroes right now. And they were—to her anyway. She didn't want to take that away from them. "No," she said. "It's fine."

"Are you sure?" Wesley asked, lowering the remote.

She nodded and looked at the screen again. Maybe one day, after enough time had passed, she'd be able to look at Bradley's face and feel nothing. In the meantime, she was going to have to get used to it. It made it a *little* easier knowing that the rest of the world would see him for who he really was now.

Hailey handed her a beer. Izzy twisted the top off and took a sip, but it felt strange to be standing around drinking a beer after everything that had happened. She felt like she should be doing something. But...what?

"Who's hungry?" Ethan asked, carrying what was left of the pizzas they'd ordered the night before out to the living room.

Several people took a slice and then sat down to watch the drama unfold on the TV.

"Do you want one?" Matt asked, holding the cardboard box up so she could reach inside.

Izzy looked down at the pizza. She felt ravenous suddenly, like she hadn't eaten in weeks. But the cold cheese and stale crust seemed so...unappetizing. Shaking her head, she looked at the kitchen—that big beautiful kitchen—and felt something stir deep inside her.

A woman's place is in the kitchen.

No, Izzy thought. A woman's place was wherever she wanted it to be. If she happened to choose to spend most of her time in the kitchen, then that was *her* choice. Not because some man thought that was where she belonged. Or that she couldn't do any better.

Fishing her phone out of her pocket, she scrolled through her list of contacts for Della's number. Della had told her a few weeks ago that if she was ever ready to cook again to call her. Not to try to do it alone. That they'd do it together.

Before she could talk herself out of it, she clicked on Della's name and typed out a message: 'Are you home?'

A few minutes later, Della texted back: 'No. I'm at the café. Prepping for another catering gig. Swamped!'

Izzy hesitated, just for a moment, then wrote: 'Need any help?'

'YES!!!'

Lowering the phone to her side, Izzy looked out at the yard. It was late, but she probably had time to get to the café before dark if she left right now. Feeling a tremor of excitement, she placed her beer back in the fridge and walked over to Paul, who was sitting on the barstool farthest away from the TV.

"I need to go to the café," she said.

He looked up at her, surprised. "Why? What's up?"

"Nothing." She wasn't ready to say the words out loud yet. She was afraid if she did, she might chicken out. "I just...need to go."

He started to stand. "Do you want someone to drive you?"

"No." She shook her head. "I'll bike. Annie can give me a ride back later." Looking around at the rest of the veterans, she bit her lip. She didn't want to seem ungrateful, or like she was abandoning them. She just didn't want to make a big deal about the fact that she was leaving. "I just..."

Paul nodded. "Got it."

Izzy let out a breath.

"Go," he said, making a shooing motion with his hands. "I'll say you got a phone call and went outside for some privacy."

"Thank you," she said, and slipped out the back door.

As soon as she was outside, and the noise from the TV had faded, she felt herself relax again. She hopped on her bike and began to pedal toward the village. The air was filled with the sweet scent of honeysuckle. She could hear the water lapping against the shoreline and the soft crunch of oyster shells beneath her tires. She passed a hedge of blackberries bursting with summer fruit and wondered how she was ever going to return to the city after this.

Pushing the thought away, she reminded herself that Colin still hadn't found her a job. And maybe there was a reason for that. Maybe, if she could start cooking again, she could find a job in a kitchen—a job she actually wanted. Of course, that might be jumping the gun a little. Just because Bradley had been apprehended, didn't mean her flashbacks were going to magically disappear overnight.

The memories were still there, lurking under the surface.

It was going to take time, and a lot more therapy, to work through those memories—the same way it had for Will and Taylor.

As she came to the outskirts of the village, it occurred to her that there was probably no one on this island who understood that better than Annie. Annie had experienced the effects of PTSD through both her daughter and her husband. She'd seen, firsthand, how unpredictable it could be. And, though she'd been friendlier to Izzy lately, she might not necessarily want her using her kitchen to get back on the horse, so to speak.

Especially if Taylor was around.

Feeling slightly deflated, Izzy slowed to a stop in front of the café. She pulled her bike onto the grass, propped it against one of the trees, and followed the tinkling sound of wind chimes up to the porch. If Annie and Della were in the middle of frantic catering preparations, it was possible that they might not have even heard the news about Bradley. Della could have assumed that Izzy's offer to help had nothing to do with any actual cooking.

The kitchen was hardly big enough for two people anyway. She walked up the steps and peered in the windows, expecting to see both women running around. But the dining room was empty. All the tables and countertops had been cleared off. And Riley was napping on the floor in front of the register.

Izzy opened the door. The dog lifted her head, thumping her tail against the tiles. But the rest of the place was quiet. "Della?"

"In here," Della said, waving a hand from behind the half-doors that led to the kitchen.

Izzy paused to give Riley a pat on the head. "Where's Annie?"

"She's upstairs with Taylor," Della answered. "They'll be down in a minute."

Izzy walked the rest of the way to the kitchen and pushed open the swinging doors. There was only a single cast-iron frying pan on the stove. The oven was off. And almost everything had been boxed up and put away for the evening. "I thought you said you were swamped."

"I was," Della said, smiling. "Earlier."

Izzy's gaze dropped to the counter beside the stove—the only one that had anything on it. A collection of bowls, in a variety of sizes, held crabmeat, breadcrumbs, fresh basil, lemon wedges, Old Bay Seasoning, dried mustard, eggs, and mayonnaise. Confused, she looked back up. She'd seen inside Della's kitchen enough times to know she wasn't a tidy cook. "What's all this?"

"Your ingredients," Della said, as if it were the most natural thing in the world. "I'm going to teach you how to make a Maryland crab cake."

BY THE TIME Izzy pulled the last crab cake out of the pan, Annie had come downstairs to join them. Ryan had arrived right after she'd started cooking with a bouquet of wildflowers. He'd given them to her, along with a kiss on the lips, right in front of the other two women—neither of whom had seemed at all surprised. If anything, Della had looked a little smug afterwards.

Will had walked in a few minutes later, followed by Becca and Colin. Everyone had heard the news about Bradley and wanted to offer their support. Even Grace, who'd been inundated with calls ever since the story broke, had managed a thirty second conversation with Izzy, saying she'd visit the island next weekend and they'd talk more then.

Colin and Becca had left again after about a half an hour to check on the rest of the veterans. The only person Izzy hadn't seen yet was Taylor. According to Annie, she was upstairs in her old room, working on a top-secret project, and she'd be down when she was finished.

"Well," Izzy said, lifting the platter of crab cakes for Della to inspect. "What do you think?"

"I think you learned from the best," Della said, winking.

Izzy laughed and carried the platter out to the dining room where Annie had set a table for the six of them. Della had whipped up a cucumber salad to have on the side, and they'd steamed a few ears of corn as well. The entire café smelled of fried seafood, Old Bay Seasoning, and summer. And Izzy couldn't remember the last time she'd felt this happy.

They were about to sit down when Taylor came running downstairs. In her hand was the oyster shell wind chime she'd been working on for weeks. The piece of driftwood was perfectly balanced now and the spiral of shells made the sweetest clinking sound as the strings swayed together. "I finished!" she announced proudly.

Ryan made a big show of walking over and kneeling down in front of her so they were eye-to-eye. "Did you make this for *me*?"

Taylor beamed and handed it to him.

He took it, held it up reverently, admiring each piece with all the attention it deserved. The chime looked smaller, more delicate in his big hand, but, somehow, it suited him. "Thank you," he said softly, pulling Taylor in for a hug. "I love it."

"It's beautiful," Izzy said, from her seat next to Della.

"I made one for you, too," Taylor said.

"Me?" Izzy asked, taken aback.

Taylor nodded and ran back upstairs. A few moments later, she came down again, clutching a shiny red colander turned upside down with several kitchen utensils suspended beneath. "It's all cooking stuff."

Taking the chime carefully from Taylor's hands, Izzy's gaze dropped to the slotted spoon, metal whisk, pair of tongs, silver spatula, and salt and pepper shakers—each dangling from its own piece of cooking twine. "I can't believe you made me a wind chime. Thank you. I...promise to find the perfect place to hang it."

"Actually," Annie said, from across the table. "We thought you might want to hang it here."

"Here?" Izzy asked, surprised. "You mean, until I leave?"

"No," Annie said, exchanging a glance with Della. "We were hoping you might want to stay."

"Stay?" Izzy's brows drew together.

Annie nodded. "My phone's been ringing off the hook with people asking about our catering services ever since you helped us with Ryan's event. I'd really like to say yes to some of them. But I can't do that without you."

Izzy's eyes widened. "You're offering me a job?"

"And a place to live, if you want it," Annie said. "You could rent the apartment upstairs. There's a full kitchen up there. I know it's probably not as big as you're used to, but if we do as well as I think we're going to, we might be able to renovate it next year."

Izzy stared at her. Annie wanted her to stay here? To work

here? And she was already talking about renovations? "Did you know about this?" she asked, looking at Ryan.

He nodded.

Her gaze shifted to Will. "Are *you* okay with this?"

"Of course," he said, smiling.

Della reached over, squeezed her hand. "Think about how much fun we'll have cooking together."

"I don't know what to say," Izzy said.

"Say yes," Taylor said.

Izzy looked at Taylor's expectant face, then back at the chime. "I think," she said, as her lips curved, "that we should go find a place to hang this wind chime."

TWENTY-TWO

TWO MONTHS LATER...

*B*y the end of September, the first touches of autumn had begun to sweep over the island. The days were getting shorter, the nights longer and cooler. Acorns were falling from the branches of the oak trees and squirrels were racing around, gathering them up. Soon, the watermen would stow away their crabbing gear for the winter. A few of them had already removed the canopies from their workboats to make room for the tongs and dredges they would use during oyster season.

From her apartment above the café, with a view of the narrow channel that threaded through the marshes, Izzy could watch them come and go. She knew the names of most of the boats now, and the stories of the men behind the wheels. In the mornings, when the sun was barely a whisper of light along the horizon, she could hear them cutting a slow path toward the open Bay.

The sound always made her smile.

The next cohort of veterans had arrived on the island a few weeks ago. They were gradually settling into their jobs and getting to know each other. Izzy wondered if they had any idea that the friendships they would make over the next three months would last for the rest of their lives.

Her own group had disbanded at the end of August. Kade had been picked up by a gardening center in Annapolis, whose customers got a kick out of consulting with the heavily-tattooed ex-Marine about what flowers to plant around their mailboxes. His wife hadn't asked him to move back in yet, but she was letting him see his children again. They were taking things slowly. She wanted to make sure all the changes he'd made in the program would stick first.

Izzy didn't blame her.

Once you'd been burned, it took a lot longer to trust again.

Most of the veterans had found jobs on the Western Shore. The only three who'd stayed in the area were Izzy, Hailey, and Paul. Hailey had gotten a job at the local maritime museum and Paul had managed to convince Ryan to let him stay on at the farm. Colin had been opposed to the idea initially, but in the end, when it came down to it, Paul had made himself indispensable.

As for Ryan, Izzy saw him almost every night. Sometimes he stopped by the café after work just to say hello; other times he stayed for dinner. He was quietly pursuing her with the same patient persistence he used to pursue everything he wanted in life. And, as usual, it was working.

She was actually starting to believe that they could have a future together—that she could be intimate with someone again. She hadn't invited him to spend the night yet, but she was getting closer to taking that step. She'd even bought something lacy and feminine to wear when she did. It was in the top drawer of her dresser, wrapped in pink tissue paper—a constant reminder of that one last fear she still needed to overcome.

At the sound of footsteps on the stairs, Izzy felt a flutter in her belly. Thinking it might be Ryan, since he usually stopped by around this time, she checked her reflection in the oven door, tucked a few curls into her ponytail, and smoothed her hands down the front of her apron. Smiling, she turned to face the person making his or her way up to the apartment.

But it wasn't Ryan. It was Will.

"Hi," she said, not quite as happy to see him as she would have been to see Ryan, but still happy to see him.

"It smells amazing up here," Will said, walking into the kitchen. "What are you making?"

"Pumpkin-seed crusted rockfish, oyster stew with fennel and chorizo, and a spicy bay scallop ceviche." Izzy moved over to the stove and lifted the top off the stew to let him have a look. "We're catering an engagement party for the daughter of a former ambassador in a few weeks. The bride's mother wanted a traditional menu, but the bride pulled us aside afterwards and said she wanted something a little different."

She picked up a spoon, handed it to him. "Care to do the honors?"

"Gladly." He dipped the spoon into the rich, creamy broth and took the first taste, groaning the instant it hit his tongue. "Mmm," he said, nodding. "Mmm-hmm."

"You like it?" she asked hopefully.

Will set the spoon down. "It's incredible, Izzy. I can't imagine *anyone* not liking this. Has Della tasted it yet?"

"Not yet," Izzy said, pleased by his reaction. "If she likes it, I'll offer to add it to the menu downstairs this winter. Though, " she added, "it *is* pretty spicy. Do you think the locals will be able to handle it?"

"Yeah," Will said, laughing. "I think they'll be able to handle it."

She smiled, glad that he thought so. She enjoyed experimenting with traditional recipes and giving them her own unique twist. But it was just as important to her to respect the sensitivities of the locals. She didn't want to push too much change on anyone too fast. Not that there was much chance of that happening as long as Della was in charge of the kitchen downstairs.

When it came to their catering services, they were able to offer the best of both worlds. If a client wanted a traditional menu, Della would provide the recipes for Izzy to cook. If they were open to something more experimental, Izzy would take the lead.

The two women had fallen into a comfortable rhythm, with both of them up and down the stairs all day long, wandering in and out of each other's kitchens, bouncing ideas off each other and tasting each other's creations.

Somehow, in a different way and with a different woman, Izzy had managed to reclaim the dream she'd once shared with her grandmother. It was hard to believe that this was her life now, that after everything that had happened, she had found her way back to the one thing she loved more than anything in the world.

"Before I forget," Will said, pulling a card out of his pocket. "Erin thinks she might have found a social worker who'd be willing to meet with your friend at no charge."

"Thank you," Izzy said gratefully, glancing down at the name before slipping the card in her pocket.

It had taken Izzy a few weeks to convince Carolina that she needed to talk to someone, and that it would be safe for her to do so, but her friend had finally come around to the idea. It would be a huge help if she didn't have to pay for it. Any extra money her friend made these days was going toward the attorney she'd hired to work on her citizenship.

More importantly, though, Carolina and her children had

finally left their apartment in Sandtown-Winchester and moved into Izzy's house on the other side of Baltimore. Every two weeks, Izzy drove across the bridge to visit them. They seemed to be settling in just fine. And Izzy could sleep better at night, knowing that Carolina and her children were safe.

When the timer binged, she pulled a tray of toasted pumpkin seeds out of the oven and set them on the counter beside the rockfish. "Do you want me to bring some of this over later, relieve whoever's on kitchen duty at the inn?"

Will checked his watch. "Why don't you wait until tomorrow? They've probably already started on dinner for tonight." He pushed back from the counter. "I should probably go, make sure no one burns the place down."

Izzy smiled. She knew he was joking...sort of.

Will headed for the stairwell, but he paused outside Taylor's old bedroom, which was still decorated with the same twinkle lights, paper butterflies, and dream catchers as it had been when she'd lived here. Izzy had left everything the same so that Taylor and her friends could still come up and play whenever they wanted.

"Thank you for not changing this," Will said quietly.

"Of course," Izzy said.

He tapped his palm against the doorframe, like he needed to leave a few emotions there, then headed for the stairs again.

Taking a deep breath, Izzy walked out from behind the counter. "Will?"

He stopped walking, looked back at her.

She'd never really gotten a chance to thank him, to let him know how much the program had meant to her. "I just wanted to say...thank you, for not giving up on me."

"Honestly, the thought never crossed my mind."

～

LATER THAT NIGHT, Ryan helped Izzy step down from the dock behind his father's house into the old wooden rowboat that had been in his family since he was a child. The air was cool and crisp. And when he handed her a blanket to stow under her seat, she wrapped it around her shoulders instead.

As soon as she was settled, he lowered himself to the seat across from her and picked up the oars. It had been a long time since he'd been out in this boat, but he remembered it like it was yesterday, and his father had kept it in good condition over the years.

Over the past two months, Ryan's relationship with his father had begun to shift. Izzy had told him what his father had said when she'd gone out on the boat with him that day in July—that he thought his wife had left him because he hadn't been enough for her. Suddenly, all his father's actions over the years had begun to make perfect sense.

His father hadn't been pushing him away because he didn't want him around. He'd been pushing him away because he didn't want his son to end up like him—to ever know what it felt like to not be enough for someone.

It had taken a few heart-to-hearts between the two men to get it all out on the table, but Ryan finally understood where his father was coming from. And his father was finally beginning to accept that Ryan actually *wanted* to be here—that this was all he'd ever wanted.

"Do you want me to open this now or later?" Izzy asked, holding up the bottle of wine he'd brought along.

"Later."

"Where are we going?" she asked curiously.

He smiled. "You'll see."

He dipped the oars into the water, rowing them toward Pearl Cove. His whole life he'd been running from this. He'd tried to turn his back on it, pretend that it didn't exist. But he didn't want to pretend anymore.

He knew what he'd seen and heard out there as a child—what he could still see and hear every time a full moon rose over this island.

There was a full moon tonight.

A Harvest Moon.

It was rising over the marshes now, painting the surface of the water a glittering gold.

Maybe he'd needed to see what Izzy had gone through to understand what hiding the truth could do to someone, how much unnecessary pain it could cause. But he'd finally decided to come clean with his father and his sister about the role he'd played—or, at least, the role he *thought* he'd played—in their mother's disappearance.

A few weeks ago, he'd sat them both down and told them the story of what had happened when he'd paddled out to Pearl Cove as a ten-year-old boy. He'd told them how he'd heard the clinking seashells and seen the trail of moonlight transform into a string of pearls, just like in the fairy tale. He'd told them how he'd rushed home and woken his mother up, thinking she'd be so excited to find out that the story she'd told them at bedtime every night was true.

Instead, the very next day, she'd left—never to be seen or heard from again.

Ryan had expected his father and his sister to be angry with him. Either that, or tell him he was crazy. Instead, they'd been relieved. Because, for twenty-three years, they'd been blaming themselves, thinking *they'd* done something wrong. When, maybe, the only thing they'd done wrong was not talk about it.

That next day, Grace had met with her editor at *The Washington Tribune* and told him she was taking a leave of absence from the paper, effective immediately. She was planning to spend the next three months in Ireland, learning everything she could about the selkie legend—starting with a small island off the West Coast called Seal Island, where she'd traced the legend's origin.

Apparently, all she'd ever wanted was a clue—just one clue—to launch an investigation of her own.

Ryan had no idea where her research would lead. Personally, he didn't have much hope that they would actually *find* their mother after all these years. But if Grace could uncover a connection between her and one of those legends, it might at least help them understand *why* she'd left.

As far as Ryan was concerned, that would be enough.

In the meantime, he was going to try to find some answers of his own, right here—starting tonight.

When they made it to the mouth of the cove, he pulled the oars in so they could drift upriver, and Izzy came into his arms as naturally as if she'd been doing it forever.

"I hope you're not planning to put me to work," she joked as they floated past his oyster lease.

He smiled and lowered his mouth to hers. She tasted like licorice. Her hair smelled faintly of toasted pumpkinseeds. And he didn't want to let her go for the rest of the night.

"I peeked at the website for Nolan Reyes' new restaurant this afternoon," she said, nuzzling against him. "Your oysters are on the menu."

"Thanks to you," he murmured, sliding the blanket off one of her shoulders and kissing her there, too.

"Thanks to Annie and Paul," Izzy corrected, pulling back slightly.

"True," he conceded, smiling again. It *was* true that Paul had done most of the legwork. But Izzy was the one who'd set the wheels in motion. When she'd found out that Annie had spent the majority of her twenties working at one of the hottest restaurants on Pennsylvania Avenue, she'd convinced her to invite the chef and his family out to the island to tour Ryan's farm.

The chef had accepted, and as soon as they'd set a date, Paul and Izzy had come up with a plan to give him and his family an experience they'd never forget. In addition to the farm tour, they'd gotten a trotlining demonstration from Jake, a three-course lunch at the café from Della—who'd charmed them with stories of what Annie and Taylor had been up to since leaving the city— a cocktail cruise on one of the island's last working skipjacks, and a decadent dinner at the inn with the rest of the veterans, which Izzy had prepared.

By the time they'd left, they'd fallen in love with the island, and the chef's wife—an editor for one of D.C.'s premier regional magazines—had promised to write a story about their trip. When it came out, it had been enough to catch the attention of several top-tier chefs, including Nolan Reyes—the celebrity chef who owned six restaurants in the city.

Before he knew it, Ryan had more orders coming in than he and his father could possibly fill.

Not that he was thinking much about oysters at the moment since Izzy had begun nibbling on his ear. "If you keep doing that," he warned, "I'm going to have a hard time saying goodbye to you later."

"Then don't," she said softly.

He pulled back, looked at her. "You want me to stay tonight?"

"Yes."

"Are you sure?"

She nodded, but her smile had turned shy and she was looking up at him with so much vulnerability and trust in her eyes that if she hadn't already brought him to his knees a dozen times, he would have quite simply handed over his heart.

It was hers now anyway.

He tipped her mouth up to his, kissing her with the same care and tenderness he planned to devote to her for the rest of the night. When they finally pulled apart again, he poured them each a glass of wine, and they sat there for a long time, wrapped in each other's arms, gazing at the moon.

"What's that?" Izzy asked as a lone structure on the edge of the marshes came into view.

"Just an old house."

She lifted her head off his shoulder to get a better look and her eyes widened. "Is that the house from the legend you told us about? The one where the fisherman lived?"

Ryan nodded. "What's left of it."

It was overgrown now, covered in a thick tangle of vines. The marshes had swallowed up the foundation, causing one side to tilt and crumble. Storms had shattered most of the windows and the torn roof had become a popular nesting spot for birds.

The story itself might have been a legend, but the fisherman *had* existed. He had lived in that house with his family for years until his wife had vanished. Whether or not she'd left him to return to the sea was still up for debate, but Ryan knew where his beliefs lay.

They were almost past it when the faintest clinking of seashells filled the air. Izzy looked back at the house, a puzzled expression on her face. "Do you hear something?"

Yes, Ryan thought. He could hear something. He'd been hearing it all his life.

Moonlight tripped over the water, hesitant at first, like a child skipping a stone. The drops of light reached for each other, fusing together, until a single strand of pearls began to form on the surface.

Izzy sat up slowly. "Is that...?"

A voice—a woman's voice—so far away it seemed like it was coming from the bottom of the ocean, drifted toward them.

Izzy turned, looked at him. "Do you *believe* in magic?"

Tilting her face up to his, Ryan whispered, "I believe in you."

THE END

A NOTE FROM THE AUTHOR

Dear Reader,

I hope you enjoyed *Wind Chime Summer*. I grew up in a small town similar to Heron Island on the Eastern Shore of Maryland and I will always consider the Chesapeake Bay to be my home. I feel so fortunate to be able to share the rich culture and traditions of this place through my stories. As with the previous Wind Chime Novels, I've included a Chesapeake Bay recipe at the end of this story. On the next page, you'll find a recipe for Della's Maryland Crab Cakes. I'd love to hear what you think if you get a chance to make them!

I am currently working on the next book in the series, which is tentatively titled *Wind Chime Cottage*. Grace Callahan's story will pick up where Ryan Callahan's left off, as she travels to Ireland to uncover the truth behind their mother's mysterious disappearance. If you're familiar with my Seal Island Trilogy, you're probably beginning to put two and two together, but for those of you who aren't...

Prior to writing the Wind Chime Novels, I wrote a series of romances called the Seal Island Trilogy, which were based on the selkie legends of Ireland. At the end of the third book in that series, I hinted at the possibility of a fourth book by introducing a new character named Aidan O'Malley. I have received many emails from readers over the years asking when I was going to write that story.

I am very excited to announce that *Wind Chime Cottage* will be a love story between Aidan and Grace! It will take place on both Seal Island and Heron Island, and it will merge the two series together. As soon as I have more details, I'll share them on my website. In the meantime, I've included a special preview of *The Selkie Spell*, the first story in the Seal Island Trilogy, at the end of this book.

Lastly, I have a small request. If you enjoyed *Wind Chime Summer*, it would mean so much to me if you would consider leaving a brief review. Reviews are so important. They help a book stand out in the crowd, and they help other readers find authors like me.

Thank you so much for reading *Wind Chime Summer!*

Sincerely,

Sophie Moss

MARYLAND CRAB CAKES

Ingredients:
    ½ cup chopped fresh basil
    1 slice white bread, crust removed
    1 pound crab meat
    ¾ cup mayonnaise
    ¾ teaspoon dry mustard
    2 teaspoons Old Bay Seasoning
    1 egg
    Juice of half a lemon
    Salt and pepper

Instructions:
Pinch the slice of bread into tiny pieces, then toss everything in a big bowl and mix together. Form into balls using an ice cream scoop and drop heaping scoops onto a platter. Sprinkle more Old Bay Seasoning on top. Be generous! Cover with plastic wrap and refrigerate for one hour. This will help keep the cakes together. When you're ready to cook, heat about ¼ inch of cooking oil in a

large pan until it sizzles when you throw a few drops of water into it. Fry the crab cakes on both sides until golden brown. Serve with cocktail sauce and lemon wedges.

For more *Wind Chime Café* recipes, visit my website at sophiemossauthor.com.

ACKNOWLEDGMENTS

Thank you to my mom and dad for your support and for always believing in my dreams. Thank you to my editor, Martha Paley Francescato, for your constant encouragement, for reading every single chapter as I wrote it, and for helping me find my voice again. Thank you to Ann Wilson for, not once, in all our conversations together, suggesting that I give up on writing this book, even though I came close so many times.

Thank you to Patricia Paris and Tracy Hewitt Meyer for helping me reach the breakthrough that got this story back on track during our writing retreat last summer. Thank you to my beta readers—Patricia, Tracy, Juliette Sobanet, and Christine Fitzner-LeBlanc—for reading early drafts and providing valuable feedback.

Thank you to Kelley Cox of Phillips Wharf Environmental Center for answering all my questions about running a nonprofit, helping me understand the overall transition that the Chesapeake Bay seafood industry is going through right now, and sharing your insights on the issues currently affecting the waterman's community.

Thank you to John Valliant, former president of the Chesapeake Bay Maritime Museum, for answering all my questions about the history of the Chesapeake Bay and setting me straight on what you can, and cannot, catch in a crab pot.

Thank you to Anna Priester of Island Creek Oysters, Jake and Irving Puffer of Wellfleet Oyster and Clam Company, and Anthony Marchetti, Patrick Oliver, and Eli Nichols of Rappahannock Oyster Company for sharing your stories with me and helping me understand the complexities of running an oyster farm.

Thank you to Vera Connolly and Merced Flores for introducing me to the plight of the migrant worker and opening my eyes to that world so many years ago. I was deeply moved by what I learned and I hope I did the subject justice. Thank you to all the men and women who have served in our military. I am so grateful for your sacrifice and for everything you do to keep this country safe.

Lastly, thank you to Elizabeth Moorshead Benefiel and Megan Trovato Jensen for being there for me when I really needed you these past two years. Your friendship means the world to me.

ABOUT THE AUTHOR

Sophie Moss is a *USA Today* bestselling and multi-award winning author. She is known for her captivating Irish fantasy romances and heartwarming contemporary romances with realistic characters and unique island settings. As a former journalist, Sophie has been writing professionally for over ten years. She lives in Maryland, where she's working on her next novel. When she's not writing, she's testing out a new dessert recipe, exploring the Chesapeake Bay, or fiddling in her garden. Sophie loves to hear from readers. Email her at sophiemossauthor@gmail.com or visit her website sophiemossauthor.com to sign up for her newsletter.

BOOKS BY SOPHIE MOSS

Wind Chime Novels

Wind Chime Café

Wind Chime Wedding

Wind Chime Summer

Seal Island Trilogy

The Selkie Spell

The Selkie Enchantress

The Selkie Sorceress

Read on for a special preview of *The Selkie Spell*!

THE SELKIE SPELL

PROLOGUE

IRELAND, TWO HUNDRED YEARS EARLIER

Ian Quigley crept toward the woman on the beach. He'd seen her from the cliffs, bathed in the moonlight of Midsummer's Eve, shedding her seal-skin and tucking it under a rock. He'd heard tales of the creatures, selkies—seals who could take the shape of a woman on land—but he'd never seen one. He'd heard accounts of their beauty, of their ability to bewitch grown men, but he'd never felt their spell.

Ian's heart beat faster as he made his way closer, for he knew that the most sensible fisherman, at a mere sighting, would abandon his curragh in the roughest of seas to get a better look. The most faithful of men would desert their wives to follow a selkie into the sea, gulping the salty waves into their lungs, forgetting they could not breathe underwater as they reached for the woman's long black hair with the tips of their fingers in their last sane breath. Others would lose their ability to speak or to eat, their need for the woman driving them mad as they wandered the beaches, waiting for her to return, their fingers rubbed raw as they dug in the sand, searching, always searching for her pelt.

For the man who captures the pelt of a selkie claims mastery over her.

Ian lowered himself from the cliff path, onto the sand. He crept toward the rock, where her seal-skin lay hidden. But at the sound of her low, throaty voice, he froze. The first notes of the siren's song twisted into the night.

Ian fisted his hands to his ears. He squeezed his eyes shut and tried to fight it, but her voice threaded into his mind and he turned, gazing at the glorious face tilted up to the star-studded sky.

The hair that rained down her back was the color of crow feathers. Her skin, as pale as the sand at her feet, seemed to glow. The pelt lay forgotten as Ian started on shaky legs toward the selkie.

Toward the voice of the woman of the sea.

He tried to fight the force that pulled him to her, the hands that seemed to push him from behind. But the song seduced his soul, intoxicated his mind, and the words in his head only moments ago —follow her, capture her, claim her—vanished and there was only that woman.

That voice.

He was almost to her. A few more steps and he'd be able to reach her, to touch her. To claim her for his own. His selkie. His seal woman. His own. Ian's hands shook. He reached for her.

A gull cawed, swooped low over the ocean, and the selkie stopped singing. Released from the trance, Ian stumbled backwards and fought off the ropes that were trapping him, tugging him to her as his feet dug into the sand.

He scrambled for the rock, tearing at the tangles of seaweed, fumbling for the seal-skin. And when his fingers found it, his *palms wrapping around the oily pelt as he pulled it to his chest, he sank to his knees, gulping for air.*

In the village, dogs began to howl. In their beds, women woke, gasping, clutching at their throats, unable to breathe. Children dreamed of drowning, calling out for their mothers in their sleep. And on the beach, in the moonlight, the selkie turned and saw what Ian held.

An anguished cry cut through the night.

Ian lifted his eyes to the woman's and a slow smile spread across his lips. *Mine,* he thought, as he pulled himself to his feet. *You are mine. You belong to me.* He held out his hand. "Come to me."

She went to him. But her dark eyes were void of passion, void of life as she stared at the bundle crushed to his chest. Her pelt, her freedom, her link to the sea; he had stolen it. He had shackled her to him.

And with every breath, every step closer to the man, she hated him.

When he reached out, threading his fingers into her hair, she closed her eyes and listened for the ocean. For the heart, for the beat of the only world she had ever known.

But there was only silence.

And him.

THE SELKIE SPELL

CHAPTER ONE

IRELAND, PRESENT DAY

Tara Moore crossed the thin wooden plank leading to the ferry. She spied the nets in the back, the wide wooden coolers and yellow rain slickers draped over the crates.

The captain eyed her curiously. "What do you think you're going to find on Seal Island this time of year?"

"Peace," Tara answered. "Quiet."

"You'll get plenty of that," the captain assured her, locking the gate behind her. "But are you sure you're not wanting to go to Inishmore, or one of the larger islands? Not many tourists on the island in April."

"I try to stay away from the touristy places."

"A single woman, traveling alone?" He took in her thin frame and threadbare sweater, the raven locks framing a pretty face with wide-set green eyes. "Isn't it safer to keep on the well-trodden paths?"

Tara glanced down at her ring finger, the faint imprint of her wedding band slowly fading. "I'm not afraid."

"Suit yourself." The captain shrugged and turned the key.

The engine gasped and sputtered to life. She smelled gasoline. Saw smoke. The dark waters churned as the ferry pulled away from the dock, cutting a slow path toward the island.

"Ever been to Ireland before?" the captain called out from behind the wheel.

Tara shook her head.

"What do you think so far?"

"It's wet."

"That it is." He chuckled, steering out into the fog. "But it wouldn't be so green if it weren't so wet." They rode in silence, until the mainland behind them disappeared and the only sound was the hum of the motor and the sea lapping against the hull of the ferry. "Course some would say it's because we're all descended from the selkies and we need the wet air to breathe."

"Selkies?"

"Aye." The captain nodded toward a shadow shifting beneath the dark waters.

Tara watched a shiny creature pop its head up and swim alongside the boat. She spotted another one, moving underneath the surface. Sleek and black it moved like a fish under the water.

"Seals," the captain explained.

Walking to the front of the boat, Tara rested her hands on the railing. The wind whipped her dark hair into her eyes as she gazed down at the animals swimming beside them.

"You've heard of the legend, I imagine?" the captain called.

Tara turned, shaking her head.

"Ah, it's a tale for the tourists." The captain's pale blue eyes twinkled. "But you're not looking for that, are you?"

Tara's eyes scanned the water, widening when more seals slid up to the surface, slicing through the ocean beside the ferry. "That depends."

"On what?"

"On how it ends."

The captain settled back, his leathery hand resting on the top of the wheel. "Now, that I can't tell you."

"Why not?"

"Cause we don't know yet."

Tara's eyes met his across the deck. "How can you not know the ending? All legends have endings."

"Not this one." The captain nodded toward the bow of the boat.

She turned, sucking in a breath as the island erupted out of the water in a slash of slick limestone and weathered quartz. Fingers of fog dripped from the soaring cliffs. Seagulls dove in and out of the jagged crevasses, their solemn cries echoing over the harbor.

"Are those...?" Tara squinted through the mists at a sliver of sand covered in seals. "Selkies?"

"Aye."

"I've never seen so many of them," Tara exclaimed. "Is it normal...for them to gather like that?"

"Tis." The captain replied. "When they're waiting for something."

"What are they waiting for?"

The captain steered the ferry into the harbor, his cracked lips curving into a grin. "Maybe they're waiting for you."

～

So she had come.

Thick mists swirled around the selkie's ankles, snatched at the tips of her raven locks as she watched the ferry dock, watched the woman step down to the tall pier and head toward the path leading up to the village.

A faint ray of light burned in her soul, chipping away at the hopelessness, the despair, the longing she'd buried deep inside. But with the hope, came the memories. And she saw her captor's face as if it were yesterday. She heard his laughter as he dragged her back to his home.

To her prison.

She squeezed her eyes shut as she remembered the first slap of his fist, the groping fingers trapping her wrists as she struggled, her desperate cry for help as he threw her onto the hard, dirty floor and pushed himself inside her.

But no one came.

And as she lay on the floor of the cottage, beaten and broken, he hid her pelt. He took her freedom and, as the years slid by, her sanity.

In her madness she believed the sea would recognize her. That, in her desperation it would accept her and take her home. But without her pelt, without the seal-skin protecting her from the cold, icy waters, she choked on the very substance that had once been her air.

In taking her life, she cursed her already-broken spirit. She trapped her soul on this island, fated to wander the cliffs, reliving her torture, her sorrow.

Seawater dripped from the selkie's fingertips, from the hem of her dress. The shells threaded into her hair clinked in the wind. She opened her eyes, dark as the splinters of a curragh lying at the bottom of the ocean, and turned them on the woman making her way up the path below.

One daughter. Only one daughter, she had managed to save. On the day she'd sewn rocks into the hem of her dress and walked into the sea, she had given that one infant child to the seals to

*protect. She pushed the crib out to sea, and watched as the seals
surrounded it, nudging the child toward the mainland.*

*She knew in her heart that the child made it, that the others
who came after her survived. But would this one, so many years
later, be willing to accept the part she must play?*

*Would she be willing to stand for the women who came before
her? Or would she run, turning her back on her fate?*

Tara felt the force, like a jolt of energy, course through her and she
lifted her gaze to the tallest cliff. Through the fog, she glimpsed
the outline of a woman with long black hair, her dress whipping in
the wind, but when the mist shifted, she was gone. In her place
was only a small house, perched on the edge of a craggy hillside.

Shaking off the strange image, she shouldered her pack,
climbing the curved road leading up to the sprinkling of white-
washed cottages. The mists slid in patches, like schools of silvery
fish around her ankles. She could smell the sea, taste the salt in
the air.

*A legend that didn't have an ending? People who were
descended from seals?* She might have believed in fairy tales once,
long ago.

She knew better now.

Her fingers brushed the advertisement in her pocket as she
spotted the Guinness sign hanging from the thatched roof of
O'Sullivan's pub. The wind pushed it back and forth; the squeak
of rusted metal hinges the only sound drifting through the
deserted streets of the village.

Two weeks, she thought. Two weeks was all she needed to
pocket enough cash for her next ticket. She walked to the door,
grasped the cool brass handle and pulled. The scent of malt

vinegar and pipe-smoke wrapped around her, tugging her into the dark, wooded barroom. A turf fire snapped in the hearth. Boots were piled up in front of it, drying from the wet day's work. Pints of Guinness—dark as molasses topped frothy white like a milkshake—cluttered every flat surface.

She strode toward the bar, focusing on the tall, dark-haired man behind it, as islanders glanced up from their tables and their conversations—a cheerful jumble of Irish and Gaelic voices only moments ago—spun out in a quiet murmur.

Behind the bar, Dominic O'Sullivan caught sight of the newcomer, a wisp of a woman in ill-fitting jeans and a worn sweater draped over sparrow-thin shoulders. "Little early in the season for tourists."

Tara pulled out the crumpled advertisement. She knew the risks, the dangers of picking a place where visitors didn't come and go unnoticed, a place where people talked, asked questions and expected honest answers. But she needed time to think, to come up with her next plan.

All it would take was one tiny mistake.

"I'm here about the job," she said, setting the ad on the bar and gazing up into eyes the color of liquid silver. Thick black hair, still wet from the shower, swept back from the bartender's ruggedly handsome face, revealing a scar etched into his left eyebrow. He'd forgotten to shave, and a shadow of stubble darkened the strong line of his jaw.

Dominic looked down at the ad he'd posted in the Galway Gazette a few days ago, then back up at the woman who wore no makeup, nothing that would draw attention to a face that made his eyes want to linger just the same.

"I'm Tara Moore," she said, extending her hand.

"Dominic O'Sullivan," he said, marveling at the soft, pampered palm that met his, a direct contrast to the second-hand traveler's clothes.

"Are you still hiring?" Tara asked.

Twisting the top off a Harp, Dominic slid it down the counter to a customer. A simple white T-shirt stretched across his broad shoulders, revealing the hard muscles of his arms and chest. "That depends."

"On what?"

"On what an American wants with a job in an Irish pub."

There were so many ways she could answer that, Tara thought. But when she looked back into his eyes, she settled on the truth. "I needed to get away."

"From what?"

"From life."

Dominic leaned his arms on the bar. "Anything in particular?"

Tara shook her head. "Just in general."

Dominic pushed back from the bar and ran a wet rag over the counter. "In my experience, life has a way of catching up with you. Wherever you go."

"In my experience, life is what you make of it," Tara countered. "Right now, I'm looking for a job as a waitress in Ireland. Are you hiring, or not?"

Dominic set the rag down. It was a compelling combination—that rich, cultured voice, those soft, sensual lips, the cool confidence of a woman used to getting what she wanted. If she'd arrived during the regular tourist season, he'd already be laying the groundwork for a long, lazy summer seduction. He was about due for one of those anyway.

But it wasn't summer. And she wasn't the first attractive woman to come to this island with nothing but the clothes on her back. He'd fallen for it once. He wasn't stupid enough to fall for it again. He turned, pulling a bottle of Jameson's off the shelf. "Sorry, but the position's been filled."

"By who?" Tara pointed to a loaded tray sitting on the bar. "I don't see anyone delivering these drinks."

Picking up the tray, Dominic smiled and slipped out from behind the bar.

Tara watched him set the drinks down on a nearby table and caught the curious glances the islanders threw at her. "I don't understand. Did you change your mind after you put the ad in the paper?"

"I changed my mind when I saw you."

Tara tensed. "What is it about me that made you change your mind?"

"You've a look about you."

"What kind of look?"

"Like you're running from something."

"I'm just looking for a quiet place to spend the summer. That's all."

"Dom," Jack Dooley called out from across the room. "Can you do us a whiskey and a Smithwicks?"

"And two more pints over here." Kevin Brady held up his empty glass.

"And what did Caitlin put in this stew?" Donal Riley yelped as a dish towel sailed out of the kitchen and smacked him in the chest.

"I never claimed to be a cook, Donal Riley! And you can keep your mouth shut until Fiona gets back next week!" The kitchen door swung open and a plump redhead stormed out, holding up seven fingers. "Seven days, Dominic! You see this. Count them. Seven more days and I'm done. And you,"—she turned back to Donal Riley—"you're going to eat what's put in front of you and you're going to like it!"

Turning on her heels, she stalked back toward the kitchen, pausing in the doorway when she spotted Tara. "Hello there." She took in the backpack and shifted direction, strolling over to the newcomer. "Don't get many travelers to the island in April." She set a coaster on the bar in front of her. "Have you been helped?"

"She's not looking for a pint," Dominic called back.

"What's she looking for?"

"I'm here about the position," Tara explained. "Are you Mrs. O'Sullivan?"

"Me?" Caitlin's face broke into a grin. "No." She wiped her hand on her apron and held it out for Tara to shake. "I'm Caitlin Connor. The *friend*. I just fill in from time to time."

"Tara Moore," Tara said, offering her hand.

Caitlin frowned. The other woman's grip was firm, but her hand was so bony, she felt like she'd crack it if she squeezed any harder. "Is that an American accent?"

"Yes."

Caitlin withdrew her hand, regarding the newcomer warily. "Excuse me for asking, but haven't you got enough jobs of your own?"

"I'm looking for a change of pace."

"Bit of a drastic change, isn't it?"

"We all need to get away now and then."

"Do we?" Caitlin angled her head. "Never felt much of a need to leave the island myself." Caitlin's gaze lifted, her eyes meeting Dominic's across the room. He shook his head, just the smallest movement from side to side. "I wish we could help you." Caitlin shrugged. "But I don't think we're hiring anymore."

Tara bit back her frustration as the front door swung open and three children burst into the room.

"Dad!" Breathless, Kelsey O'Sullivan rushed to the bartender's side. "Ronan kicked the ball over the edge again!"

"It wasn't me!"

"It was, too!"

Dominic arched an eyebrow. "Ronan?"

"Okay," Ronan muttered. "It was me."

"How far did it go?"

"I heard a splash," Ashling piped in.

Dominic crossed his arms over his chest.

Kelsey tugged at her father's sleeve. "Ashling and I were winning."

The slightest smile tugged at the corner of his lips.

"Dad, this is serious. Ronan threw the game on purpose."

"What do you want me to do about it?"

"I think you should help us find the ball."

"You want me to scale the cliff wall?"

"I bet you could if you wanted to," Ronan muttered.

Dominic smiled and mussed his daughter's hair. "I'm sure there's another upstairs."

"That was the last one."

"What about the one I gave you for Christmas?"

"We lost it."

"What about the one your grandmother gave you?"

"We lost it."

"What about the one Ronan's mum gave you a week ago?"

His daughter's eyes lit up.

"It's on top of the fridge."

Her face fell.

"You found it?"

"That's the one we just lost."

Dominic hooked his arm around her daughter's waist and swung her upside down so her blond curls just brushed the floor.

"Dad!" she protested, giggling and trying to wiggle free.

"You know what you are?" he asked, still holding her upside down.

"What?"

"Trouble." He flipped her right-side up and set her back on

her feet. "Now go upstairs—all three of you—and wash up. I'll ask Caitlin to fix you something to eat."

When Ronan stuck out his tongue, Tara couldn't help but laugh. Dominic's eyes snapped to the sound, his smile fading as he caught the wistful expression on the newcomer's face.

"They're adorable," she said, her gaze lingering on the stairs after the children clamored up them. "Are they all yours?"

"No." Dominic stepped back behind the bar. "Just Kelsey."

"How old is she?"

"She turns eight next month."

Caitlin poked her head through the window connecting the kitchen to the bar. "Did I just see Ronan O'Shea stick out his tongue at my cooking?"

Dominic tossed an empty bottle of whiskey into the trash and glanced at Caitlin. "I don't know, but I think you could take him." He ducked as a dish rag flew past his head. Smiling, he twisted the cap off a bottle of stout, slid it down the bar and turned, pulling another bottle off the highest shelf.

Tara picked up the plates Caitlin slid through the window. "Where do these go?"

Dominic took the plates from her hands, set them back on the counter. "Like I said, the position's been filled."

"Why don't we treat it as a test run?" Tara offered. "If I do okay tonight, you'll hire me. If not, I'll leave first thing tomorrow."

"I've made up my mind."

"It's one night," Tara protested.

"Then why not enjoy it? I'll bring you a pint. You can sit here and listen to the music that'll start up soon enough. Then you can be off in the morning and find work somewhere else. There's other islands to choose from. Coastal villages on the mainland if all you're looking for is a quiet place."

"I want to work here."

"Why?"

"Because...it feels right."

"Right?" Dominic started another pint of Guinness, then leaned back from the taps. "Is that how you live your life, then? Doing what feels right?"

"Yes," Tara replied slowly. "Recently that is exactly how I've been living my life."

"Well, I'm sorry to disappoint you." He finished the pint and set it on the bar. "But the only thing I've to offer at the moment is a bar stool and a pint. You'll have to look for work somewhere else."